The Space Between Notes

Sinéad Tyrone

Copyright © 2019 by Sinéad Tyrone

The Space Between Notes/Tyrone 1st Edition

All rights reserved. No part of this book may be replicated or transmitted on any form or by any means, electronic or mechanical; including photocopying without permission in writing from the Author.

ISBN: 978-10863814-2-9

1. Fiction. 2. Music. 3. Irish Heritage.
4. Western New York. 5. Band/Music. 6. Poetry. 7. Tyrone

Cover design by Beth Bales Ostrowski

NFB/Amelia Press
<<<>>>
119 Dorchester Road
Buffalo, New York 14213
For more information please visit
nfbpublishing.com

Also by Sinéad Tyrone:

Fiction:

Walking Through The Mist

Crossing The Lough Between

Poetry:

Fragility

A Song Of Ireland

For all of the musicians
who have traveled a very difficult road
in order to follow their passion
and to bring us their glorious songs
and especially for all of those
who have lost friends
along that very difficult road

Life inspires art.

The novel and poems
contained in this book
were inspired in large part
by the stories of Savatage
and Trans-Siberian Orchestra.

This book is not about them,
nor about any real life musicians,
but is, rather, a composite of many musicians
blended to create the characters
you are about to meet.
Any similarities between my fictional musicians
and real ones is purely coincidental.

However,
this book is most of all
dedicated to
Paul O'Neill,
Criss Oliva,
Jon Oliva,
and all of the past and present
cast and crew of
Savatage
and Trans-Siberian Orchestra.

Thank you for your incomparable music,
for the joy you bring to so many of us,
and for inspiring me
to write this material.

Foreword

I first met the author, Sinead Tyrone, at one of the largest Irish Festivals in the world. We were both attending as guest authors. It did not take long for me to realize the deep passion she has for writing. This passion shines through in her latest novel, "The Space Between Notes."

My father was a song writer in Ireland and as a young teen I had the privilege of experiencing musicians and their life on the road. It was the Showband era in Ireland during the '70s and I spent most weekends backstage watching my father play his songs on a hand-held cassette player for the leading singers in the country at that time. It was a fascinating glimpse into a world not afforded to many other music lovers.

Despite being quite star struck, I was aware of the tough life these musicians led as they took to the road to reach fans in far flung dancehall corners of the country. In "The Space Between Notes," the author gives us much more than a glimpse into the lives of a heavy metal rock band. Seldom do most of us stop to consider what it takes to create the music which touches deep into the soul and which often takes a heavy toll on those who gift us with their genius.

"The Space Between Notes" does just that. We become involved in the lives of the musicians – inner band relations, marriages, divorces and even death at such an intimate level, that we cannot help but feel empathy for the pain and suffering of those involved.

I feel that musicians everywhere would join me in applauding the way in which the author brings us behind the scenes of the music business. Sinead Tyrone writes with such authority and passion that we are not merely drawn into their trials and tribulations as a reader, but we feel as if we have become part of the road crew. The fact that this story was born out of a collection of richly inspired poetry makes it all the more intriguing and a windfall for any reader.

J.P. Sexton, Author "The Big Yank – Memoir of a Boy Growing Up Irish" and "Four Green Fields: Wild Irish Banter and Stories, Shenanigans & Poetry."

Introduction

This project started with a poem. I had attended a concert, and been so moved by the program and the performances of the musicians involved that I could not sleep afterward. Instead, in the middle of the night, I wrote a poem ... Faith Walking ... about stepping out in faith to accomplish what you must even though you don't know how you'll achieve it.

The next day I wrote another poem, and one after that. In two weeks time I had written a dozen poems.

Then the story line hit.

I didn't act on it right away, imagining the story line was just me processing my emotions over what I'd experienced in the show. The story line remained stuck on my heart though, and in time I realized it had been given to me to write.

While inspired by actual musicians, none of the characters in this book are based on the musicians who inspired the book, nor any other actual persons. The characters exist only in my imagination and on these pages. Any similarities between the characters and any living persons is pure coincidence.

As I wrote the novel, the poems continued to come my way. In the end I had almost sixty poems. As I considered the best approach to releasing this material, I debated whether the novel and the poems should be two separate books. However, since the project started with a poem, and since the poems are so intrinsically connected with the novel, I knew I could not separate them. Thus, you have in this book a novel which tells a story of musicians bound by their craft, brothers in art connected by a common passion and drive, whose commitment to each other helps them navigate life's often troubled waters; and after the novel a collection of poems that are tied to the story.

I hope my words here move your heart as deeply as the musicians who inspired them have moved mine.

The Space Between Notes:
The Story

We Dream

We dream
we believe in our dreams

Sometimes they soar
and we along with them
high among clear blue skies
invincible
indestructible
world at our feet
stars within easy reach
we fill our hands and pockets with them

sometimes our dreams
crash to the ground
shatter on hard cement
a million shards of glass
glistening through our tears
impossible to reassemble

We sweep the shards
into a dust pan
throw them into the refuse bin
and pray for the strength
to start over

One

Look beyond the stage . . .to the hearts and souls of those who craft the music of our lives
—Sinéad Tyrone, *Beyond The Lights*

The crowd in St. Louis stood in a double file line, tickets in hand, waiting for the doors to open and admit them to the venue where Odysseus would play that night.

"Have you ever seen them before?" one fan asked.

"No, this is my first time," the person next to him answered.

A third fan joined in. "I've seen them several times. Marner and Morgan are monsters! Never seen anyone attack guitars the way they can."

"They're all gods," the first fan confirmed. "Delaney on drums is a man possessed!"

"Walkowicz owns the bass. I've never seen the bass played with such power."

"Cardinale's keyboards shine for me, like he's throwing handfuls of stars out against a dark night."

Back and forth the conversation ran, with others around them joining in, each new participant extolling the virtues of the heavy metal musicians they had come to see and hear. Listening to their albums at home was never enough for these ardent followers. Watching their heroes perform live was to witness gods come to earth, bestowing brilliant light upon the common masses before moving on to the next city on the tour list to further spread their light.

Inside the arena security guards took their positions, some to check tickets, others to scan and inspect packages and people entering the venue. Concession vendors finalized food and drink preparations, while the team working the official merchandise booth for Odysseus braced themselves for the crush to come as the band's fans pressed for t-shirts, cds and programs, souvenirs of the momentous event they were about to experience.

While all these visible activities took place, invisible to the rest of the world in the bowels of the arena, the members of Odysseus prepared for the evening's show.

Fourteen years earlier, Odysseus was five musicians in search of a new band. Steve Marner and Rusty Morgan had met backstage at a concert in New York where friends were performing. They had both seen each other play on the metal music circuit, but had spent little time in serious conversation with each other.

Both at loose ends after the show, Steve suggested, "Why don't we grab burgers and beer around the corner and catch up with what's going on with our lives?"

They entered a late night diner Steve had frequented a number of times, a dingy looking place from the outside, but with warm amber lights and fifties and sixties music playing in the background, a relaxed place where comfort food reigned and conversation was easy.

"You've been without your band for what, three months now?" Rusty asked after the waitress had taken their orders.

Steve corrected, "Five months. Greg's giving up music altogether, I think his wife's pushing him to go back to college and get his business degree."

"Ugh. I can't believe he wants that."

"I don't think he does, but his wife's being pretty stubborn about it. Well, with a baby on the way and all I can't blame her; we haven't exactly been pulling in big money."

"Greg's a great drummer, though. He could do session work, or get in with another band."

"Maybe he will in time. John's arm was broken in three places in his motorcycle accident a couple months ago, it will take a long time before he can play bass again."

"That's tough. I heard about his accident; you're all lucky he's even alive."

Steve agreed. "What about you? What's the latest with your group?"

Rusty shrugged. "Terry and I are looking around. Carl's in rehab, third time around for him, I don't think he'll be back on the scene. At least I hope he isn't; he can't say no to the drugs all around for the taking. Rob's got a potential job with another band, so Terry and I are in limbo."

"What a crazy business, huh?" Steve ordered fresh beers for them both, while an idea formed in his mind. He turned it over several times before sharing it with Rusty after the waitress had delivered their refills. "Ever think of you and me joining forces?"

Caught off guard, Rusty didn't answer right away. He studied Steve, and drank half his beer before responding, "I hadn't thought of it before, but tell me what your idea is."

Steve watched Rusty's eyes as he laid out his plan. He would know by watching them whether Rusty liked the idea or he was wasting his breath. "You and Terry are already looking for a new band. I am too. We'd need a bass, I know Rick Walkowicz is looking for work."

"Rick's good. I'm surprised he's not signed up by anyone else."

"He won't be free long, that's for sure." Steve thought he saw a glimmer of light in Rusty's eyes and, encouraged, continued, "I'd also like to get Dave

Cardinale, I think he's still open. He'd do a kick ass job for us on keyboards."

"Keyboards?" Rusty gave his first indication of objection. "I've never worked with them in my bands. Kind of outside the metal realm, don't you think?"

"I used to," Steve admitted, "but I've heard a few groups utilize them, and it opens up a whole new dimension to the music. I think you'd like the sound if you tried it."

Rusty considered the idea. He was willing to bend to Steve's will on this. They had a larger issue to resolve. He studied Steve a full minute, weighed what he knew about the guitarist who sat across the table from him, his temperament, his talent, his reputation. He couldn't judge how Steve would react, although he felt he had a good idea. He could not move forward on Steve's proposal until he knew where they both stood on one thing. "How do you propose we split guitar duty? We both play lead and with similar styles."

Steve already had an answer prepared, although he doubted it was the solution Rusty wanted. "You're a better rhythm guitar player than I am. I play lead, you can play both. I'd set a new band up with me as lead guitarist, you as rhythm."

He held his breath, waiting for Rusty's reaction.

Rusty had anticipated Steve's decision. While they both could play either style of guitar, the truth was Steve reveled in the limelight the lead guitar's solos always drew, while Rusty was content to remain in the lesser light as the rhythm guitarist. Steve could throw out all the flashy, imaginative, exciting shredding anyone could want. Rusty could lay down a solid foundation, a balance between drum and bass and the flash of lead guitar. Let Steve have all the glory; in truth Rusty preferred the challenge of holding the rhythm line of a song, of the complex chord progressions and riffs in a rhythm guitarist's arsenal, and of providing part of the framework upon which the lead guitarist could let his magic shine.

On the other hand, he wasn't about to give in to Steve without putting up a fight for at least a share of the glory.

"I think I should at least have three or four songs where I play lead."

He was no pushover, Steve thought, eyeing Rusty with closer scrutinization. He liked that. It was hard to respect anyone who always gave in, who didn't stick up for himself. Steve knew from hearing others rave about Rusty and from watching him first hand that Rusty could play any kind of guitar thrown at him. No doubt he could lead on any number of songs. The only question was, how much was Steve willing to give up?

Rusty waited on Steve's decision. Playing lead wasn't critical to him, and the idea of forming a band with the great Steve Marner, one of the top metal guitarists around in those days, sent his mind whirling in multiple directions for all the possibilities the venture could hold. He wondered what he would do if Steve rejected his idea straight off. Would he walk away from what looked like a golden opportunity? Or cave and let Steve have his way?

Rusty released a long, slow inner breath when Steve agreed, "I'd be willing to trade off lead with you on two or three songs a show, would that work?"

That night Odysseus was born.

Their first gigs were played in small bars and clubs with fifty to a hundred people in attendance. In time they built their way up to the old theater circuit, playing for one to four thousand people per night. As their albums climbed the charts and their online videos were viewed more and more, their shows sold out and second shows or return engagements were booked.

They all remembered the day Larry, their manager, announced, "It's time we started booking Odysseus into arenas."

"Are you kidding?" Steve had asked, stunned.

"That's insane!" Dave had declared.

Rick and Terry had just laughed, finding the whole idea incredulous.

Rusty alone digested Larry's announcement as if it was their due, a well deserved reward for their years of hard work. They had watched a number of their peers rise to the level of blockbuster popularity, and had wondered when it would be their turn, when all their efforts and sacrifice would pay off.

Now Larry, who had always believed they would reach this level in time, was handing them their dream. Rusty, seated closest to where Larry sat in the conference room where they had gathered to strategize what they would do in the coming year, told him, "You were always so sure we'd make it this far. Thank you for never giving up on us."

Larry had just waved Rusty's thanks off. "You all did the hard work rowing this ship through the waters, rocky seas and all. I just pointed the ship in the right direction from time to time."

Several years on, their tours continued to fill arenas, album sales continued to soar, and they found their lives running at a non-stop pace.

They prepared now for their St. Louis show using the same patterns each of them had found worked best.

Dave Cardinale, the band's keyboard player, ran through the set list for the third time that night. Even though he had the sequence of songs memorized backwards and forwards, he over-prepared for their shows, as he did for everything else in his life. His classical music training had taught him to be precise in all things, especially the music he played. In all the years he'd worked with Odysseus he'd never broken his habit of being extra cautious with everything from the care of his keyboards to his pre-show preparation. Now, at the age of forty, he'd settled into a comfortable routine he was loathe to change. He checked the set list against the photo of it he kept on his cellphone's camera, a copy of which he knew was taped to the right-hand side of his keyboards. Satisfied that the lineup hadn't changed in the twenty-four hours since their previous show, he set his phone and the piece of paper aside and ran his hands and arms through their customary pre-show limbering exercises. Exhilaration built inside Dave as he warmed up; soon the curtain would be raised, he would take his place behind his keyboards, and another show would be underway.

Rick Walkowicz played imaginary notes on his air bass guitar, running through the night's songs in his mind once more before the curtain rose. He could have played each song in his sleep but he followed this routine anyway, both as a form of focusing on the show they were about to embark on and a way to relax before the fun started. Each song carried with it a personal meaning, some piece of his heart he'd woven between Steve or Rusty's words and tunes, a habit he'd developed over the years, affixing a connection to each composition that reached deep inside him and drew out intense feelings which carried through to the notes he played. Most of the thoughts and feelings that flowed through him were of his wife Laurel, his seven-year old son Ryan, and his five-year old daughter Christine. Some days he wished he could rent a second bus and bring them on tour with him, although he knew it was no environment for kids. He forced his mind to focus back on his job, and ran through another air song.

Terry Delaney couldn't remember a time when playing drums didn't thrill him. He was five years old when he'd started, sitting behind the drum kit at his uncle's house. Even that young, Terry felt the rhythm of the drums resonating inside his heart, his pulse quickening as he raised and lowered the sticks, as he discovered the various sounds he could produce. Something inside him came to life every time he sat at the drums when he was young; over the years, rather than diminishing, that sensation had increased. Now, waiting for their show to start, Terry felt the same excitement. As he watched his Odysseus brothers prepare for their show, he thought of how far they had come in the fourteen years they'd been together. While their success sometimes surprised Terry, what impressed him most was that, while so many metal groups they knew had gone through personnel changes over the years, Odysseus had never varied any of its members; they remained the same tight core of brothers bound by their passion for music. They even looked like brothers to a large degree, wearing the same leather pants and black t-shirts with lightning bolts emblazoned across them for shows, and long hair that fell halfway down their backs. They each bore tattoos that read Odysseus, with a lightning bolt underneath, on their upper right arms, one more token of brotherhood, souvenirs of a hard drinking evening in their earlier days.

Steve Marner pulled each of his guitars, one by one, off the rack where they stood at attention, waiting for their turn to shine under his masterful hands. Even though Bryan, the band's guitar tech, had already inspected and tuned each one, Steve rechecked each now, making sure the strings were secure and in tune, studying the hairline crack in his black guitar to make sure it hadn't grown worse. While he treated each one of his guitars like they were children, giving them tender loving care, the jet black one, which he'd named Sylvia after his grandmother, was his favorite. She was the one person while he was growing up who always believed in whatever dreams he dared to hope for. Each time he held this guitar in his hands he felt her spirit inside him giving him the strength to reach for one more piece of his dreams.

Strength was something he needed an extra measure of that night. That afternoon his wife, Sascha, had served him with divorce papers.

He should have been surprised; but in his heart he'd known it was coming. If a musician's life was hard for the musicians themselves, it could be twice as hard on the wives and families who had to struggle through long absences and support from a distance. Sascha had warned him often enough over the past several months that she could no longer bear the burden of raising their four year old son Kody all on her own, to say nothing of how much she missed Steve herself. She'd made her decision, not even waiting for the tour to be over a few weeks from now so they could talk things over. Probably on purpose, he thought to himself. She would find it far easier to start the process to terminate their marriage when he was miles away and had little time to fight back.

No time to think of it now, he ordered himself. You have a show to focus on.

Satisfied that Sylvia was in top working condition, Steve returned her to her place of honor in the rack, ran his hands through his long, thick black hair, letting it fall fresh and free down his back. He then closed his eyes and tried to force his mind and heart into a state they called performance mode, where all the problems and stresses, physical, mental, or emotional, were pushed into the background and the music they were about to perform was the only thing that mattered.

Rusty Morgan, whose long, wild, rust colored hair fit his name, paced the backstage area. The youngest Odysseus member, at thirty-seven, and the most full of nervous energy which he burned off in part by running back and forth across the stage during their shows, he always hated the minutes just before the curtain went up and he and Odysseus could do what they came for. He was ready to hit the stage and pour out on the fans who had come to see them all the passion for music that had built up in him since their prior show. It always seemed to him that no matter how much music he gave away, there was more to release, a spring always bubbling up from somewhere deep below, a well that never ran dry. Killing time, waiting for the concert to begin, was torture to him.

While he waited, Rusty turned his thoughts to the four musicians who, along with him, formed Odysseus. Right from the start Dave, Rick,

Terry, Steve and he had meshed, forming a tight bond among themselves. Fourteen years later, they had become brothers in every sense of the word except blood, with a musical bond stronger and more enduring than any bond he'd had with his own blood family.

He wished his biological family could see him now. His parents had both been furious at his decision to follow his dream to play music, and not just any music but the heavy metal he'd fallen in love with. They hated the looks of the musicians he called heroes, and what they perceived to be a wild, drug-filled, sex-filled lifestyle. If they hadn't severed all contact with him once he'd made his choice final, he would have been able to prove to them that not every metal musician lived that way. If they were still a part of his life, he could have shown them how the music he and Odysseus generated so deeply moved their audience, how the power of some songs brought the audience to their feet, cheering and singing along, while other, softer, deeper songs moved their listeners to tears. If his family could see him now, maybe they'd be proud of him after all.

There was no more time to think of his family. The announcer for the radio station that had promoted their show was speaking to the crowd, his clear, booming voice echoing throughout the arena. Show time was here at last.

Metal music audiences come in a variety of ages and backgrounds. Where its followers were once young, disillusioned and alienated from society, they now run the gamut from young to middle age, and from a wider range of socioeconomic levels. Some are drawn to the pounding drums and background rhythms and blistering guitar solos, others to lyrics that reach into a listener's soul and immortalize in words what the listener's heart struggles to say. While so much of popular music focused on songs about love and failed or successful relationships, metal groups including Odysseus focused on more universal themes of life and death, dreams and unfullfilment, and current social issues, topics mainstream music at large ignored. Whether the audience attending Odysseus shows came for the powerful instrumentals or intense lyrics, they were never disappointed.

Attendees new to the show that night were struck at first by the Greek style pillars at the sides and rear of the stage and Greek landscape image that spread across the graphics screen behind the band's setup. As Odysseus took their positions among the pillars, the screen faded to black, lightning flashed across the screen, and thunder echoed loud enough to shake the floor seats, reaching a crescendo as the band struck their opening notes. Concertgoers who had seen Odysseus perform before anticipated the explosive start and cheered wildly as the first song of the night broke out, as pyrotechnic flames and laser lights flared across the stage. Alternating between hard driving songs that incited the crowd to react and slower paced songs whose plaintive lyrics and stunning guitar and piano exchanges mesmerized those who watched, Odysseus held their fans riveted to the stage. New fans were enthralled not just by the music, but by the visual effects as well, as back screen graphics and pyrotechnics played in alternating succession, dazzling viewers.

Some special kind of magic filled the arena's atmosphere that night. Newcomers to the show weren't aware of it, they only saw that the musicians onstage were as on fire as the occasional pyrotechnics that exploded in front of them.

Fans who were familiar with Odysseus shows, however, noticed the difference. While the band always performed with great passion, that night they reached a new height, notes soaring and slicing through air with laser precision at times, at other times throwing out a solid wall of sound so thick and heavy all the pyrotechnics in the world could not blast through. The crowd watched, mesmerized, hanging on every word and sound.

If the sea of faces in front of them felt magic in the air that night, the band noticed it even more.

Dave felt as if an extra, invisible pair of hands played across his keyboards, adding a depth to them he'd always imagined but had never fully achieved. Tonight the ivories underneath his fingertips danced on their own, elevating to new heights the foundational support his playing gave all the band's songs. While every concert was unique and carried its own feel, he couldn't remember the last time a show caused the hair on his arms and the back of his neck to stand on end, and shivers to run up and down his spine as he played. This was the rare kind of night every musician he knew dreamed of, when the music took on a life of its own and the players were just along for the ride. As Odysseus moved from one song to the next, Dave watched his brothers play their guitars and drums. From the looks on their faces, he could tell they were experiencing the same thing.

Rick felt his bass guitar come alive that night to the point where he could barely keep it reined in. It begged to run wild, like a stallion penned up far too long who suddenly saw an open gate and broke free. Like a herd of wild horses stampeding over hard ground, on the band's heavier songs Rick's bass thundered through the background, sending vibrations through his arms and body. On Odysseus' slower songs, he forced his bass to hold a steady line, like a stallion forced to walk, submitting while still yearning to race through the air. Rick hadn't sensed this much passion in his instrument in months. They were in that special zone where the music seemed to play itself. He was sure his bass would transform itself at any minute into Pegasus and carry him and his brothers through the stratosphere to the heavens themselves where their music would echo across celestial skies.

Rick smiled at Dave and ran through a keyboard-bass line in their song Beyond The Highway which always generated a special bond between them, one of the moments in all their music where their two instruments alone shone like diamonds against a dark background. While all their band brothers were tight, he and Dave had formed a special closeness, borne in part by the supporting roles keyboard and bass held in Odysseus' songs, bouncing off each other various ideas for bass and keyboard passages before sharing them with the others. Terry and Rusty had been close friends before Odysseus formed, they already had a tight bond between them. Steve, well, he was everybody's brother, but he often held himself apart, separated from the rest of them by an invisible wall. Over fourteen years they'd each learned when to push past that wall and when to leave it unchallenged.

Rick turned and nodded to Terry as a new song began, one that opened with a blistering drum and bass passage that had the crowd cheering three bars in.

From the raised platform upon which his drums had been set up, Terry could watch his bandmates and a good portion of the crowd. The audience had remained on their feet, an ecstatic, singing, adoring sea of humanity, ever since the show started. The same rapture he saw on the crowd's faces he could feel in his bones, a feeling of completeness, wholeness, as the music poured out of his arms and legs as he spent every ounce of energy he possessed in raising and lowering his sticks and hitting his drum pedals. He was not only doing what he loved, he was living out just what he'd been created for, fulfilling a destiny that had been planted inside him long before he had been born. Every cell in his body had been formed to make music that touched and moved its listeners, and that night he moved them more powerfully than ever before.

For one flash of a moment, Terry recalled the voices that had always encouraged him to follow anything other than music. His father had insisted he become a banker, a worthy profession guaranteeing he would never be out of a job. His mother, seeing he held no desire to join his father, had tried to convince him he would be a natural at law, with his quick analytical mind and excellent academic skills. He'd ignored them both, as well as his aunts and uncles who pushed more sensible paths, insisting he needed to follow his dream of heavy metal music, the same pounding, shouting, headbanging music his heroes played. He'd rather live a broke, starving life doing what he loved than take any job that provided security but killed his soul.

In the electric, fully charged, enthused arena that night, he was grateful to the gods he'd followed his heart. He glanced at Steve, recognized the same joy on the guitarist's face he was sure played across his own, and wished somehow this night would never end.

Steve felt the energy the crowd gave off, a palpable force that he could reach out and grab handfuls of if his hands hadn't already been glued to his guitar. Something special was in the air that night; he couldn't put his finger on exactly what, or where it was coming from, he only knew from the exhilaration that coursed through his veins that this was one of those rare nights every musician dreamed of but few fully experienced, when the music came together in just the right way that the songs fairly flew through the night on their own. He was sure if he took his hands off whichever guitar he played at any moment that night that guitar would carry on playing notes without him. Nights like this, Steve wanted to play forever. The hell with the rest of the world, with all its stresses, fears, and pain. Let it all fall away. If he could lock the doors to the world outside and remain here with these ecstatic fans and his band brothers forever, sharing music that somehow reached the deepest parts of all their hearts and either soothed the pain so many hid there, or released their fears and gave them license to be as crazy as they dared, he would gladly do it. Doors never remained locked, though. Nights like this never lasted long enough. Soon the outside world would force its way back in. All he could do was soak up every moment of this special night, gather it into every pore, every cell, every fiber of his body like one hoarded diamonds. On harder days to come, when the world was its ugly, cruel self again, he would have this treasure to return to, to soothe him and once again help him find hope.

Throughout the show Steve exchanged looks with his Odysseus brothers, catching the visual cues they always sent each other to keep their songs and their show on track. While they always played as a tight unit, that night they performed as one, reading each other's minds, knowing where each other would take their music next, improvising here and there yet never losing each other along the way as if they were in truth one mind and body, and not five individuals who performed music because that was their job.

Show after show, month by month, for years Odysseus had plied their craft. Rusty had grown accustomed to the routine of strapping on a guitar, taking his place on stage, and running through single notes, chords and riffs, at times making his guitar sound sad, soulful, sweet, other times turning it into a raging monster. He'd grown used to giving and taking cues with his bandmates, accepting applause from an audience of appreciative fans, then moving on to the next show. Each night he and his brothers on this musical journey gave their best, each show they strove to reach the highest mark they could, to leave everything on the stage, to hold nothing back.

Some rare nights they exceeded anything they thought they were capable of. The show in St. Louis was one of those nights. They soared higher than Rusty had ever experienced before. Some supernatural force had swept in, as if the gods themselves had taken over and Rusty and his brothers were just puppets going through the motions the gods dictated. The notes and words seemed to live and breathe on their own as if each were alive. He could see from the audience's reaction and interaction that the words they sang hit deeper within the crowd's hearts than he'd ever witnessed. For the second time that night he wished his family and all the people who had doubted him, who had never believed in his dream, could see how the music they played touched so many lives. He wished they could see how high up in the music world he had risen. He wished they could watch as he proved them all wrong about the choice he'd made.

Rusty closed his eyes as he danced his guitar through Reason To Fly, the title track from their latest album. On this song he played lead guitar while Steve took one of his infrequent turns playing rhythm. Rusty loved, in particular, the exchange between his guitar and Dave's keyboards in the center segment of the song, both instruments so powerful it felt to him that they pulled each other back and forth, not just instrument-wise but physically as well, their bodies swaying and long hair flying. Tonight, when their music soared higher than he'd ever felt, Rusty knew this song was on fire, each note a glistening spark, an explosion of fireworks that held the crowd on its feet, almost breathless, the reverberations of all Odysseus' instruments and amplifiers vibrating through them all.

Towards the end of their show Odysseus performed Thin Line, Terry's favorite song, the one that still floored him no matter how often they'd played it over the past four years since its release. The longest song in their repertoire, it started out simple and slow, built very quickly to a full heavy metal beat with complex lyrics exploring the fragile separation between life and death. Terry loved the delicate keyboard line that ran through the song, how the bass entered and laid down a strong foundation that carried the rest of the song through to its soft, gentle end, how Steve and Rusty alternated lead guitar on this song, how the vocals bounced between Steve, Rusty, Rick and Dave, each of them taking the lead at some point while others held the backup positions.

Rusty, who had written Thin Line, found this to be his favorite song as well. Each time they performed it, he reveled in the rich tapestry each of them wove with their instruments and vocals. That night, Thin Line shone so brilliant it rivaled a full moon illuminating a midnight black sky, each note, each word, hanging like crystal prisms through which the story of life and death was reflected. Some nights Rusty played parts of this song with his eyes closed, absorbing the magic of the song into the depths of his soul. On that night, the magic was in the air already. Eyes open, he caught the enthralled looks on the faces of the front row audience, some of whom he recognized from previous shows. He caught sight of Rick, Dave, Terry, and Steve's faces, each reflecting the same ecstasy he was feeling. That night they soared as high as the Hubble space telescope. If he had it within his powers, they would never come back to earth.

By the time the show ended, the people who'd filled the arena felt three things: their ears would never recover, they were physically spent, and they'd experienced one of the most magical, powerful, emotional shows ever. Walking to their cars, catching cabs, or grabbing spots on one of the city's public transportation options, they all spoke the same words.

"They were on fire tonight!"

"Best show I've ever seen!"

"Now you know why I never miss their concerts!"

Within a day their hearing would be recovered, their bodies restored, but the brilliance of Odysseus' show would remain in their memories for months to come.

Two

We give the audience what pleases them, make it look so easy, they have no clue.

—Sinéad Tyrone, *Brotherhood*

Rusty woke earlier than the rest of Odysseus. The resident insomniac on their tour bus, he'd slept very little that night. At first exhilaration from their St. Louis show left his mind buzzing long after the others had given in to sleep. Then the sound of rain beating on the bus's roof over his bunk kept him awake.

Even sleep, once it settled over him, was fragile, disturbed by nightmares borne of worries and unresolved issues from recent days.

In the past few weeks Steve had been prickly and gruff with each of the Odysseus members, most of all Rusty, so much so Rusty has given him the nickname "Old Porcupine" in his mind, although never to any of their band brothers, and certainly never to Steve's face. In sound checks, in preshow warmups, even in down time on the bus, no matter what Rusty did he was on the receiving end of icy glares or disapproving looks or, worst of all, a reprimand such as "Why are you playing that song that way," or "What the hell are you doing now?"

In his dreams that night Rusty saw a dark, shapeless, nameless shadow hovering over every step he took, every task he set his hands to. Everything he and Odysseus touched in that dream fell apart and a thick, oppressive spirit hung over them. Everywhere he turned the dark spirit pursued him. Rusty woke, panicked, just as the dark shadow threatened to crush him.

He slid off his upper bunk, careful to not disturb Terry in the bed below, and stepped back to the lounge area where he made a cup of coffee then settled on one of the bench seats where he could view the world rolling by in early morning light. No dawn broke on the morning's horizon; instead, the same steady rain that had fallen all night cast a soft drumming against the bus's roof and windows, and the bus's wheels on wet pavement played a satiny underlying hum. Judging by the weather maps he pulled up on his cellphone, he saw the rain would track along the same direction they were headed; the gray skies that hung low over the road they were on now would accompany them throughout the day.

As he drank from his steaming black coffee, Rusty revisited the show from the night before. Awake, with no night demons chasing him, he could still feel the high off the St. Louis audience, and the majestic brilliance with which Odysseus had performed. He hadn't felt that level of magic in their shows in so long he'd almost forgotten they had ever possessed such ability. Now it all flooded back to him, the exhilaration that performing could raise when all the elements combined just right, and along with it memories of when he'd first experienced that musical high with Odysseus.

It had been in the early weeks after he and Steve had joined forces.

After their late night burgers and beer meeting, Steve and Rusty had wasted no time in enlisting Terry, Rick and Dave to join their venture. The first few days they experimented with each other's music, feeling their way through various songs and styles. Within a week they had adjusted to each other's manners of playing, each of them fitting in with the others like parts of an engine aligning with other components just right so the engine would hum.

"You were right about Dave," Rusty admitted to Steve one night as their first week of working together came to a close. "He adds a whole new dimension to the metal sound I've always generated."

"The whole band's gelling, alright," Steve agreed. "I think we're ready to move away from the songs we're all familiar with. What do you think of these?"

Rusty looked over the sheets of music Steve had handed him. "These are good. Your lyrics rock! Do you mind if I play around with the notes a bit?"

"No, I want you to."

Steve and Rusty tested out various pieces, working between themselves at first then drawing the other Odysseus members in, experimenting with keyboard and bass, lead guitar, rhythm guitar and drums, searching for the combination of each that would bring out a new, dynamic sound, a cross between metal and progressive rock that none of the bands around them had yet developed.

Rusty remembered the day their sound clicked. They'd been testing out one of Steve's new songs. After the first verse, Steve held a hand up to stop them.

"Dave, that passage you played, could you start the song with that?"

Dave complied, giving the metal song a classical piano introduction. Next, Steve brought Terry's drums in, gentle at first, adding Rick's bass lines and then Rusty's guitar, building the sound by layers before he entered with lyrics and lead guitar. They ran through the song that way three more times.

By the end of the last round, Rusty and Steve both looked at each other, eyes bright with excitement.

"What do you think?" Steve asked, exhilaration tinged with nervousness at what Rusty's reaction would be, the same nervousness he felt whenever he stood on the edge of realizing a dream. Dreams were fragile, one negative opinion could crush any confidence he felt. Confidence was sometimes a rare commodity in his world.

A slow grin spread across Rusty's face. "I think you've found the sound you're looking for!"

Rusty was so lost in thought now, remembering Odysseus' early days, he didn't hear Terry open the cupboard next to him, select a coffee mug, and brew fresh coffee for himself. Rusty jumped when Terry asked, "Refill?"

"Good God, you scared me!"

"Yeah, you were miles away!" Terry laughed as he slid onto the bench seat across from Rusty. "Anywhere interesting?"

Rusty selected a toasted coconut donut, a variety they rarely got, from the box Terry had set on the table between them. "New York. Years ago, when we first joined up with Steve."

"I remember when you called me about the idea. You were so damn excited," Terry remarked in between bites of a glazed donut.

"You were too!" Rusty recalled.

"Hell yeah, I was! I would have signed up with any band at that point, but Steve Marner, man, that was the biggest draw anyone could have offered us."

"Someone that high up in the business could have been a real challenge to work with, but he wasn't. Right from the start he was agreeable, easy to get along with, didn't push any of us around."

"Yeah, back then." Terry cupped his hands around his coffee mug, absorbing as much warmth into them as he could, and thought not of earlier days but of more recent weeks, of sound checks, gigs, and countless hours riding their bus, each day it seemed punctuated by Steve's moody glares or angry outbursts. "He sure has changed."

Rusty pulled a jelly donut out of the box, then pushed the container towards Terry's side of the table. "You better keep this by you or I'll eat the whole damn box!"

"What I don't understand," Terry continued as he chose a jelly donut as well then set the box back on the counter away from their reach, "is why he's taking so much out on you. He doesn't bother much with the rest of us, but you, it's like you can't do anything right anymore. What's that all about?"

Rusty shook his head. "Damned if I know. I think he's just tired."

"We're all tired. None of the rest of us are taking our frustrations out on each other."

Rusty watched several cars pass their bus, spray from the passing cars' wheels in the now heavier rain trailing behind like comets rising out of the pavement. "Do you think we've reached the end of the road?" He asked after a while.

Terry knew what Rusty meant but didn't want to think in that direction, and instead went for the obvious laugh. "Hell no! We've got six or seven hours ahead of us."

Rusty shook his head and allowed a slight grin to cross his face. "You jerk! You know what I mean."

Forced to face the question, Terry studied the grain of the oak table in front of him, noting how in places the lines were straight and neat, in others swelled as the grain moved around a knot or scar in the wood. Maybe Odysseus was just shifting around some invisible knot. Maybe all the turmoil, the moodiness, the conflict this tour had been plagued with was just some natural sifting through process they would soon move past. "I don't think we're breaking up," he answered Rusty. "Do you?"

Rusty focused on the outside view again. "Fourteen years is a long time. Most bands don't make it this far. Maybe Steve's bored, maybe there's something else he wants to do but he just doesn't know how to tell us." He decided there was no further point in dissecting a problem they weren't sure of. "Whatever it is, he'll let us know when he's ready."

He turned back to the view outside the window beside him. They had moved overnight from cityscapes to rural regions; now he watched a procession of farmhouses and barns roll by, an odd cow or horse left out in falling rain, one barn so dilapidated Rusty thought one brisk wind would bring it down. He'd seen that barn a half dozen times in the band's travels over the years, and felt sad now at the thought it might not survive another winter.

Landscapes always changed. Rusty knew that. Fields became parking lots, housing developments, or shopping and business strip malls. He thought again of the barn they'd just passed. How many harsh storms had it endured? Did its bones feel as fatigued as it looked? Did it ever feel empty and alone, with no animals to shelter or people buzzing around tending to chores? He wondered if he would feel that way, empty and aimless, if Steve had in mind stepping away and Odysseus disbanded.

Rusty shook his head to jolt himself out of the gray mood that had begun to fill his mind. "Enough of that," he ordered himself. "Find something else to fix your thoughts on before you drive yourself and the rest of the guys crazy."

Even as Rick and Dave joined Rusty and Terry at the breakfast table and the sounds of general talk and laughter filled their bus, Steve remained stretched out on his bunk, staring at the last photo he'd taken of Sascha and Kody earlier that year in front of the lilac tree he and Sascha had planted. She'd chosen a dark purple variety, her favorite flower and color, with the thought that every year they would take a photo of Kody in front of the tree and be able to trace the growth of both over time.

Viewing Sascha's divorce request, Steve wondered who would take those photos now, and if he'd ever get to see them.

He forced depressing thoughts back to the corner of his mind where he kept them locked away. "You're running too far ahead of things," he told himself. "Call her. You can work this all out."

His phone call went to Sascha's voicemail. "Sasch, it's me. I got your papers. We need to talk. Call me."

After he'd left the message, he thought of a dozen better ways he could have said things, but it was done. When she called him back he could refine his approach.

Each of the Odysseus members had developed their own ways of dealing with long hours on the bus. Dave passed the time reading, with a focus on classical literature although in recent months he'd started to include more current bestseller novels. Books had always transported him to other worlds: when he was young and in school and not a member of the popular, athletic set they kept him company; when he was in college and surrounded by party animals they kept him sane; and now, on a cramped bus with too many miles to cross before he could get out and stretch his legs, they occupied his mind. While stories always fueled his imagination, now they also laid the foundations for Odysseus songs, as he shared the gist of the stories he read with his Odysseus brothers, inspiring themes and lyrics from them.

Rick spent part of every bus day reviewing videos Laurel had made with Ryan and Christine, catching him up on what they were learning in school, keeping him involved with their family as best as possible despite the distance between them.

Some days Rick wondered what life would be like if he had a regular job, the kind where he went to an office by day and spent evenings home with his family. Sometimes, especially when bus life seemed its most tortuous, the idea felt like paradise, the luxury of countless hours with his wife and children so appealing he was tempted to let go of the traveling musician lifestyle and settle for any job, no matter how mundane, that would allow him that heaven.

Then music would call to his heart once again, and he would let go of his home life dream. Music would always pull him back to the road in the end.

Eventually Rick would log off his computer, Dave would set his books aside, and they would start a new chess game, Dave the ever patient teacher and Rick the eager student absorbing as much of Dave's instructions as he could at each sitting.

Chatter from the chess lessons drifted to where Terry sat writing in his journal. At the start of every tour, the band always presented Terry with two new notebooks and a dozen pens. Ever since they'd all joined together as Odysseus, Terry had journalized their path towards the pinnacle of success they'd eventually reached, earning him the nickname "The Historian." Every day he covered what had happened at shows the night before, various conversations they'd all shared, thoughts for new music and hopes and dreams of each of his brothers not just for Odysseus' future, but for their personal lives as well.

When his journaling for each day was complete, Terry turned to drawing. He tried a number of styles as he drew or painted, from caricature, to impressionism, to realism. He preferred the discipline of realism, capturing details in as accurate a manner as possible. He drew from cellphone photos of places they visited, or photos he took of Odysseus members at various moments, but time after time he returned to drawing what he loved best, the ocean. Sometimes he would work from photos, other times from memory, capturing through water color or colored pencil the myriad blues and greens of the ocean waves he had memorized, sometimes placid in early morning or late evening light, sometimes wind driven with huge swells and whitecaps. While he worked, his heart ached with a deep longing to stand at his favorite viewing post, an outcropping of rocks above a stone crusted beach where he would watch for hours as the mighty Atlantic tossed about below him. On long bus days Terry's need to stand by his beloved ocean gnawed at him like a giant fish out of water too long; at least through drawing or painting he could feel some connection with her, no matter how tenuous.

Rusty would have loved to pass his free time carving and creating wood pieces, from tables and trays to wall art and bird houses. He loved the smell of sawdust and fresh cut wood, and the silky smooth feel of sanded, finished pieces. On some items he would carve intricate designs, on others he would fashion a simple heart or thin basic lines.

Woodworking on the bus was too hard. Small electric tools were not easy to use on a moving vehicle. Even hand carving with the fine set of tools his Odyseus brothers had given him last Christmas was a challenge; one pothole or unexpected swerve could cause his hands to slip and ruin a piece.

Instead, while riding the bus Rusty passed his time formulating plans. He wrote out ideas for designing various gardens on his property, a vegetable garden here, a rose garden there, a pond stocked with goldfish or koi, a patch of berry bushes. He designed on paper some of the woodworking projects he would like to create when time allowed. Free time never seemed to come around anymore; when it did he was too tired or too busy catching up on house and property care to get to any side projects, and his design file grew more voluminous with each passing tour. Still all of the planning helped the bus time go quicker, and someday when the time was right he'd be grateful he'd captured and stored so many good ideas.

They arrived in Baltimore for their next show and jumped right into pre-show preparations, with each of the Odysseus members participating in radio interviews and other media contacts, then showers and backstage warm ups at the venue where their show would be held that night.

While the others spent their time getting ready, Steve tried calling Sascha twice more. The second call went to voicemail. The third time he thought someone answered, then they were cut off, or the person at the other end hung up.

Sascha was home when Steve's first call came through. She recognized his number, allowed it to go to voicemail, then played the message back.

"I told you." She turned to her best friend, Kit, who sat in the family room enjoying coffee and their favorite cinnamon twist pastries while Kit's four year old son, Garret, played with Kody. "Now he wants to talk! Six months I've tried to have this conversation and Steve couldn't be bothered."

"Are you going to call him back?" Kit asked.

Sascha sent her a steel emerald-eyed glare. "I've given him all the chances I can. He can go to hell now."

She let the second call go to voicemail as well. When the third call came in, she accepted it then terminated the call before he had a chance to say a word.

Rusty thought the Baltimore show that night went well, Odysseus sounded tight, the crowd responded with enthusiasm. To him it was much the same as every other show they'd done.

He was stunned when Steve stormed off the stage after the encore and headed straight for him.

"What the hell were you playing tonight? It sure didn't sound like any song we rehearsed!"

Confused, Rusty glared back at Steve. "I played all our songs the same way I have all through the tour."

"You sounded like shit tonight! You better get it right in Columbus."

With that, Steve stomped off to their bus.

Radio station and newspaper personnel witnessed Steve's outburst, as had a number of crew members and venue employees. As incensed as he was at Steve, Rusty didn't want to make matters worse. He handed the guitar he'd carried offstage to Bryan, then gathered his belongings in his duffel bag, each movement slow, deliberate, demonstrating great restraint in the presence of those outside the band.

Terry, Dave and Rick all took their cues from Rusty and wrapped things up with a minimum of chatter, then followed Rusty to the bus.

Once they were all on board, away from the public eye and with the door locked behind them, Rusty turned to Steve, eyes blazing.

"Don't you ever do that again! Don't ever ream me out in front of others. Even if I'm in the wrong, which I wasn't tonight, if you've got a problem with me you wait until we're alone before you come after me! You got that?"

Steve didn't back down. "Do your job right and I won't have to have a go at you, in public or in private!"

"There's nothing wrong with my playing or anything else I'm doing. I don't know what the hell you're on about!" Rusty turned to the others. "Do any of you know?"

Rick and Dave, hoping a neutral stand would diffuse tensions, refused to answer. Rusty understood and didn't hold it against them. Their taking his side would only make matters worse.

Terry, though, backed Rusty all the way. "Your playing sounded fine to me."

"I should have known you'd take his side," Steve snapped at Terry.

Rusty exploded, "Don't you go after him!"

Afraid that tempers would rage out of control, Terry stepped between Rusty and Steve. "Both of you stop it. You've said what you had to say. Back off now and cool down."

He held his ground while Steve glared at him and Rusty glared at Steve. After what seemed forever, Rusty turned away, grabbed a beer out of the refrigerator and a deck of cards from the drawer under the counter. He set the deck down hard on the table. "Poker. Terry, you deal."

Glad for the diversion, Rick and Dave slid onto the bench seat across from Rusty. "Hey Terry, grab beers for me and Dave!" Rick called out.

Steve watched as the others settled into their game. Even if he wanted to, after the outburst between himself and Rusty there was no way he'd be welcome in the game. He headed for his bunk and whatever movie he could pull up on his laptop, listening through his earphones so he couldn't hear the laughter and light banter he was missing out on.

Three

I wish at times we could have landed somewhere in between
—Sinéad Tyrone, *Somewhere In Between*

Steve rose before dawn the next morning. Between his inability to reach Sascha by phone and his blow up with Rusty he'd slept very little; any sleep he fell into was disturbed by odd dreams, one where he'd been a baseball pitcher and had shown up for a championship game to find he was in the wrong city, one where he was driving somewhere and was so beset by wrong turns and highway accidents he never reached his destination. Realizing at last sleep was not meant for him, he surrendered to the day, moved with his laptop to the front lounge where he would not wake the others and, fueled by his inner relentless drive and multiple cups of high octane dark roast coffee, within a couple of hours had completed lyrics and the first layer of music for one new song and drafted a schedule for Odysseus' next round of studio work after this tour was over.

Rusty, the first of the others to wake, ignored Steve and took his coffee and tablet to the rear lounge to work. Dave and Rick joined him soon after. Steve did his best to ignore the conversation at the rear of the bus. He waited until Terry had joined them, then stepped back to where they had gathered.

"Check your e-mails when you get done here," he ordered. "I've sent you all a new song to start learning and a schedule for us to dig into recording after Christmas."

No mention of the night before. The others exchanged glances, not sure whether they should bring the prior night's incident up or let it go.

Rusty took the initiative, "Schedule already? How soon after Christmas did you have in mind?"

"Mid-January." Steve caught the disappointment on their faces but chose to ignore it. What the hell did they think? That the next album would generate itself without them?

"I thought we were going to take a longer break. I was planning a trip to the Pacific Coast with Renee." Terry saw any plans he hoped to arrange with his girlfriend evaporate.

"I was counting on more time with my family." Rick's let down came through in his voice. "I thought that's what we all agreed when we started this tour, that we all needed a longer stretch at home."

They all looked to Dave, the one member who hadn't spoken yet. He could have cared less, an extra few weeks in an empty house meant nothing to him. For Rick's sake though, if for no one else's, Dave told Steve, "Mid-January doesn't seem much of a break to be honest."

"Fine!" Anger flashed in Steve's tone again. "You know our contract calls for another album next year. If you don't care about breach of contract issues, we can cancel the studio time."

As Steve turned to walk away, Rusty grabbed his arm. As soon as he realized what he'd done, he dropped his hold. "Let's not start where we left off last night. No one's saying we don't want to do the next album. We're just tired. Good God, we've done three albums and six tours in five years. Even you must know that's a hell of a lot. We're all burned out, even you must feel that."

An idea occurred to Terry. He was sure Steve wouldn't like it, but he offered it just the same. "Technology has changed so many things. You know most groups record tracks at home, then have them mixed and mastered with much less studio time. Why don't we record as much of the album digitally as we can. We can do our individual parts that way, give each of us more time at home, then finish it in the studio."

Steve shook his head. "We've never taken shortcuts before. Our albums always have that in-studio sound; it shows in the quality of our work. You know this business. New music. New shows. High quality in both. If we want to stay on top, that's the game."

"Is staying on top that important?"

Steve looked at Rusty as if he'd been asked whether breathing was vital, whether a heartbeat was necessary. "Isn't the point of all our work to stay ahead of the pack?"

Rusty looked away from Steve, away from them all. His eyes peered through his surroundings to Odysseus' early days, when money was tight and all that kept them going was their dream. They'd reached their dream and in fact had surpassed any hopes or goals they'd set. When was it all enough, he wondered. In a quiet voice he answered, "I thought the point of our work was to make the best music we could, regardless of standings and album sales."

Steve held his harsh glare on Rusty a full minute before telling them all, "Our best music is recorded in the studio, not in our homes. Mid-January. Be ready."

Tension between Steve and the rest of the band remained so thick the rest of the day a chain saw would not have cut through it. Sound check and meals were subdued, no one dared crack jokes or tease each other. They dressed for the Columbus show in silence. Whatever magic had graced their music in St. Louis was nowhere to be found now. They played all the notes and sang all the words with perfection, but even they sensed something was missing.

Reviews of the Columbus show the next morning noted that while Odysseus' music itself was as solid as ever, the band seemed disconnected, each member distant from one another.

The next day was a day off, which meant a coveted hotel night after the show. Their normal routine on those nights would be late dinner and drinks together before going separate ways for the night.

Still fuming over the band's failure to understand the necessity of cutting their January break short and returning to the studio, Steve left after the Columbus show without a word to the others. "I'll see you on the bus tomorrow afternoon," he texted Terry so none of the others would worry. As if any of them would miss him, he thought.

Rick knew his brother and sister-in-law would be at the Columbus show. They showed up backstage with a surprise, Laurel, in tow.

"I know you'll be home soon," she told him, "but I couldn't wait!"

He hugged her tight. "I'm so glad to see you! Did you bring the kids?"

She wrapped an arm around him and whispered in his ear in her most sensual voice, "They're staying with my parents. I thought a night to ourselves would be a treat."

Rick's brother laughed. "You two go ahead! We'll see you at breakfast tomorrow."

As always, a number of girls hung around the venue after the show, hoping to catch one of the Odysseus guys for more than an autograph or a photo. Dave recognized one of them, a dark haired girl with too much makeup and danger in her eyes. He steered clear of her. Instead, out of the corner of his eye he spotted another girl, one with long rust brown hair and enormous blue eyes. She seemed to be alone, and nervous judging by the way her eyes darted from the doorway that led outside to the crowd congregating around the band, as if gauging whether it was worth her time to wait in line for a brief bit of conversation with one of the guys or perhaps more if luck was on her side.

Dave was intrigued by the girl. She wasn't the most beautiful of the backstage horde who had gathered that night, although she was pretty enough in her jeans, lace top and leather jacket. Something about her eyes drew him in; when not darting around, they were intense, inviting him to explore what lie deep behind them.

Dave and each of the Odysseus guys had fallen victim from time to time to the temptations groupies held. The road took a toll on every aspect of life, including the desire for sex. They were human, after all. They had needs and desires like other men; God knows they had more than their fair share of opportunities to have those needs met. He was divorced, a free agent with no one to answer to in the morning. The music tonight, although as powerful and eloquent as always, had not assuaged the emptiness that echoed through the chambers of his heart. Dave was sure a night with the blue eyed girl would ease his longings, even if only for a while.

"How about a drink in my room," he offered. "We can order a midnight snack if you'd like, get to know each other better."

The girl smiled, slipped her arm around Dave's and headed for the hotel, leaving a number of jealous girls behind.

Rusty turned to Terry, "What'll it be? Pizza around the corner, or are you just heading to bed?"

Terry wanted nothing more than a peaceful night away from the public, but he was keyed up, as they always were after a show, and knew he wouldn't sleep right away. "Pizza to go," he suggested. "We can take it up to my room and talk."

An hour later, he set aside the remains of his fourth piece of cheese, pepperoni and mushroom pizza. "This confirms it! Officially the worst pizza ever!"

Rusty laughed so loud he was afraid whoever was in the next room would hear him. "It took you four slices to decide that? I gave up after two!"

"You always were faster than me!" Terry leaned back against the headboard and pillows propped up there. "That had to be one of our worst shows in years."

Rusty popped open a fresh beer and settled into the lone chair in Terry's room. "It was awful alright."

"At least the fans didn't seem to notice."

"Or care. They were thrilled to see us, and we didn't play bad. They might not have caught onto any problems we were having."

"We might as well have been playing from different countries." Terry finished his first beer and opened a second. "Is this all down to Steve and our last twenty four hours? Or is that just a symptom of a deeper problem between us all?"

"Steve sure isn't helping. God, I don't want to rush back into the studio so soon." Rusty studied the carpet on the floor, the faint gold diamond pattern against brown meant to brighten the room, noticed the stains the pattern failed to hide and the threadbare path along the foot of the bed where too many people had walked, and searched his mind for an answer. "Maybe after he's been home a couple of weeks he'll see things in a different way. Maybe Christmas will soften his heart."

Terry laughed, "Have we been good enough this year to deserve a Christmas miracle?"

"If we're basing it on that, we're already screwed!"

After so many years of friendship and brotherhood, Terry could read through Rusty as if his mind were encased in glass instead of flesh and bone. Rusty was so much better at seeing a whole scenario, not just what was happening at the moment or what had occurred in recent days. "What you asked me a few days ago, about reaching the end of the road, is that what you think?"

"I don't know. We've all been so close, but this year the fun has gone out of it. We don't laugh like we used to, and if we have another night like last night . . . ." He let his thoughts trail off, afraid to speak into air words that might self fulfill.

Terry let the conversation end there as well. Most times he pushed a conversation to its conclusion, pulling out of whoever else was speaking what lie buried deep within them, what he knew they most wanted to express but held back. He often had to dig deep to get Rusty to open up, something Rusty always thanked him for later.

Tonight, he sensed pushing deeper wasn't what Rusty wanted. The tour would be over soon. They would have plenty of time after to dissect the band's problems and debate possible solutions. If he pulled out the feelings Rusty was so cautious with now, he might hear things he wasn't ready for. No, tonight he'd let the conversation end as both of them wanted.

Terry rose from the bed, yawned, stretched, and closed the pizza box on the remains of their late night meal. "Call me when you're ready to go down for breakfast."

Rusty rose and stretched as well. "Nope! I'm sleeping straight through until lunch!"

Before falling asleep Terry texted Renee, "God, I miss you! Counting down the days until I'll be home. Can't wait to see you. Love you!" He dreamt that night of sitting on the ground at his favorite oceanside lookout point, Renee next to him and his arm around her, both he and Renee wrapped in a blanket for warmth, a full moon casting golden light on the waves below and a million stars shining overhead.

Rusty stretched out on his hotel room bed, reveling in the spaciousness and comfort of it compared to his tour bus bunk. Any other night he would have found a good movie and fully relaxed. Tonight the show and his conversation with Terry still churned in his mind. He hated problems for which he had no solutions; he sure as hell had no ideas for how to deal with Steve. He could only pray they'd be able to hold things together for the remainder of the tour, and that a much needed break beyond that would sort them all out. Realizing he could do nothing about their problems tonight, he turned the television on at last, flipped through the channels until he found a home repair show which would either give him ideas for how to deal with various fixes needed in the old country house he had bought years ago, or lull him to sleep.

Dave woke early in the morning, dawn casting a pale light through the window whose curtains he had forgotten to close the night before. The girl next to him in the bed was still asleep. What did she say her name was? She'd been a good choice the night before, responsive, almost inspirational in her lovemaking prowess, requiring very little conversation before or after.

He only wished the satisfaction he'd felt then he could still feel now. Instead, he felt empty. Nothing seemed right this morning. Not with Steve, who seemed to have so isolated himself from the rest of Odysseus there was no way to reconnect with him now. Not with the band itself, having somehow started on a downward spiral he didn't know how to pull them out of. Certainly not with the girl lying next to him. Single status or no, what had seemed right the night before now seemed one more colossal wrong step.

"You're a fool, Cardinale," he told himself. "You're too old for this crap. Do you never learn?"

Dave dressed, gathered the few belongings he had brought with him, stuffed them into his overnight bag and left, removing the do not disturb sign from the outer handle as he closed the door behind him. He slipped his bag into the cargo hold of their bus and informed Andy, their bus driver, that he'd return to the bus by noon. Grabbing coffee to go from a nearby coffee shop, he walked the streets around the hotel not caring where they led, incognizant of whatever shops or buildings he passed, only aware of an inner need to keep moving physically, mentally, emotionally. The repetitive motion of setting one foot in front of the other on firm concrete at least soothed the physical need. The mental and emotional emptiness would take more time to heal.

"I love waking up next to you!"

Laurel had waited a good half hour to say those words to Rick. She'd woken to find him still sleeping, worn out from the show the night before and from weeks of touring. She had watched him as he slept, noting how the tired lines she'd seen around his eyes the night before had smoothed in his sleep, how a bit more gray had crept into his long brown hair, how much he needed a shave.

Rick woke at last, blinking his eyes open and closed a few times before leaving them open, inhaling deep then releasing the air he'd taken in, stretching his legs to full length underneath smooth, clean sheets. Then, fully awake, he saw Laurel and smiled. Under the sheets he ran his hand over her skin, as soft and smooth as he remembered, still carrying a hint of her signature perfume.

"I love waking up to you too." He grinned and drew her closer. "Know what I love even more?"

After they made love again, they turned on their backs and studied the ceiling. "I'll be home soon," he stated. "I can't wait."

"Good! I'll start making a list of chores to keep you out of trouble!" Laurel teased.

"Don't make it too long," he teased back. "We still have some catching up to do!"

Laurel turned to face him again, her smile replaced by a look of concern. "What was wrong with you all last night? You played like you were total strangers, not the band of brothers you've been for years."

Rick chewed his inner lip, a habit he fell back on whenever troubled by something too complex to fathom. "I wish I knew. We've hit a rough spot. Steve's been a bear the past several days. I think we can work through it, but let's not waste our time worrying about it today."

"Are you okay?"

"Yeah, babe. I'm fine. I'll be even better once I get home."

The sun had almost reached its zenith above the city by the time Steve rose. Two things had nagged at his mind most of the night: Odysseus and Sascha. He had no excuse for the anger he'd displayed in recent days. He knew none of his bandmates understood where the rage came from. They'd always held to a code of mutual respect among them all, yet now he was breaking that code. He knew they were all worn out from constant work; he was too, but he didn't see anyone else taking on the responsibility of mapping out their next steps. It all fell to him, or at least that's how he felt. If he drove them all too hard now, they'd thank him later when the album was complete.

Then there was Sascha. Springing divorce papers on him then refusing to discuss things was cruel. He had to make her see she at least owed him a chance to resolve issues between them.

He reached once more for his phone, praying this time Sascha would answer. When she hadn't answered by the fourth ring he was ready to hang up; just before he did, her voice came through.

"Stop calling me. Have your attorney call mine."

"Sasch!" he called out loud before she could hang up. "Give me five minutes anyway. You can't just file for divorce and not give me a chance to talk with you."

She shouldn't, she knew. He'd have nothing new to say, nothing she could believe anyway. He was Kody's father though, and if for that reason alone she would give him a few minutes now, then let all future contact go through their lawyers.

"Five minutes," she granted him, "starting now."

With no time to waste, Steve dove right in. "I know you're upset, you have every right to be. I ignored everything you tried to tell me. I'm listening now. Can't we work things out between us?"

"Steve, you always promise you'll change, but you never do. I'm tired of the lies. I can't do this anymore."

"One chance. That's all I'm asking. Give me time to sort things out with you. If I don't, say in six months' time, I'll give you your divorce."

Sascha was almost persuaded, not wanting any more than he did to give up on what they once had. Then her common sense took over. He would say anything now; but later he'd go back to the same insane schedule, leaving her and Kody behind.

"No, Steve. I've tried to be patient. I've hoped for, prayed for change that never came. Now the only change I want is a fresh start for me and Kody."

Angry that he couldn't persuade Sascha to see sense, Steve vowed, "If this is the road you want to go down, I'll fight you all the way, alimony, child support, custody, whatever. You'll wish you never started this fight!"

"Fine! Have your lawyer call mine!" With that, Sascha hung up.

Steve stared at his phone for several minutes. Calling Sascha had failed. He couldn't try that again. He had only one option now. He called Jake Terhune, his attorney.

"Sascha's filed for divorce. How do I stop her?"

Four

I do not want to travel this road I am on
  —Sinéad Tyrone, *This Road Carries No Outlet*

"Damn it! Don't ever do that again!" Sasha scolded herself after she hung up on Steve. "Don't talk to him anymore! He only makes you mad."

She was so unnerved by his call, so focused on her anger, that she didn't see the street light change from yellow to red, drove through it, and had to slam on the brakes to miss a car entering the intersection from another direction. A shrill horn and angry shouts from the driver in the other car brought her back to the present.

Glancing in the rear view mirror, Sascha saw that Kody was undisturbed, watching the world through his passenger side window, oblivious to the near accident. Whispering a quick prayer of thanks, she pulled away from the intersection, driving slower, eyes fixed on every moving object around her. She arrived at her parents' house a half hour late to find lunch already laid out and them starting to fill their plates with her mother's specialty chicken and rice casserole.

"We tried calling you." Her mother, Renata, turned an exasperated frown on her. "We thought maybe your schedule had changed or some other problem had come up."

"I'm sorry." Sascha slipped Kody's coat off and hung it with hers on the tree rack that stood by the front door. "Slow traffic on the way here. Kody, go sit by your grandpa."

Renata watched as Sascha microwaved chicken tenders for Kody, then dished up some of her mother's casserole for herself. As they ate, Renata read the agitation in her daughter's face, how Sascha focused on her plate at the exclusion of any conversation around her, and noted her flat, almost businesslike communication with Kody as she tried to get him to eat the chicken tenders in front of him rather than the macaroni and cheese he begged for.

After all her efforts with Kody failed, Sascha snapped, "You're not getting anything else! If you're not going to eat your chicken, you can leave the table!"

Kody slid off his chair and wandered into the family room, a large frown clouding his face.

"Go with him," Renata ordered her husband, Glenn. He complied, and Renata turned to her daughter.

"Alright. What's wrong?"

"Nothing. It's just been a stressful morning." Her mother's face indicated she didn't buy the excuse. Sascha knew she had no choice but to be honest. "I talked to Steve on the way here. I wasn't late because of traffic; I was so stressed by his call I almost got in an accident."

Shocked and scared, Renata ordered, "You can't let that ever happen again! Stay off the phone when you're driving!"

Like a child admonished, Sascha defended, "I know. I just had a weak moment. I was curious about what he had to say."

Renata's face was stone cold. "And what did he say?"

"He wanted to work things out, of course, without the attorneys, without the divorce."

"What did you tell him?"

"That from now on I won't argue with him, he has to go through his lawyer."

Expert at seeing through her daughter like no one else could, Renata waited for the elaboration to come.

"I hate this, Mom. I don't know if I'm doing the right thing. I mean, what's the biggest thing he's done wrong?"

Renata defended her daughter. "Abandoned you, left you to raise Kody alone. You know that."

"He hasn't abandoned me, he's just doing his job. That's what he'll say anyway."

"Doing a job is one thing; but he's away from home more and more. And when he is home he might as well not be, always stuck in his studio, or on the computer, hardly giving you or Kody a glance or a word. Do you want to keep living like that?"

"He hasn't always been that way. You know that."

"But he's that way now; and getting worse, not better."

Sascha had to agree. When Steve had been home at all during the last several months he'd been snappish, impatient, and self absorbed. She could deal with that. What she couldn't take was his increasing temper, lashing out at Kody if Kody interrupted him in the middle of writing a song, yelling at Sascha when she tried to persuade him to join her and Kody for family dinners or outings, or just watch a movie with her at home after Kody had gone to sleep.

"Mom, I know he's been impossible, and he's not going to change no matter how many times he promises. I'll go ahead with the divorce, but I know he'll tell me that's what I signed up for, I should have known right from the start what his life would be like, what our marriage would be. And you know what Mom? He'd be right."

"He's not right. . . ."

"Yes, Mom, he is. He's hard at work trying his best to keep his music going, fighting to stay on top in an unpredictable industry, never knowing what turn it's going to take next, knowing there's a limited time for any band to remain afloat. I'll do what I have to do, but in the back of my mind I feel like a horrible wife who should be showing her husband far more support and understanding, should be standing by his side instead of walking away. For better or worse, that was the vow we made. I feel like I'm violating those vows."

Laughter rose from the family room where Kody and Glenn were playing with toy cars and trucks. Sascha watched them having fun without a care in the world. "Steve's missing out on so much, Mom. He never sees Kody laughing like this anymore. He's missing Kody's childhood."

"He's making his choices." Renata watched Glenn and Kody race their toy cars. "You aren't responsible for what he's losing out on."

"I know that. But am I taking the easy way out by pushing for divorce instead of working through our problems?"

Renata spotted the family photo hanging on the family room wall of Steve, Sascha and Kody taken last May during one of Steve's rare weeks off. Her daughter had smiled that day. She hadn't seen Sascha wear that bright of a smile in weeks. "Divorce is no easy way out," she told her daughter. "Anyone who's gone through it will tell you it was far harder than they thought. You haven't been happy for months; and don't forget, vows are a two way street. Steve hasn't kept up his end of his promise to always be there for you."

All the way home and well into the evening, while watching Kody play, while giving him dinner, then bathing him and preparing him for bed, Sascha's mind waged war with itself as to whether she was on the right course.

Renee sorted through the stacks of books that crowded her already cramped office, some waiting to be cataloged and shelved, others to be sent to partner libraries for circulation, a third group to be taken out of circulation and stored in the central library's archives. While she loved her library assistant job overall, some days she found it harder to face the mundane tasks her job entailed.

She was crazy for books! They filled every corner and shelf of her apartment, and spilled onto tables and chairs when she ran out of shelf space. She loved the feel of them in her hands, covers inviting her to open them and explore new worlds, pages crying out to be turned and reveal their magic language, the heft of them, their structure and sturdiness. Even the smell of them, some fresh and clean, others musty, having lived many lives over the course of their years, filled her senses with excitement and wonder. Electronic books never thrilled her the way physical ones did.

Today the books that surrounded her were mere nuisances, demanding attention while her mind preferred to be elsewhere.

She missed Terry so much it almost suffocated her. She could think of nothing else, he held her mind captive, rendering her unable to focus on, or even consider, the tasks she'd promised herself she would accomplish.

Two hours and three cups of coffee later, having catalogued a total of ten books, Renee turned from her computer to her cellphone and again scrolled through the latest series of photos Terry had sent her, a couple from backstage at a recent show, a few from the bus as they once again traveled from one gig to the next, and one selfie of him seated at a coffee shop. "Lest you should forget how I look," he'd captioned that photo. As if she could ever, in a million years, forget his face, his eyes, his smile.

"That's it," she told herself. "Enough pretending I'll get anything done today! Terry will be home in a few weeks, time to start planning a proper welcome home for him."

She knew by now the first thing he'd want would be sleep, two or three days' worth at least, no schedule or commitments. That was fine with her. She would meet him at the airport, collect his luggage and drive him back to his apartment. Thankful she had a key to his place, she would gather groceries enough to get him through the first week, eggs, bread, milk, the cheese and crackers he was so fond of, and chicken breasts and burgers for his freezer. She would open his apartment windows for an hour before shopping so his rooms would have a clean, fresh air scent when he returned home. With Christmas fast approaching, and him being away so long, he would have no chance to decorate; she would set up a small tree with tinsel and multicolored lights and a few other touches so his apartment would contain at least some festive spirit.

Clean sheets on his bed and fresh towels in his bathroom would complete the picture.

She would stock champagne in his refrigerator so they could celebrate the end of another tour once he was caught up on sleep.

Mrs. Clarke, her supervisor, interrupted her planning. "Can I speak with you?"

"Of course." Renee rose, cleared a pile of books from the chair by her desk, and offered it to her boss.

Mrs. Clarke lowered her trim frame onto the chair and surveyed the stacks of books surrounding the room. "Think you can get all this cleared up in two weeks?"

"Two weeks?" Renee repeated, puzzled. "I'm sure I can, but may I ask why that soon?"

A smile played at the corners of Mrs. Clarke's mouth. "Because that's when I'll be losing you."

Now Renee was completely confused. "I'm not going anywhere, am I?"

"There's an opening for a head librarian at our branch in Candler. I'm recommending you for the position." Mrs. Clarke caught the unsettled look on her assistant's face. "I thought you'd be more excited."

"I am," Renee was quick to assure her. "I just … I'm surprised, and there are a lot of things to think about."

Mrs. Clarke rose to return to her work. "Don't think on it too long. The job posting will be listed tomorrow. I'm sure they'll receive many applications for it. Let me know before the end of the day today if you're interested; with my recommendation you'd almost be guaranteed the position."

Head librarian. Renee watched through her doorway as Mrs. Clarke returned to the front desk and greeted patrons. The doorway to her office afforded a substantial view of the library itself. Small in size, the room's central area held four tables at which patrons could research books, write notes, or wait while others finished their book selections. Three computer stations stood off to one side, and a card catalog with electronic search terminal atop it on another side.

The library in Candler was twice this library's size, more modern, and with a much more up to date catalog. Any librarian or assistant would be thrilled to work there.

So why wasn't she?

Renee knew the answer before the question even entered her mind.

Taking the position in Candler would mean either a forty-five minute commute, or a move. Neither option thrilled her. In good weather the drive would not be bad, but winter, with it's ice and occasional snowstorms could be a nightmare. Renee knew she could find an apartment in town, at a higher rent rate of course. Candler itself was charming, with a main street lined with cute shops and cozy eateries, which would be fun.

Moving would put her farther away from where Terry lived; the twenty minute drive between her place and his now would become an hour's drive, in good weather, and would no doubt hinder their relationship. They had survived four years of his constant travels, but they were almost inseparable when he was home. She wondered if they could survive living in different towns. When he was home, as infrequent as that was anymore, they could squeeze quick visits in every day, or stay at each other's apartments and still allow her to get to work with ease. A move would mean a drastic cut to their already limited time together.

On the other hand, head librarian was a hard job to find, and harder to win with so many applicants searching for that gold nugget. Her relationship with Terry held no guaranties. For all she knew, with the complexities of his lifestyle and limited home time, he was content to leave things as they were. She wanted more. She wanted someday to hear those magic words, "will you marry me," to buy a house and build a life with the man of her dreams, to raise children and share in the same family joys so many of her friends were discovering. What if Terry didn't want the same thing? No matter how much they loved each other, he'd never even hinted he wanted any more of a commitment than what they already shared. Should she risk turning down the job of her dreams for a future that might never happen?

The rest of the day, as she pushed her plans for Terry's return to the back of her mind and worked with renewed fervor to clear through the books in her office, she wrestled with the choice Mrs. Clarke's announcement represented. By five o'clock, as the library closed, she approached Mrs. Clarke with the only resolution she'd been able to reach.

"I know you had hoped I'd have an answer by now, but I have a number of issues I have to resolve first. Can I think on the head librarian position overnight and let you know in the morning?"

Mrs. Clarke could see conflict written across Renee's face, and felt sorry for her. "Of course. Tomorrow morning will be fine."

Luke Morgan turned on his laptop and pulled up the latest Odysseus reviews he could find. He glossed over mention of everyone else in the band, zeroing in on any word of Rusty. He saved every article that praised Rusty's talents, absorbing every word as if the words were gold, the only link he had with the uncle he'd never met.

He remembered the day three years earlier when he'd learned Rusty Morgan was his uncle. He came across Odysseus' music by accident, scanning through radio stations in their car while his parents stood in the driveway chatting with neighbors. Every station sounded the same, top 40s pop, country, or, God forbid, classical, all of it boring, repetitive, and completely uninteresting, until he found the hard rock station playing a three for Thursday run of Odysseus songs. At eleven, his first taste of metal music resonated with something he didn't even know he'd carried inside, pounding drums and soaring guitars grabbing hold of his spirit, infusing his cells with a thrill he'd never imagined could exist in this world. From then on, metal music was all he would listen to, vibrating the walls of his bedroom until his parents yelled for him to turn the volume down, blaring the songs in his family's car until they switched the radio off. Of all the metal music he listened to, Odysseus held him the strongest, the first band he'd heard, the one that had captured his heart.

The day he learned Odysseus was coming to a nearby arena he begged his parents to let him go, vowing he'd do extra chores for weeks to pay for his ticket, threatening to run away and go to the show on his own, even staging a short-lived hunger strike hoping that would force them to cave. The day before the show, he read in their local paper that Rusty Morgan had been born in Averill, and went to the same high school he now attended. "Did you know that, Dad?" he asked, astonished that his hero could have walked the same halls or sat in the same classrooms as he.

His father didn't even glance up from checking e-mails on his cellphone.

"Yes."

"You knew? And you didn't tell me?"

"Uh huh."

"How could you do that?" Luke demanded. "You know I adore his work! I can't believe you wouldn't tell me something so big!"

His father, Harold, didn't care that his son was so angry. He would have ignored Luke altogether except for the information he carried inside. He knew if he didn't reveal the truth now, Luke would never forgive him when he someday found out.

"It's worse," he told Luke, not even bothering to cushion his news. "Rusty Morgan is your uncle."

Luke could only stare at his father in utter disbelief. "What?"

"He's my younger brother," Harold confessed.

Luke just about screamed, "Invite him over, Dad! Call him up! Can he spend the night here? He can sleep in my bed! Dad, now we have to go to his show for sure!"

Harold let his son run on and on until he ran out of steam, then he admitted, "I don't have his phone number. He will never come over, and you're still not going to the show."

Stung as if he'd broken open a beehive and fallen victim to the inhabitants' wrath, Luke sank into the chair across from his father. "Why not?"

"He's not the hero you think. You see a guitar god. Growing up, he was anything but. He was demanding, disobedient, and disruptive of everything in our home. I would never let you talk back to your mother and me the way he did to our parents. He fought with them so much it turned our entire household upside down, created all kinds of chaos, so much so that your aunt and uncles and I refuse to have anything to do with him. He made your grandparents' lives unbearable."

Luke could not reconcile the image his father portrayed with the image he'd built in his mind of the musician he worshipped above all others. His father had to be wrong. From all he read in interviews and articles, Rusty Morgan was a kind, considerate person. No, his father must have the wrong end of things, his memories must be blurred. Knowing he'd never get his father to relent and the concert would go on without him setting foot anywhere near the arena, Luke spent the night in his room, music blaring louder than ever.

Now Luke reread all the reviews and articles he'd gathered, his heart swelling with pride for his uncle. He was bursting with a desire to tell the guys at school that he was related to Rusty Morgan, especially with a new Odysseus show coming to nearby Denver. That would elevate his status among them! They'd be so jealous they'd probably trip over each other trying to get in good with him, hoping for tickets, or autographed CDs, or even a chance to meet Odysseus.

He couldn't tell them though. He was forbidden to say a word. His father had made it crystal clear three years earlier that any mention of Rusty Morgan to anyone inside or outside of their house would result in severe punishment. Sometimes Luke wished he wasn't so compliant. Why couldn't he be more like some of his friends who snuck behind their parents' backs to do what they wanted regardless of the risk of grounding or worse if caught. Still, he had kept his word and not spilled the secret. For him, though, the secrecy surrounding his uncle had only enhanced Rusty's mystical aura. He wondered if he could order a ticket, travel to Denver, attend the show and make it back home without his father finding out. He'd learned early on in his life the consequences of disobedience, knew if he was caught at the very least he'd be months without his cellphone or tablet, and in the end decided the price for going against his father would be too high.

Renee prepared her favorite grilled chicken salad with sharp cheddar cheese and olives for dinner, but picked at only a few forkfuls before storing it in a container for lunch the next day. Her appetite lay buried under too many layers of anxiety to surface.

Settling on the sofa with a cup of tea, she spotted the photo album she'd made for herself with pictures of herself and Terry at dinner, on picnics, at her apartment or his, and especially by the ocean where he loved taking her best, memories of so many happy times they'd spent together. She had made a duplicate album which she'd given him before he left on the current tour, for which he'd thanked her but had said nothing else.

She wondered about that now. He'd seemed happy enough to receive the gift, but on reflection she realized he hadn't been over-enthused. She told herself it had just been the distractions of pulling everything together to hit the road. Wasn't it? Or was it something more?

In past tours, Terry had texted or called her almost every day, sounding cheerful, asking for details about her life, how her work was going, how she was filling her time without him. He had shared with her details of the shows and his touring life, and said a number of times how he couldn't wait to get home and see her.

This time around the texts still came as often but the calls were fewer, and Terry's questions about the everyday details of her life came with far less frequency.

Something nagged at the back of her mind now. She and Terry had known each other four years. In all that time he enjoyed the fun they had, but never gave a hint about moving their relationship to the next level. Maybe he was content to leave things just as they were. Maybe commitment was a four letter word to him. Maybe what they had now was all he would offer her.

She wished she could call Terry, tell him of her dilemma and judge by the tone of his voice and his reaction whether there was any hope for a future with him. She wished she could hop a plane and fly out to where he was playing, see his face, feel his strong arms wrapped around her in a hug that would confirm for her they had a future together.

Renee had never been one to take risks. She was great at daydreaming, but when reality knocked on her door she answered its call and tucked her dreams away. If she waited for Terry only to discover marriage wasn't a road he cared to travel, she would have lost out on a job so many other librarians would snatch up in a heartbeat. The wise thing, the safe thing to do would be to take advantage of the opportunity Mrs. Clarke had presented her. Setting her thoughts of welcoming Terry home aside, she weighed the pros and cons of accepting the library position then made her choice.

As she cleaned her kitchen and prepared for bed, Renee wished she felt happier about her decision.

Sascha sat at the desk in the downstairs office of the house she and Steve had bought the year before Kody was born and sorted through papers, making notes on a lined pad before her. Alimony, she wrote. Child care for Kody. Mortgage or rent. Utilities.

Those were the easy categories, she thought. The harder ones to figure out would be health insurance, life insurance, and savings for emergencies.

I'll have to get a job, she realized. That would mean day care though, and would have to be added into the child care amount.

She would sell the house, of course. She could not possibly remain there, surrounded by memories at every turn. He would get half the money from the sale. She'd use her half as a downpayment on a new place for Kody and herself.

As she juggled figures and made notes on paper, sounds came from Kody's room, soft and low at first, increasing in volume and frequency until he cried out in a loud, frantic voice, "Daddy!"

Sascha rushed upstairs to comfort him. "Kody! Kody, wake up!" When he woke to the world around him, she hugged him tight. "Hush, Kody. You had a bad dream. It's okay now." She rocked him for several minutes until he was relaxed, his body limp against hers, eyes once again heavy with sleep. After she'd settled him back on his bed and tucked his blankets in around him, she watched several more minutes until she was sure he was deep in sleep.

"That's just because Steve's been gone so long," she scolded herself as she tiptoed back downstairs. "That has nothing to do with the divorce. He doesn't even understand what the word means."

Sascha stepped in the kitchen to pour herself a glass of chardonnay. As she carried the glass back to her desk, she noticed a dozen things that made the house special. The curve of the staircase, reflecting on polished hardwood floors, and the carved crown molding Steve had searched for weeks for, knowing it was her favorite style. The rose hued flagstone fireplace in the living room, teardrop crystal chandelier in the dining room, and glass door cupboards in the kitchen that had all been her desires. They'd not only made the house their own, but had done so largely in the colors and styles she wanted. The only place Steve had asserted his wishes was the deck they'd added off the dining room French doors, a large, triple layered affair with hot tub at one end and fire pit at the other. The deck had been his pride and joy, until he'd become too busy to spend much time relaxing on it.

She remembered the day she and Steve had closed the deal on the house. They'd spent the first three years of their marriage in a townhouse, planning and dreaming of what their first home would be like. This house was huge and far more elegant than anything she'd ever dreamed.

"This is insane," she'd told Steve, panicked, when they first pulled up in front of the spacious two story English manor style house with gleaming windows and warm honey colored stone. "We don't belong here!"

With all the swagger of a rock star who'd hit it big, Steve had assured her, "Baby, this house was made for us!"

After they'd closed on the house Steve had carried her over the threshold, danced her around their massive furniture-less living room, and promised her, "Sasch, this will be our love nest forever! We'll watch our children grow up here, and we'll grow old together in this place."

Maybe she could keep the house after all, she thought, running her hands along the curved staircase bannister. Just because he'd blown their marriage didn't mean they all had to do without what they loved. He could find himself an apartment somewhere. She would keep the house. It was the only home Kody had ever known. There was no reason to undo everything they had built up in their marriage.

She found herself starting to entertain the thought of keeping the house. She had to shut the idea down, she knew, or she'd let her imagination carry her away, making a move that much more painful when reality settled in. No, the house carried too many memories. She needed a clean break. She would list the house as soon as the divorce was finalized, and would start fresh someplace else.

Five

Not every broken item can be repaired
—Sinéad Tyrone, *Unrepaired*

Halfway through Odysseus' Denver show, during their song Light In The Darkness, it happened. Most of their songs veered away from the topic of romance; this one glorified the comfort and security of having someone in your corner, the thrill of being with a person you love, the agony of leaving that person behind even if only for a short while. The song's music and lyrics glistened like stars on a clear night under which such love was ignited, like the ring placed on a hand that symbolized such love.

In the middle of the song, a young man in the front row turned to the girl next to him, offered her a ring, and proposed to her. When she said yes, the crowd around them cheered.

The Odysseus musicians all spotted the moment. After the song ended Steve announced, "Looks like a couple of people here have something special to celebrate tonight! Let's bring them up here so we all can congratulate them." He pointed to the two lovers, directing the lighting crew to turn spotlights on them. At first the intimidated couple refused to come onstage, but Steve kept calling them up and the rest of the band refused to play until the two lovers came forward.

"What are your names?" Steve asked once the crowd's applause died down.

"Mike," the young man replied, "and this is Janice."

"Well Mike and Janice, you've got a whole arena of witnesses here so there's no backing out now! And we all expect invitations to your wedding!"

By now Mike had recovered his nerve and answered, "Only if you'll provide the music!"

Even Steve laughed at that. "You never know! Give us a date and we'll see if we're free."

To the crowd he said, "Let's all give Mike and Janice another round of applause while they head back to their seats. Mike and Janice, this next song's for you."

Whenever they had time after their shows, the Odysseus group would meet fans and sign autographs. When Mike and Janice appeared and presented their concert program to be signed Rusty asked Mike, "What made you choose our show as the time you'd propose to Janice?"

Mike wrapped an arm around his now fiancée's shoulder. "We met at an Odysseus show three years ago. Every year since, we've gone to one of your shows. It just made sense to propose tonight."

Eliza sprang into Rusty's mind, just as she had ever since Mike and Janice's proposal had occurred, a haunting memory he could never fully eradicate. He wondered where she was now and whether he ever crossed her mind. Not wanting her memory to dampen the joy of the night at hand, he pulled the iron gate of his mind down on Eliza. In Mike and Janice's program he wrote, "Best wishes always." As he handed the program back he told them, "Love is a hard thing to find. Hang onto each other. I hope what you have lasts forever."

"That's the first proposal we've ever seen at one of our shows," Rick remarked later as the band enjoyed tacos and beers while their bus carried them to their next destination.

"That was cool, alright." Dave turned to Terry. "Speaking of proposals, when are you and Renee finally going to commit to each other? You've been going together for what, ten years now?"

Terry laughed. "Four. And I don't need any help from my brothers here! I can handle Renee just fine by myself."

Rick joined Dave's teasing. "I don't think you can. If you haven't made a move in four years' time, maybe we should do it for you."

"The hell you should! You leave me and Renee alone. I know what I'm doing."

Their good natured teasing continued until the food and drinks were finished. Rick, Dave and Steve headed for bed, while Terry and Rusty, not yet ready to end the night, remained at the table, lowering their voices so the others could sleep.

"All kidding aside, what are you going to do about Renee? The last time we talked you were all ready to pop the big question. You haven't changed your mind have you?"

Terry remembered the conversation, two weeks before their tour started. Rusty had met Terry, Renee, and mutual friends for a concert in Boston, then he'd returned to Terry's apartment for a few days. While Terry cooked breakfast the next morning, scrambled eggs because his fried eggs never turned out, frozen diced potatoes because he rarely had fresh ones on hand, he asked Rusty, "So what do you think of Renee?"

Rusty had cocked an eyebrow and stared at Terry. "You've been going with her four years. Isn't it a little late to ask now?"

Terry turned his attention from the frying pan to Rusty. "Your opinion didn't matter as much before."

The light bulb in Rusty's mind didn't click on right away. When it did, a wide grin spread across his face. "You're going to ask her to marry you, aren't you?"

Terry had looked both excited and terrified. "Yeah, I think this Christmas I am. What do you think?"

Rusty pictured Renee, the woman his best friend was so in love with. It wasn't her wavy, shoulder length blonde hair and brown eyes he thought of, it was the way those eyes lit up whenever she and Terry were together. It was how they both smiled, how they were both so often head to head deep in conversation, in laughter, in discussing every aspect of their lives, no matter how big or small. How many times had he heard them supporting each other through difficult challenges, one shoulder always there for the other to lean on? How many dreams had he heard Terry and Renee build through their conversations, certain they would carry those dreams out? In his heart he felt they were so right for each other, so well matched, he had no doubts about the course his best friend wanted to take.

"Terry, I don't think you could ever find anyone better suited for you. If you're still sure she's the one, go for it."

Instead of the smile Rusty expected, Terry looked scared stiff. "What if she turns me down?"

Rusty would have laughed if Terry hadn't looked so serious. "For some reason the rest of us can't fathom, she's so deep in love with you she's drowning, despite our best efforts to save her from you. She won't say no."

"I hope you're right."

Terry fell silent then. Rusty could tell there was something else on Terry's mind, and was sure he could guess what it was. He could wait for Terry to gather the courage to bring the topic up, or he could let his friend off the hook by raising the issue himself. He chose the latter.

"Terry, if you're proposing to Renee at Christmas you don't need me hanging around. I was thinking I'd go to Cancun for the holiday. You don't mind, do you?"

Terry thought of the four past Christmases he and Rusty had shared, twice at his apartment and twice at Rusty's house. The memory of why they'd started the tradition haunted Terry, just as he knew it preyed on

Rusty's mind. In three years they hadn't brought the subject up, but Terry did now.

"If you think I'm letting you spend Christmas alone you're crazy. You can just cancel any plans you had for Cancun. You're coming to my place."

"You ass! You're spending the day with the girl you love, the one you're going to marry! What makes you think I want to be the third wheel in the middle of that scene?"

Terry still had his worries. "Why don't you go to Dave's then? He'll be alone, you two can keep each other company."

Rusty gave Terry the same look he gave his parents decades ago when they'd tried to run his life. "You know you don't have to sort my holidays out for me. It's been four years. I'm over her now."

This time Rusty could not block Eliza's memory from flooding his mind.

He'd met her five years earlier, the week before Christmas, at a fundraiser wine and cheese tasting event to benefit a local hospital. Captivated by her long legs, waist length black hair and smoky blue eyes, he'd fallen fast and hard.

"You all tried to warn me about Eliza," Rusty admitted to Terry now. "I just didn't want to hear anything bad about her."

His own memories of her awakened, Terry felt all over again the contempt he'd had for her while she was dating Rusty. "We all saw what she was doing, cheating on you and talking trash about you behind your back. We were shocked you couldn't see it for yourself."

"I had blinders on. I didn't want to see."

"We tried to talk you into dropping her, but you never wanted to hear what we were saying. If we'd known you were going to propose to her, we would have stopped you."

Terry's eyes involuntarily scanned Rusty's arms, searching again for the scars he knew lie hidden among the various tattoos Rusty had acquired in the past few years.

Rusty glanced as his arms as well, better able to spot the white lines along his arms and wrists he now carried as permanent reminders of his failed romance. As he looked, he relived in his mind the events as they had unfolded.

One year to the day after they'd met, Rusty had booked a table at the same restaurant where the fundraiser had taken place. Snow had fallen all day, covering the ground in a fresh, clean blanket of white, frosting tree branches and roof lines like icing on so many cakes. The skies had cleared by evening; in the moonlight and street lights the snow glistened, mirroring the stars shining out against the deep blue sky.

He had a bottle of the restaurant's best champagne reserved for them, his best black suit and white shirt on and the navy and gold striped tie Eliza claimed was her favorite. In one pocket, in a blue velvet box, was an emerald cut diamond ring.

Eliza was due in on the four-twenty flight. When she didn't appear, he checked the airline's schedule, saw three more flights she could have taken, and waited. When she failed to show for any of them he texted and called her, but all his messages went unanswered. He returned home, changed into jeans and a flannel shirt, tucked the velvet box into a drawer in his dresser, and waited for a call from her that never came.

Rusty learned through social media the next day that Eliza had married her boyfriend in Paris.

"People think I'm the confident, positive thinker of the group." Rusty's voice now was hushed, somber. "If they knew anything about that week they'd know the truth about me."

"Everyone has a breaking point," Terry defended. "She treated you like shit. You couldn't help what happened."

"No, Terry. I caved. I let my pain drown me. At the very least I should have called you. You would have talked me through the hurt. But no, I let it swallow me, I went down a dark hole."

Terry closed his eyes to block the scene from his mind, but the visions appeared anyway. When Rusty had failed to call the day before Christmas, as he'd done for over a decade, Terry had grown worried. Rusty was always faithful in keeping traditions. When all his calls to Rusty went unanswered, Terry panicked. He drove through the night, arrived at Rusty's house the next morning, found the house too quiet, Rusty's car in the driveway, and the kitchen light on despite the morning's brightness. Sure now some crisis had occurred, Terry busted the back door open, searched downstairs, ran upstairs, and found Rusty unconscious on the bathroom floor, blood from deep cuts on his arms and wrists covering his clothes, the floor, the sink, and every other surface in the vicinity.

"Oh my God!" Terry cried out. "Rusty, no! What are you doing? Why?"

Terry had tied towels as tight as he could around Rusty's arms and called for an ambulance. Later, after Rusty had been stitched up, released, and was sleeping, Terry scrubbed away as many blood stains as he could. Some would only fade with time. He called their Odysseus brothers and filled them in on what had happened. He notified friends he'd planned to spend Christmas with that plans had changed, he'd had a family emergency, although he knew they knew he was estranged from his family.

Terry stayed with Rusty through New Year's Day. Every year since then he'd made sure Rusty didn't spend the holidays alone.

He looked straight into Rusty's eyes now. "I don't want you going to Cancun or anywhere else alone. Spend the time at my place. Even if Renee's there, you're family, you'll fit in."

Rusty met Terry's gaze. "You can't babysit me forever. Someday you'll have to let me go. You need to start now. I promise I won't do anything stupid over the holidays. I had one bad stretch. I'm in a better place in my life and my mind now."

Terry knew Rusty was right. Rusty seemed to have moved on, although he shied away from serious relationships, never venturing beyond a brief fling here or there. Still, Terry found his fears for Rusty, borne that one horrible night, hard to let go of. No matter how much he wanted to, he could not safeguard his best friend from every hurt life would throw at him. He could not watch over Rusty every day, year after year, could not encase him in a bubble where he would be forever protected. Christmas this year would be the first test. Terry would have to face that. Hell, he should be elated that he'd spend Christmas with the girl he loved most celebrating their relationship and planning the next steps in their future! Rusty would be fine, he told himself.

He wondered at what point his heart would believe what he told it.

Every morning while his coffee brewed Rusty checked the copy of the tour schedule they'd taped to a cupboard door by the bus's coffee machine. Keeping track of days and cities when highways and venues all seemed so similar was impossible without the schedule to keep them oriented. After each show someone, most often Dave, would cross that day off. What had started as a long, exciting list three months ago was now reduced to less than a dozen days.

Even without looking at the schedule, Rusty knew the end of the tour was approaching by the way his body felt. Like every other tour, he'd started this one full of energy and enthusiasm. By now his shoulders and back ached. Worse, he was desperate for a long break from the bus and venue confines. Their built in days off were still restrictive, too far from home to hang out with friends, too short to afford true relaxation. By this time on any tour the walls of the bus started to close in on Rusty, and he counted the days until he could stretch his legs walking the open land around his house, and share a few laughs and beers with friends with no schedules boxing him in.

Rechecking the schedule while his coffee finished brewing, Rusty realized the next day was Thanksgiving. Another holiday on the road, he thought. One more thing he and Odysseus would miss out on.

The only solace Rusty found was in performing. Each sound check his blood started to rush faster. As the curtain rose for a new show any tiredness, physical or mental, evaporated. He fed off the energy of the crowd, losing himself in the notes and words, in the applause and ecstatic response from the sea of nameless faces before him. He held nothing back, but gave away every ounce of energy and emotion through his songs. Rusty could never explain how it worked, but in every show Odysseus took to the stage to pour out all they possessed inside through the vessel of their music, leaving on the stage floor all of the beauty and power of the notes and words they carried, and along with that all of their dreams and emotions, all they carried in their hearts. Somehow the more they gave to the crowd, the more the crowd gave back in applause and appreciation, the energy flowing through their response refueling Rusty and the rest of Odysseus, enabling them to play even louder and harder.

The continual give and take transference of energy and power was part of the magic each show contained, part of why Odysseus and other bands took to the road instead of just releasing album after album. Albums were vital, spreading music in a format through which it could be played time after time and shared. Concerts, on the other hand, held the real key, connecting musicians with their followers, forming a bond that kept both performers and listeners hooked on each other. Even on the night before a major holiday the venue in Wichita was packed, the concertgoers enthusiastic in their support, the band showering on them all the artistry it possessed.

"Thanksgiving dinner at Andy's brother's house tomorrow!" Rick's eyes shone with excitement as they gathered their gear after the show.

Dave started listing all the foods he looked forward to, "Mashed potatoes, pumpkin pie, gravy."

Terry added, "That cranberry bread Andy told us about last night. Can't wait to try that!"

Even Steve joined in the fun. "What was that sweet potato dish dripping with butter and pecans he described? I want lots of that!"

They stepped out from backstage to find the snow flurries that had started to fall in the afternoon had become a raging storm. A half foot of snow covered their bus and all roads around them. Andy helped them store their instruments and gym bags in the bus's baggage compartments, then followed them onto the bus.

"I've been studying road maps and weather forecasts. I'm afraid we'll have to change our plans. Heavy snow is falling all the way to my brother's house. We'll have to detour around it if we hope to make Friday's show."

Steve and Rick pulled weather sites up on their phones and confirmed what Andy had said.

Dave scanned the disappointed faces around him. "There's no choice. If we don't leave now, we might get stuck in snow ourselves." He turned to Andy. "Think you can scout out a restaurant along the way where we can still have turkey and trimmings?"

Andy tried, but the majority of restaurants they passed on Thanksgiving Day were either closed or fully booked with hours' long waits. The best he could offer the boys was a grocery store.

"I'm sorry," he apologized. "It looks like microwave dinners are all I can do for you."

Rick surveyed the plate of sliced turkey, gravy and mashed potatoes he'd heated. "Almost as good as home," he lied, trying not to think of another holiday he wasn't spending with Laurel and his kids.

"At least we won't get dirty looks for parking ourselves in front of the football games!" Terry slid his plate into the microwave and set the timer. "Renee's mother has a rule, no football until the table is cleared."

"You better hope she doesn't become your mother-in-law," Dave teased. "She sounds like a nightmare already!"

"We're rarely home on Thanksgiving anymore," Terry reminded him. "It wouldn't be an issue."

Steve, who had set his songwriting aside to join the others for dinner, recalled the Thanksgivings they'd spent in hotels the past couple of years. No amount of first class environments could ever replace being home, but they'd always made the best of the situation. Hoping to distract them from focusing too much on family, he asked, "Think Andy could find us a swimming pool like we had at last year's hotel?"

Rusty remembered the hotel, a five star establishment Larry had treated them to to alleviate the pain of missing home on such a family oriented holiday. "That was one fancy place. That Thanksgiving buffet, good Lord, they had everything!" The plate before him all of a sudden looked cold and uninviting.

"That hot tub. . . ." Terry felt again how relaxing it had been, a far cry from the day on the bus they were stuck on now as Andy maneuvered them through snow clogged highways.

They joked and teased their way through dinner, although they each felt the laughter forced and artificial. This was the side of their life the band's followers never saw. Performing on stage, playing to thousands of adoring fans night after night, people imagined all the glory of fame, the grandeur, the high life Odysseus must have led. They never saw the empty days and nights, never felt the ache inside the musicians' hearts as so many holidays, birthdays, and other special times were spent away from home.

To the uninitiated, life on a tour bus seemed like a constant party. To the musicians who lived the life, though, any fun was tempered by a constant sense of the distance between themselves and their loved ones, and the kind of normal life everyone else enjoyed. Not that they would have changed anything; they were following a passion for creating music that permeated every cell and fiber of their bodies, that ran as deep within each of them as the need to breathe. Still, they were not gods, they were human. By this time in every tour, no matter how much they loved their work, no matter how much they enjoyed connecting with their fans, they'd had enough of the bus and the distance and were ready to return home.

While they watched football, images of Stacey and Jessica floated across the back of Dave's mind. He knew Stacey had met someone else; Jessie had rubbed that information in the last time he'd tried to talk to her. He wondered if Stacey would be cooking dinner for the boyfriend today. Jealousy burned hot within him, although he knew he had no one to blame but himself. If he hadn't given in, more times than he could count, to the temptation of girls on the road, Stacey and Jessie would still be his.

Rick drew pictures for Ryan and Christine of the outline of the bus they were riding in, his bass guitar, the lounge area where he and his bandmates sat, and wrote a short story to go along with the drawings, all of which he e-mailed with a special note to Laurel. She would be with her family for Thanksgiving; he wouldn't interrupt their meal with a call but knew she'd call him later so he could say goodnight to Ryan and Christine.

While Terry watched the game, he researched honeymoon destinations. Aruba looked very appealing, or Belize, or St. John's. Or maybe Europe; he could show her around Germany, he'd spent enough time there and knew his way around fairly well. Or Ireland, where he'd visited once with Rusty and had long since wanted to return.

He wondered if Renee would be willing to move to the countryside with him after they were married. He'd had enough of city living, and would love nothing more than to enjoy the same peace and quiet Rusty surrounded himself with. Maybe they could find a house with a view of the ocean. She wouldn't like leaving her library job, but he was sure she'd be able to find something wherever they moved.

He had to laugh at himself. Here he was planning their future, and he hadn't even proposed yet.

Rusty enjoyed watching football as long as his teams were winning, which they almost never did. Today was no exception. One after another, all the teams he'd bet on went down.

"I don't know why I put myself through this torture every year!" He muttered to the rest of the guys.

With nothing else to focus on, Rusty thought beyond the Thanksgiving dinner they'd just shared to Christmas, and his recent conversation with Terry. At least with turkey day he had his brothers around him. They'd all have gone home by Christmas. There was no way in hell he'd horn in on Terry and Renee's day, especially knowing now that Terry planned on proposing.

He wondered for a moment what would happen if he went back to his hometown, walked into his parents' church for Christmas Eve mass, or showed up on their doorstep in time for dinner. They would be stunned, to say the least. So stunned his father would probably drop dead on the spot from heart failure. There was no sense causing that. As much as he'd love to shock the hell out of them all, he didn't want to be the reason for anything quite that drastic.

No, he thought, he would just stay home. He'd force himself to put a tree up and string lights around his house. He'd research new recipes and create a sumptuous feast for himself, maybe pork tenderloin and sweet potatoes. If he had to spend the day alone, there was no reason he couldn't make the most of it.

Steve tried his hardest to not think of Sascha and Kody and the Thanksgiving dinner they'd be sharing with Sascha's parents. He left her a voicemail message and texted her in hopes of talking with Kody, but heard nothing back. In years past Sascha and Kody would have started the day with a call to him, texted him throughout the day sharing bits of conversation and photos, and ended the evening with a goodnight video chat. Their silence today was deafening.

He tried his best to get through the day. Thanksgiving dinner for all of Odysseus had been disheartening at best. They'd made the most of their microwave fare, and the rest of the guys had enjoyed watching football, a sport he could have cared less about. While they were glued to the TV, he chose to fine tune some of the lyrics he'd written for songs they would record once Christmas and New Years were over. The boys had fallen silent now, unless some spectacular play occurred on the field which brought either cheers or outcries from one or another of them, depending on who was cheering for which team. Despite their best attempts to get through the holiday, a heavy mood had begun to permeate the space inside the bus. Between the threatened loss of his marriage and his son, and the dark mood surrounding them all, he was ready for a good whiskey binge or whatever pill he could pop to make the dark mood go away. Days like this, he understood why so many musicians he knew fell into drugs or alcohol, or passed their down time with as many girls as they could entice to share their beds. The loneliness of touring could be overwhelming at times; anything that helped ease that pain was welcome.

They'd all served their time in the war of drugs and drink and come out of the battles alive. Even if they had drugs or alcohol on the bus, Steve wouldn't go back down that road. There were no ladies along on the bus. That left no escape or relief from the battles that raged inside him.

After football, the guys cut into the apple and pumpkin pies they had bought at the store. Conversation was low key, each of them just biding time until they could go to bed and let sleep carry them through to the next day. By now Steve had had enough of the somber atmosphere.

"Good God! If this is how bad you all are over Thanksgiving, it's a good thing you'll all be back with your families for Christmas!" Steve zeroed in on Rusty. "Except you! What the hell are you even sad about? It's not like you have family to miss. I'd think you'd be happy today. And what about Christmas? You don't ever have to worry about missing. . . ." He stopped himself. He'd almost been about to let the divorce issue slip.

The others stared at Steve, stunned, except Rusty who kept his eyes focused on the plate before him.

"Shut up, Steve!" Terry ordered. "I've had it with you going after Rusty. What the hell's wrong with you?"

"Quit defending him!" Steve shot back. "You don't see it! Rusty's the weak link here anymore. I'm tired of carrying him through all our shows!"

"Weak link? He hasn't played a weak note this entire tour! You're not carrying him through anything! If anything, he's covering for you!" Terry slammed his coffee cup down so hard on the table some of the coffee in it splashed out.

"Stop it, both of you!" Rusty broke in. "We're all tired, we've all had a shitty holiday. Let's all just put it behind us before anyone says something they'll regret in the morning." He stepped away from the table, picked up his acoustic guitar, and started playing, no song in particular, just a series of quiet notes meant to soothe the atmosphere. After several minutes the others cleared their plates away and settled in for computer or music time themselves.

The next morning Steve stayed in the front lounge area while the others had breakfast in the back lounge. Rusty watched as Steve stared at the landscape passing by the bus windows. If Steve just wanted quiet,

Rusty would respect that; but he sensed Steve was avoiding the rest of them because of his outburst the night before. He cut a piece of coffee cake, put it on a plate, and brewed a cup of Steve's favorite pecan flavored coffee. He took both up and sat on the bench next to Steve.

"Here. Better take this before the others polish it off."

Steve shook his head. "I'm not hungry."

Rusty set the plate on the counter across from Steve. "You might be in a little bit." He handed Steve the coffee mug, which Steve accepted after a moment's hesitation.

"Why are you being so nice to me?" Steve wanted to know. "I treated you like crap last night."

Rusty shrugged. "Yesterday was a hard day for all of us. You were just frustrated. And tired, we're all tired this week."

"Don't be so damn understanding! Can't you just once be real?"

"Do you want me to yell at you? What good would that do?" Rusty saw in Steve's eyes that his friend was struggling with something more than their battle the night before. "Look, I don't know what's going on inside you. It must be big, you've been on edge for weeks now. I don't have to know unless you want to talk, but last night is behind us. It was just brothers blowing off a little steam. In my book, it's over. Don't let it hold you back from the rest of us."

Rusty let his words sink in, then returned to the table with the others. Steve stayed up front, but after a few minutes Rusty saw him pick up the plate, eat the coffee cake, and finish his coffee.

"It's a start," Rusty told himself. "It's enough for now."

Six

You are my solace when the rest of the world has retreated
        —Sinéad Tyrone, *Behind The Mask*

Rusty breathed the open, empty vistas of New Orleans' Audubon Park, allowing fresh air and the park's uncluttered, unconfined spaces to seep all the way through his soul which had too long been bound by hotels, venues, and the tour bus he'd called home for the past three months. Always scheduled towards the end of their tours, over the years New Orleans had become a favorite destination for Odysseus, filled with dozens of alluring attractions from the historic regions to the endless offerings of music filled bars and night clubs. This time out, Rusty was determined to scope out the labyrinth at Audubon Park. After months of touring, a year full of the pressures their demanding schedule wrought, and the growing tension between himself and Steve, he hoped walking the labyrinth, as he'd discovered through research the past several days, would restore a sense of centering and calm inside him.

Rusty was surprised to find Terry seated on one of the benches overlooking the labyrinth. "You too have escaped the madhouse?" he asked as he settled into the empty seat next to Terry.

"The thought of one more hour in a hotel room or lobby was enough to make me vomit!"

Rusty nodded towards the open book in Terry's lap. "What are you reading?"

Terry left a thumb inside to mark his place, and held the closed leather-bound book up. "Recognize it?"

"Isn't that the one I gave you last Christmas?"

"One and the same."

"Haven't you got those stories memorized by now?"

"You'd think I would!" Terry replaced his thumb place holder with the leather strap bookmark sewn into the book's binding and closed the book so he could more fully focus on Rusty's presence. "You know this volume of Homer's *Iliad and Odyssey* is my favorite, don't you?" Without waiting for an answer, as his fingers caressed the soft brown leather and intricate stitched cover design he told Rusty, "This is the best Christmas gift anyone has ever given me."

"I remember you almost cried when you opened it." Rusty changed the topic, "Don't let Steve catch you reading that instead of going over the new songs he's given us!"

"Don't tell him, but I didn't even look at the e-mail he sent this morning."

"I won't say a word! You better glance at them before dinner tonight, though, in case he asks."

"Is Steve going to want to try the songs out this evening?"

Rusty weighed Steve's hard pushing in recent weeks against the draws of the city around him. "He won't catch Rick and Dave anytime after dinner; I think they had a watering hole or two they wanted to check out."

"Can we pay them to take him with them and give us all a night off?"

Rusty laughed at the thought. "Hell no, they're going to be paying us to keep him away from them after dinner!"

"I saw the e-mail Larry sent," Terry admitted. "What's with him, reminding us we have an album due next year to fulfill our contract while we're still finishing the current tour? Good God! Do they never get enough blood out of us?"

Rusty released the sigh of one exhausted in both body and mind. "No, they don't. No matter how much we give, they always want more. Always have, always will." Rusty watched a trio of twenty-something guys in suits, coffee cups in one hand, briefcases in the other, heading off to whatever firm they worked at, heads together as they discussed whatever business they were involved in. He could sense their determination to reach the top by their quick, purposeful strides and energetic conversation. He wished he could pull them aside and warn them of pitfalls they would no doubt run into. Eyes fixed on them, he asked Terry, "Do you ever wish we hadn't made it so big?"

Terry didn't respond right away. He knew Rusty wasn't looking for an instant answer. He thought way back to Odysseus' early days, when they were so hungry for success they spent every waking hour pursuing their dreams. In those early years they fed off every good show, every album sold, every building block that moved them closer to their goals. They forged their bonds of brotherhood in those early years, encouraging each other when times were rough, celebrating with one another when album sales went through the roof and shows sold out. As their popularity rose and the challenges of maintaining their higher rank multiplied, they helped each other through the stresses and increased demands, humor and camaraderie the tools that saw them through.

"Do I ever wish?" Terry turned to Rusty. "Life was so much easier in the old days, wasn't it? It's too bad we couldn't have found some sweet middle of the road spot and stayed there longer."

Rusty nodded. "That's what I mean. We love what we do, and we're fortunate enough to have reached the heights where we are now, most musicians don't reach that level. Some days the road is so hard, though, I wonder sometimes if it's worth it."

Terry held his book up. "That's why I'm so obsessed with these stories. At the end of the day, all Odysseus wanted was to get back home, to peace and quiet and loved ones around him. He faced so many obstacles on his way, but he overcame them all in the end." He pointed to the sprawling oak tree nearby. "It's like that tree. They call it the tree of life. It's hundreds of years old, survived all kinds of devastating storms, any number of threats to its survival, and yet look at it, thriving despite all the things that could have brought it down."

Rusty studied the massive oak, its thick, sturdy trunk, its powerful limbs spread out in every direction. It had not only survived, he thought, it continued to offer shelter to anyone and anything in need, lowering branch arms out for easy access to its sanctuary, rising tall and proud against any challenges that might throw themselves at it.

"Think we'll make it home like Odysseus did?" Rusty asked at length.

Terry watched Rusty pondering the tree, thought of the many times lately he and the rest of the band had witnessed Steve throwing word arrows at Rusty and how many times Rusty had taken those wounds in without retaliating. "Of course we will," he reassured Rusty. "That tree has scars, Odysseus did as well, and so do you and the rest of us. But we've still got strength inside us. We'll make it through to the end."

Rusty let Terry's assurance sink in, then rose. "Alright. I'm going to test that labyrinth out. Care to join me?"

Terry felt the draw of the characters in the book in his hand, and recognized Rusty's inner need for something deeper than words. "No, thanks. I think that's something best done on one's own."

Bright sun shone down on Rusty as he stepped into the labyrinth's path. He felt the sun's warmth penetrate through his skin and the cells and bones within him absorb its healing powers as he focused on following the stone path. He'd read much over the past several days about how circles were a source of strength, a symbol of completeness, wholeness. As his feet traveled over the stones, testing various paths, holding his progress to a slow, steady, meditative pace, he found a peace settle over him that he hadn't felt in days.

Midway to Odysseus' next destination they stopped in a small southern town, similar to a dozen they'd passed that day with a dozen more ahead, for a bite to eat and a chance to stretch their legs. Main Street in that town carried only three restaurants: a fast food hamburger place, a breakfast style diner that looked closed by this time of evening, and a family type restaurant, which they all agreed was their best option.

As soon as they stepped inside, they regretted their choice.

Seated at a corner table were a husband and wife and two toddler age children. At a second table, by a large window, was a late teen- early twenties couple so engrossed with each other they didn't notice the Odysseus band enter. A waitress stood behind a counter pouring coffee for two men, thirty something, well built with strong arms outlined underneath their flannel shirts. Rusty guessed they were construction workers or roofers.

"Let's get out of here," he whispered to Terry, hoping to avoid what he was sure would come next.

They were too late. The construction workers had spotted them and now studied the Odysseus guys head to toe, frowning at their leather jackets, worn jeans, and long hair.

"Will you look at what just crawled across our doorstep!" The taller of the two said in a tone that carried both amusement and danger.

The second one, shorter and stockier in build, answered, "Damn long haired freaks!" As he approached he told his friend, "Look, this one's wearing earrings!"

"This one too." The first stood before them and sent them a menacing glare. "We don't want your kind around here."

"We're leaving." Rusty would have turned to carry out his words but Steve grabbed his arm and held him in place.

"No we're not." Steve turned to the two construction workers. "We just came in for some dinner. We'll leave after that."

The taller of the two workers locked eyes with Steve. "You won't get any service here. Get out now while you can."

Steve ignored the warning, took a step towards the closest empty table, and pulled a chair out to sit down.

A viselike hand grabbed his arm and stopped him. "I mean it. You and your ladies here get the hell out."

The other four band members all recognized the signs of a brawl about to break open. Rusty and Terry grabbed Steve and pulled him back, while Dave and Rick rushed to open the door and hurry them all away from danger. They scrambled onto the bus, Steve cursing and protesting all the way, and ordered Andy to speed off.

"Why the hell did you stop me?" Steve demanded of Rusty.

"Seriously? Did you want to end up in jail? Or the hospital? You know we never win in towns like this."

Rick agreed, "Even five on two, if we'd all stepped in, they would have beat us. And the local law would have taken their side and thrown the book at us."

"God! How many times have we gone through that?" Steve slammed a fist down on the bus's counter. "How many more times?"

"We don't very often, thank God." Rick felt an involuntary shiver run down his spine as he remembered the few times they had refused to back down in the face of threats. They'd learned their lessons the hard way years ago, each of them sporting occasional black eyes or other colorful bruises. "We should have known better than to choose that restaurant."

Each of the Odysseus members fell silent, reflecting on the brawl they'd averted and the level of hatred they had encountered so many times over the years.

Steve was still furious. He hadn't intended to allow a minor incident to escalate. When the two restaurant patrons started in on his brothers and himself he felt a rage boil up inside him he couldn't turn off, as if all the times he'd been bullied or ridiculed over the years pooled together into an overflow of emotions as impossible to hold back as too much water against a dam. He'd had enough. He'd be damned if he'd let anyone push them around. He'd come into the restaurant for a meal, and by God he was going to have what he wanted. If Rusty and Terry hadn't intervened and hauled him out of there, he knew he'd have ended up eating that meal and more through a straw with jaws wired shut.

To settle himself, Steve turned to the one constant thing in his life, the one thing that always soothed the surge of emotions within him. He picked up his guitar and started playing, just a bunch of notes at first, nothing planned, impromptu notes and chords as his heart and mind moved him. Soon Rusty had picked up his guitar as well, and Rick his bass, three guitars blending together in unplanned harmony. Dave added keyboards from his tablet, Terry drummed his sticks against the table's edge, and music filled the bus.

This was what Steve had dreamed of so many years ago when he first picked up a guitar after seeing numerous videos of musicians playing songs that stirred their audiences. The songs they performed so resonated within him that he fell under some sort of spell, following pied pipers, only the pipers were singers and their instruments guitars. The spell they wove forever hooked him. He followed where his heart dictated.

While all forms of music moved him, he was captivated by metal music, by guitarists who shredded notes like they were shredding ribbons, pounding through invisible walls, who ran riffs of notes that screamed and wailed, thousands of unspeakable cries against a dark night. He devoted all his time and energy to learning how to recreate their magic.

The path had been hard. No dream worth following was ever easy. He'd faced opposition from most of his family and friends, and the occasional bouts of self doubt and insecurity that went hand in hand with the pursuit of an artistic goal. He'd won in the end, although the tracks of scars the chase had left inside him sometimes caused him to wonder what, in the end, he'd really won.

While they all jammed together, Steve scanned the musicians seated or standing around him, his brothers sharing the pursuit of a dream, chasing after the same magic. They achieved it that night, the music they created as sweet and powerful as anything they performed in public. He could tell by the looks on their faces they each felt the joy of letting the music take them wherever it wanted. Hell, let the outside world come at them however it wanted! He had his music, and his brothers. At the end of the day that was all that mattered.

Dave wondered again why, in this day and age, they still ran into opposition and outright hatred at times. It didn't happen very often anymore. In most places they were either casually accepted or ignored, hardly given a second glance at best. In some places they were treated like adored heroes. Still, especially in pockets in the South or Midwest, they and their fellow musicians were looked down on or, like tonight, threatened. He tried to make sense of why people still hated them so much. Because they were outsiders? Because they were different? If they were just minding their own business, what difference was it to others? He and the others had gone through it enough to know, like tonight, how to remove themselves from trouble at the first sign. Still, it was never fair.

They'd all known what they were heading into when they chose this lifestyle, Dave reminded himself. The metal musicians he'd grown up idolizing had each gone through the stares, the sneers, the ugly remarks. What had driven him, or any of the Odysseus members, to follow this path, knowing they'd be outsiders in some circles?

Dave had grown up exposed to various forms of music, from the classical pieces his parents, both classical musicians, had filled their house with, to the popular music his two sisters always played in their bedrooms, to the band music he dabbled with in junior and high school. None of them excited him, though, the way the pace and power of metal music did. While his parents were disappointed at his choice, they stood behind him and encouraged him to follow his dreams.

He remembered the early, lean years with Odysseus. They'd had plenty of run-ins like the one tonight; on the other hand, they'd had a faithful, energetic core group of followers whose support and encouragement kept them going. As they'd risen in popularity and their touring travel vehicles and accommodations had improved, they'd had fewer incidents. Tonight's was rare anymore. Thankful they'd avoided serious trouble, Dave let the impromptu music he played now seep into his spirit, calming and restoring a sense of inner peace.

Growing up, Rick had dreamed of becoming a builder, enjoying working with his father's tools, creating first a dog house, then a tree house, after that a table his mother still used by her living room window. Each created item gave him a sense of accomplishment, seeing something he'd imagined come to life and witnessing how happy the items he created made the people who saw them.

Rick would have followed his builder dream if music hadn't crossed his path. A high school friend of his had an extra ticket to a rock show in town, invited Rick along, and that night Rick found something he wanted more than to work with power tools and lathe. He was mesmerized by all of the musicians that night, especially the bass guitar player. Rick was captivated by the player's rapid fire notes, by his stage presence as he stalked the space between the drummer and lead singer, by how the steady line of bass notes anchored each song the group performed, like wood framing anchored whatever was built upon it.

The next week Rick withdrew money from a savings account he'd started when he began selling some of his woodwork, bought a second hand bass guitar and started taking lessons at the music shop in town.

He'd never regretted the road his choice had led him down; but on nights like tonight he couldn't help wondering what life would have been like if he'd followed his original dream. He thought of all his friends back home who had breakfast with their kids every morning and dinner with them every evening, sleeping in the same bed with the same woman next to them every night. What would it feel like to be home for every birthday and holiday? He'd be bored in a matter of months, he realized, but for one brief moment the thought did have its appeal.

Terry studied his band brothers as they jammed together, wondering why some people still felt so threatened by them. What about their long hair scared folks? Their earrings, tattoos, and leather jackets? Thank God that evening they'd had those jackets on; if the two construction workers had seen their multiple tattoos they'd have really gone after the Odysseus guys.

He thought back to when he'd announced to his parents that he wanted to be a drummer, and not just any drummer but one in a heavy metal band. Far from mainstream, the music genre he'd chosen flew in the face of so many of his parents' values, or so they thought. They were furious with his career choice at all, and more so with one they viewed as so diametrically opposed to the way of life they'd raised him on. What did they think all the time he'd spent holed up in his room beating away on his drums was for, he wondered. Did they really think he'd set his sticks aside for college and a chance to spend his life like they did, chasing the next financial deal, working endless hours for nothing but a paycheck? No. He wanted more.

If they'd asked him why he chose heavy metal as his music of choice, he wasn't sure he could explain it in a way they'd understand. Metal music had a pounding, addicting drive, but that wasn't all. He liked the raw honesty in the songs, musicians pouring words out from the depths of their soul, their open passion, nothing held back, pushing beyond every boundary set in front of them. He loved that he could be as wild as he wanted on his drums, each beat he played another strike against those who sought to hold him back, those who refused to support him, those who mocked or scorned him as his hair grew longer and his clothing more rebellious. He threw all his emotions into his playing, adopting a lifestyle his parents shunned.

Now, as Odysseus' tour bus drove them farther and farther away from the town where their confrontation had occurred, Terry thought of every person who had turned their backs on him as he pursued his career, and most of all his parents. He wondered if they ever regretted closing the door on any contact with him when he'd failed to bow to their expectations. Probably not, he realized. Part of him still hurt that they could be so cold hearted. The larger part of him drew closer to the brothers he had now, united by their common bond of music.

Steve had started the music that night. After the first song Rusty decided to jump in, but found when he first tried to play that his hands were still shaking, lingering effects of the confrontation they'd managed to escape. In time his hands relaxed, and the music he and the rest of the band played calmed him inside and out.

They played everything that night, from acoustic, folk and classical, to blues, then metal, with the metal being his favorite, just as it had always been from when he was ten and first listening to music, straight on through. At first his parents dismissed it as a temporary phase he was going through. When he reached his teens and started fighting to let his hair grow long they forced haircuts on him until he started running away. When he first had an ear pierced they insisted he at least not wear the earring in their house. They forced him to practice his guitar away from the house, and did everything they could to dissuade this foolish dream of his.

He told others he didn't care, but in truth their lack of support was a ghost rattling chains inside him every now and then, memories and scars he had to constantly battle. There were other memories as well, middle school and high school bullies who hated him because he was different, who felt it was their duty to force him to conform to their standards. For every bullying incident, every shaming incident, every beating he took his resolve only grew stronger: someday he would rise to the top and they'd regret they had ever treated him with such contempt.

Now, as he improvised music with his Odysseus brothers, all those ghosts stirred again and rose within him, rattling their chains so loud he poured extra effort into his playing in order to drown them out. He succeeded for a while, until the others one by one retired and gave in to sleep. He played a few more songs for them, quiet acoustic tunes based on lullabies he'd heard over the years. In so doing, he hoped he would lull his ghosts back to sleep as well.

It was well into the early morning hours before Rusty fell asleep. In his dreams the ghosts rose again, and three in particular.

He'd been fifteen at the time, old enough to have won the hair war with his parents, devoted enough to his musical heroes to have adopted their style of dress as much as possible, with faded jeans, t-shirts, a leather vest he'd found dirt cheap, and a denim jacket. He'd grown wise enough to ignore the insults hurled at him in school hallways. Most of the time his refusal to react wore the school bullies down; there was no game when the intended victim didn't play along.

Some bullies, though, were not so easily placated.

It was winter, January, and cold winds whipping through town as a storm front swept in. Rusty was walking home from a garage where he and a friend had been practicing music. As he hurried along, he wished he hadn't turned down his friend's offer for a ride home.

In the howling wind, he hadn't heard the footsteps behind him. Caught off guard, he was unable to stop himself from being shoved to the ground, nor to fend off the fists and feet that pummeled him and kicked at him. Each blow stung deep but he willed himself to keep quiet, gritting his teeth so he wouldn't cry out, steeling his body to minimize the pain as more blows were inflicted. The last thing he remembered was a kick to the head that blackened everything around him.

He had no idea how long he was unconscious. When he came to he was covered in snow, freezing cold, with a head throbbing and nose and cheekbones aching. The fingers on one hand refused to bend when he ordered them to. His ribs on one side felt like they were on fire.

He would take the pain. He didn't care about that. What hurt more than any physical wounds was the shattered guitar lying next to him. Someone had snapped the neck in two and smashed their feet into its body to ensure it would never be reassembled. He would have cried at the sight if he'd allowed himself the luxury of tears.

He didn't remember how he got home that night. He remembered his parents were angry when he walked in the door, not at his attackers but at him for allowing himself to be so vulnerable, to be such an easy target, for making choices that all but ensured he'd receive this kind of attack.

The night came back to him now in a dream that forced him awake and left him shaking, cold, and insecure all over again. Unable to return to sleep, he listened to the rhythm of the bus wheels whirring over pavement toward their next destination and created a mental checklist of things they would need to do in the morning, anything to focus his mind elsewhere until the ghosts had slipped back into their graves.

Seven

I try to keep realistic perspective although occasionally shadows creep in
—Sinéad Tyrone, *Calming Voices*

Any glimmer of hope Rusty had that the near miss of being beat up, and the unity of the music they'd shared on the bus after, might have tempered Steve's harsh criticisms towards him and the rest of Odysseus was crushed during sound check before their Jacksonville show.

Rick watched Steve as they entered the venue where they would be playing that night. While Dave, Terry and Rusty entered laughing, chatting, and in general good spirits, Steve walked in alone, unsmiling, his mind a thousand miles away. Something was different about him these days, Rick thought, something deeper than the pressure of working out their next album, or their current tour. Steve's eyes carried an emotion in them Rick couldn't identify. Fear? Pain? Whatever it was, Rick had never seen it in Steve before and it worried him now. They'd all avoided asking Steve what was wrong, but now Rick saw an opportunity while the other three were ahead of them and preoccupied. Pretty sure he'd rather enter a tiger's enclosure than approach Steve these days, he nevertheless walked over to Steve and asked, "You've been quiet the last few weeks, not your usual self. What's going on?"

Startled that any of the Odysseus guys even asked, at first Steve was tempted to confide in him, to let everything out, to share his divorce dilemma and not have to carry it all alone. He opened his mouth to speak then changed his mind, closed it, and shook his head. "Nothing. I just want to get this tour wrapped up, get home, catch my breath, clear my mind, and then get us back into the studio for our next album."

Dave watched each of the Odysseus members prepare for the show ahead. Soon the tour would be over and they'd each retreat to their individual worlds.

He wasn't in any hurry to return home. His house, no matter how luxurious and well furnished, felt so cold and empty without his wife and daughter around. Oh, he could fill the space with any girl he wanted for a night here or there, but they always went home in the morning, or after a few days, and then the emptiness returned. Christmas would be unbearable at best. He knew he would pass the time with friends at a beach house in California, but all while relaxing in the sun and sand half his mind and his heart would be on what he had lost. Oh well, he thought, that's the price to pay for too many indiscretions, too much drinking and too many wild parties over the years. He'd completely blown his marriage, now he had no choice but to serve his time as an absentee father, and hope his daughter would someday forgive him.

As he watched Rusty and Steve examine the guitars Bryan had rolled out, as Rick picked up his favorite bass and start running through notes, as Terry tested out cymbals and skins on his drums, Dave allowed his closeness to each of them to hold his Christmas blues at bay. He wished he could spend Christmas with all of them. Thanksgiving, for all its home cooked food let down, had been a great holiday for him; he'd spent it with the people he was closest to in this world. His Odysseus brothers were more family to him than anyone else. He often thought how wonderful it would be if they all bought a series of houses together, a compound of sorts, or like a commune where they could all live separate lives yet remain together, be there for each other off the road as well as on. While the others protested Steve's over-ambitious January schedule, Dave was grateful the Christmas break would be short and they'd be back together in the studio in no time.

Sound check commenced, and Dave set aside all worries of how difficult Christmas would be. At least he and the band had a few more shows before the break. He would just focus on them.

"Damn it, Morgan!"

Steve's use of Rusty's last name froze Terry, Dave and Rick mid-action. Dave caught the annoyed look that flashed across Rusty's face, replaced in an instant by one of great patience.

"You're late again coming into that song!" Steve complained. "What the hell's wrong with your timing?"

Rusty inhaled deep and slow. "Let's just try over."

Rusty looked and sounded to Rick the way he felt when he had to explain something over and over to one of his children. He gave Rusty a surreptitious nod of support, as if to say, "We know he's a pain in the ass, just hang in there!"

Rusty took deliberate care on the next songs to make sure his timing was perfect, his notes were on cue and in tune, his movements were tight and concise, just the way Steve liked.

Two songs later, Steve complained again, "Morgan, if you're not going to play that bridge right, sit that part out. I'll handle it all."

"What's with the use of my last name all of a sudden?" Rusty challenged Steve. "You know my first name. Just use that."

Steve glared at him a full minute, then backed down. "We have three shows left. Can we please just have one of them go right?"

"They've all gone right so far," Rusty spoke under his breath, intending no one to hear, but Steve caught the words and exploded.

"They've been crap! Every show on this tour we've missed notes, misconnected in places, and completely screwed up at times."

"Why is it you're the only one who feels that way?" Rusty was in full mutiny now. "The rest of us all think the tour has gone great. Why do you feel it's been a complete disaster?"

"Maybe I'm the only one paying attention! The rest of you have your heads anywhere else but on the show."

Rusty snapped, "Don't you go after the others! They've all played just fine, in fact they've been damn near perfect! Your problem isn't with them anyway! You've got some grudge against me. Well the hell with this! I don't need your harassment every time I step on the stage. I'll do my part the next three shows, then we're done. I've had enough. As for sound check, my guitars and I will be fine. I'm through with your attitude, and I'm through with you!"

Rusty stormed off stage before any of the others could stop him.

"What the hell's gotten into you?" Terry demanded of Steve, coming around from behind his drums in a flash. "Why are you going after Rusty all the time? He's not doing anything wrong and you need to cut it out!"

He followed Rusty and found him back stage, leaning against a wall, kicking his foot against the cement.

"Come on back. If Steve gives you any more crap the three of us will stand by you."

Rusty shook his head. "You know in all my career I've never missed a sound check. I've never walked out on anything. I've never let a band down."

"I know."

"I've taken everything Steve's thrown at me. I don't know what the hell's going on inside him, but I'm tired of him ripping me apart when I'm not doing anything wrong. I just can't take it anymore. I've hit my breaking point."

Terry caught the ragged edge in Rusty's voice and the tormented look in his eyes. "I know Steve's wrong. But we've only got the three shows left. Come on back and finish sound check. We'll get through tonight's show, and the rest of the week."

Rusty shook his head. "He's crossed the line too many times. I want to know why he's so angry these days, and why I'm the only one he's calling out. I can't just let it slide anymore. I'll be back before the show starts."

Rusty strode down blind sidewalks until he came to a nondescript greasy spoon diner. He wasn't hungry, but he'd walked off a good deal of his rage and now wanted a quiet hole in a wall where he could just sit and think.

The diner held a handful of patrons: a delivery person, a bus driver, a couple of construction workers whose presence caused Rusty's heart to race, recalling the band's near miss. These construction workers, though, paid him no attention; they were more focused on the burgers and fries before them. No one in the diner seemed to recognize him; in fact, the only one to notice him at all was the waitress who carried a coffee pot over to the booth where he sat, poured a cup for him without asking first, and waited to take his order.

Even though he wasn't hungry, the aroma of burgers and fries enticed him. Maybe a little comfort food would ease the hurt from his latest run in with Steve.

Where had it all gone wrong, he wondered after he'd given the waitress his order. Odysseus had fought their way through so many internal and external demons on their rise to the top. Why, now, was it all falling apart?

It was easy to blame Steve for all their turmoil. He was the most vocal about what bothered him, right or wrong. Hadn't they all, though, found this tour the hardest? Blaming it all on their tiredness wasn't the answer.

He thought back to Odysseus' early days. They were excited, and united in their dream. Well, they'd succeeded. They'd climbed to the top of the mountain. While the vista from there was breathtaking, below them treacherous mountain paths and jagged edges lie waiting to pierce them if they fell.

Rusty knew Steve's pushing the band so hard the past few years wasn't just down to Steve himself. Odysseus' fans constantly clamored for new music, and label execs with dollar signs in their eyes always demanded more either in the way of album sales or tour revenue. If the band failed to produce, the fall from the top could be excruciating.

Rusty told himself he would go back as promised for the show ahead and the last few gigs of their tour. He would try to remember Steve was under intense pressure from the outside, and that if Odysseus could stick together through this storm they would be that much stronger in the end. Still, as he paid his bill and headed back to the arena, part of him longed for the days when the dream Odysseus shared shone like gold, when their view hadn't been tarnished by the realities of life at the top.

"I didn't think you'd be back," Steve told Rusty when he showed up back stage. No apologies, no glad to see you.

"I told Terry I would be." Then Rusty cautioned him, "You better get over whatever the hell is bothering you, or you won't have a band left for the next recording session."

Renee waited on Terry's calls, which she'd learned over the past several weeks could be sporadic. While he would text every day, sometimes three or four days would go by before they talked with each other. The past few weeks the texts had grown shorter, and a week or more might pass before his calls came through.

By the time he called on Thursday of the last week of the tour, she had accepted the head librarian position Mrs. Clarke had offered. She'd researched and settled on an apartment, and started packing her books, dishes, and other personal items to take with her. The only detail not handled was telling Terry.

"Hey babe," he started the call with. In just those two words she could tell by his flat, monotone voice, he was tired, or stressed, or both.

"You're in the home stretch," she said, keeping her tone light to try to cheer him. "How are you doing?"

"Glad it's almost over." Terry debated telling her the truth, decided they had always been open with each other about everything in their lives, and chose to be honest now, while none of his Odysseus mates were within earshot. "It's been rough, babe. Steve's out of control, pushing everybody around, micromanaging, he's coming down really hard on Rusty. Rusty's just about ready to walk."

Renee's heart sank. With whatever problems he was facing now, she would not tell him tonight about her new position. He had enough worries on his mind. "What's with Steve? Rusty wouldn't really quit, would he? Steve's not treating you bad is he?"

"Whoa, girl!" Terry laughed. "One question at a time!"

"Is Steve coming down hard on you personally?"

"No, mostly Rusty. But he's insistent that we're hitting the studio with new material come January."

"So we won't have much time together." Not that it mattered, Renee thought. With her new job she wouldn't be able to take any days off; but any hopes she had that they could spend evenings or weekends with each other were now crushed.

"We'll have Christmas and New Year's," Terry reminded her.

She forced a light laugh. "Oh sure! If it's like any other year you'll be worn out from the tour and you'll spend most of the holidays sleeping."

The rest of the band had returned to the bus and Andy had revved up the engine, so Terry ended his call. After he'd hung up, Renee realized he hadn't once asked how she was or what was new in her life. Looks like I made the right decision, she thought. Maybe Terry's gone off me; maybe we're hitting the end of our road.

"Steve should be home, what, next week?" Kit asked as she and Sascha sipped wine and dined on fettuccine alfredo in front of Sascha's fireplace. Kody had been tucked into bed a half hour earlier, and they had a chance at last for a serious talk.

Sascha nodded. "Their tour finishes Saturday night. He should be home Monday."

"He's not coming here, is he?"

"No, he has something else worked out."

"Is he still opposing the divorce?"

"Of course. I knew he would." Sascha recalled the conversation she'd had with her attorney earlier that day. "Steve wants full custody of Kody and he's balking at the alimony amount I've requested."

"Things could get nasty," Kit cautioned. "Are you prepared for that?"

Sascha took a long drink of her wine. "For Kody's sake I hope it doesn't get ugly, but I'm prepared to do what I have to."

"Don't let him off light! Make him pay for what he's put you through!"

Surprised by the ferocity of her friend's reaction, Sascha turned to Kit. "I won't be mean to him. He hasn't been bad, just absent." Not like your husband, who put you through such horrible mental cruelty you needed therapy for three years after your divorce, she almost added, but held back. She couldn't afford to make an enemy of Kit now, when she would need her support the most. "I just want a fair settlement and then to move on with my life."

Kit studied Sascha's face and body language, the uncertainty in her friend's eyes, the constant clenching and unclenching of her hands. "You don't really want this divorce, do you? You're still in love with him."

Sascha glanced at the diamond engagement ring and gold band she had not yet removed from her left hand. She could still remember as clear as if it had happened yesterday the day Steve had proposed to her, a sunny day in May, at her favorite stone bridge in the countryside. She could still see their wedding day, the satin and lace dress she wore with scattered rhinestones across the appliqué roses, and the black tuxedo with royal blue cummerbund he was attired in, the scent of his aftershave, the feel of his firm hand on her bare back as they danced their first dance. She could still feel his touch as he'd slipped the wedding ring on her hand, and knew by now those impressions would never fade.

"I'll always love him," she admitted to Kit. "We never stop, do we? Even years after a marriage is over they still have a way of turning our hearts."

Tim Caldwell was dead. The Odysseus members learned the news after their Jacksonville show, from a series of texts each of them received from other friends throughout metal music world. Early texts hinted at a possible heart attack.

Metal bands often interchanged members over the years. A top notch guitarist, Tim had started out in one band, moved to another, then when the second band broke up, to a third. He'd substituted for guitarists with other bands when their members had had to cancel due to health or family issues. Odysseus had been on the same tour with him a number of times, either opening for one of the bands he was in, or co-headlining on shows where two or three bands shared billing. At fifty-eight Tim had made noise over the past several months about hanging his guitar up for good and retiring, but no one believed him. His passion for music ran too deep. He would play forever.

Forever ended far sooner than any of them expected.

Terry slumped onto the bench in the bus's front lounge area. "I can't believe Tim's gone."

"I just talked with him last week." Rick sat across from Terry, numb with shock. "He sounded fine."

"Remember the time we all played near Naples, and he took us out to the swamp on an alligator hunt?" Dave had to laugh in spite of his sadness. "I never thought we'd get out of that swamp alive!"

Rick recalled, "That alligator moved so fast it scared the hell out of Tim!"

"I went fly fishing with him once." Terry could still smell the river water and feel its cold embrace. "Something bit his leg; I've never seen anyone run as fast as he did. We never did see what bit him but he had a mark on his leg for weeks after."

Rusty focused on his guitar case standing by the bunk section of the bus. Tim had not just been a fellow guitar player, to Rusty he'd been a mentor of sorts as well. Every guitar lesson Tim had taught him over the years, every specialized technique, came back to Rusty now.

"I wouldn't be half the guitar player I am without him," Rusty told the others, his voice choked with emotion. "There's still so much he could have taught me. Now I'll never have the chance to learn."

They all shared memories of Tim, except Steve who listened to their stories while his mind swirled with memories of his own, times he and Tim had jammed together backstage, times they'd partied long into the night after shows, and most clearly the last time they'd seen each other, six months back when they'd both been in Chicago and met up for dinner.

"I don't know, Marner," Tim had confessed back then. "I don't know how much longer I can live on the road."

"You and your guitar are still red hot," Steve had pointed out, aware Tim needed no such confirmation.

"Yeah, I know, but it's taking a heavy toll on me."

Steve had understood. Tim had twelve years on him age-wise; already Steve felt aches and tiredness he hadn't felt five years previous. Good God! Twelve years on he would really be struggling. He didn't know how Tim kept going.

"Why do you keep at it?" Steve had asked that night.

Tim had looked far away in responding; whether far back into the past or way ahead into the future Steve couldn't tell, or perhaps he'd set his sights on something deeper, some place inside the universe where music originated from, a place so deep within the soul or the universe, or both, it could only be tapped into by those who were driven to find it.

"It's never enough to just create songs, is it?" Tim had responded. "Playing for an audience, that's where the real power's at. Feeling that connection with the crowd, seeing their faces, how music impacts them, their joy, their angst, sometimes even their tears. If I left the road I'd miss out on that, and I'm just not ready to give that up."

Steve recalled Tim's words now and spoke to an invisible spirit he hoped would hear, "You made it, my friend. You stayed true to your calling."

He ran his eyes around the musicians before him, his band brothers, his friends, studying each one surreptitiously so they wouldn't know they were being scrutinized. He'd traveled so long with each of them he'd begun to take them for granted. As he reached Rusty, seated across from him, his heart turned to ice, ashamed of how he'd treated his brother.

Life was short. Tim had died without warning. Anyone could be here one minute and gone the next. Now, before it was too late, he had to make amends.

"I have to say something," Steve announced, cutting into the flow of memories. The band turned apprehensive eyes on him, wondering what bombshell he would drop now. He knew he deserved their looks, and hoped his words would make amends, at least in part. "I know I've been a real jackass lately. I've taken things out on you all for no good reason. I'm sorry."

The others all looked to Rusty, waiting to take their cue from him.

Rusty didn't respond right away. While the show had gone well, the sound check disaster still overshadowed his feelings towards Steve. One short apology, no matter how sincere, could not go far enough to set them back on the right course.

"I appreciate that you're sorry, but I'd like to know what's behind your moodiness. It didn't just come out of nowhere."

"You're right," Steve agreed. "We've always been up front with our lives, we haven't kept secrets from each other. I haven't been up front with you on one thing. Sascha wants a divorce. I haven't wanted to deal with it myself, so I haven't told you guys. It's tearing me up inside, and I've taken it out on you all. Especially you, Rusty. I was wrong to treat you all that way."

"You jerk! Why didn't you tell us?" Rusty reached his foot across the aisle between them and gave Steve's leg a playful shove, the way brothers do, the way he and his brothers did long ago before he became the family pariah. "We could have listened and given you some support."

Terry considered the journey he was about to embark on with Renee. So many people he knew had marriages that hadn't survived the myriad absences and pitfalls of a musician's world; Rick and Steve had been inspirations to him in that regard as he'd watched them both stay with their wives despite the many challenges. To learn Steve and Sascha were in danger of their marriage failing caused his confidence that he was on the right path with Renee to waver. "Maybe it's not as bad as you think," he offered as much to support Steve as to keep his own hopes alive. "Maybe you and Sascha can still work things out."

Steve considered Terry's words. Sascha wouldn't even take his calls or respond to his texts. He knew the wounds he'd cut through her heart ran far too deep for her to change course. They both had lawyers, negotiations had started, and he and Sascha had both drawn their battle lines.

"I don't think so," he told Terry. "I've treated Sascha worse than I've treated you all; she wants out, and I can't say I blame her."

Dave recalled his own divorce, how a sense of failure hung over him for months, how his anger towards Stacey ate away at him, how depression robbed any joy in his life for far longer than he'd anticipated. He hated knowing Steve would suffer that same agony. "Don't give up hope just yet," he told Steve. "Keep trying. And if you need anything, just holler. You know we're all here for you."

Drained from the show and the emotional upheaval of Tim's passing, the Odysseus boys retired hoping sleep would provide some relief. One by one they drifted off and fell into deep sleep, except Terry whose sleep was punctuated by nightmares.

In one scene, Steve and Rusty went at it full out, Steve throwing guitar cases, microphone stands, folding chairs, anything he could get his hands on, towards Rusty, who stood there taking all the hits, eyes glowing red like the dragons in so many of the video games he'd played when he was younger. A maniacal smile spread across Rusty's face as Steve exploded, like he knew he had the upper hand and when Steve's fury was spent Rusty would rise up and pay him back, blow for blow, curse for curse.

In another, Terry and Renee stood at a storefront on the street near the library where she worked. Snow fell, dancing through the wind like myriad fairies being whisked away before their task was fulfilled, never touching ground, never hitting their target. In his hand he offered a box to Renee but that, too, was pried away by the wind, vanishing into the wall of snow behind them. In the next scene Terry wandered through the blizzard alone, calling for Renee, his voice lost in the howling gale that separated them.

In a third nightmare, while the others were out hunting down lunch, their tour bus took off with Terry still on board, speeding through cities, careening around sharp curves, bypassing venue after venue where Odysseus was scheduled to appear. He tried alerting management and authorities by cellphone but could not pull in cell tower service as the bus whizzed by. He pleaded with their driver to stop, to pull over and let him out; he even tried wrestling the steering wheel away from the driver and shoving his foot off the gas pedal. Nothing worked. He was on the bus ride from hell. Terry awoke from that dream in a panic, not sure, as the bus crashed through a guard rail and rolled down the side of a mountain, whether his piercing scream was a part of his dream or had shattered the silence around him as the rest of his band brothers slept.

Terry glanced at the time on his phone. Three-forty a.m. He knew from experience he would be a long time falling back asleep after repeated bad dreams. Careful to make no sound, he slid off his bunk and stepped to the front of the bus where Andy navigated night quiet roads with only a late night radio talk show to keep him company.

"Mind if I join you?"

Andy lowered the radio's volume. "Not at all. Have a seat."

"What's the topic tonight?"

"Alien abductions, terrorism from deep space."

Terry shook his head. "You believe all this crap?"

Andy laughed. "No, but it's great entertainment and keeps me awake."

"By all means, keep listening then! We don't want you falling asleep at the wheel!"

Andy maneuvered the bus around a slow moving semi, as conscious of the schedule they needed to hold to as he was of his passengers' safety. "And what's stealing the sleep from your eyes tonight?"

"Too much on my mind, I guess."

"Steve and Rusty?"

"You could tell?"

"I've been driving you all around for what, six, seven years now? I have a pretty good handle on who's down, who's struggling with things, who's on top of things in their lives."

Terry drew his eyes from the road to the middle aged driver so expertly guiding them through another night. "They seem to have sorted things out between them now, but do you think it will hold?"

Andy sought Terry's face in his peripheral vision, read the worry there, and tried to ease the drummer's mind. "They might have some more work to do, but they have a deeper bond between them than even they realize. They care too much about the music to let Odysseus fall apart for very long."

"God, I hope you're right."

"Brothers is an overused term," Andy told Terry, "but in Odysseus' case it fits. You all are tied to each other by invisible threads. You're more of a family than the loved ones you leave behind when you're on the road. A bit of wind blows between you at times, but you always find your way through, and when you do you're that much stronger for the storm."

Andy turned the radio volume up a notch then, allowing Terry time and space to work through whatever thoughts still preyed on his mind.

The next caller in to the radio talk show told an incredulous tale of being physically transported to a location in space, not the moon, he was sure of that, but some other physical place from which he could see the earth, although not in full detail. He was clear, insistent even, on the minute details of the vehicle that transported him to space and back, the control panels, the size and speckled black metal it was made of. He described the aliens as asexual, neither male nor female, and was sure they were shape shifters, appearing as close to human form before him, but when gathered among themselves, off to his side, taking on the form of large blobs with thin arms, tiny hands, and compound, hexagonal lens eyes reminiscent of what flies see through. While Andy was ninety percent sure the caller was a crackpot, enough curiosity remained in him that he wondered if the story could possibly be true.

Terry turned his eyes to the dark night around him, radio chatter fading to the background as he sorted through the thoughts that had clouded his mind and disturbed his sleep.

Part of it was Steve and Rusty, and the fear that even though they'd had some sort of breakthrough earlier that night trouble between them could still erupt; but something else nagged at him as well.

The past couple of weeks, in the few phone calls between them, Renee had been quieter than usual, listening as he described for her the chaos of all he was dealing with, but offering no fresh glimpses into her life. She'd offered a general support for him, but had stopped short of deeper, more personal communication.

Had she fallen away from him?

As Andy guided their bus through the dark, Terry noticed pockets of light appear to their left or right, small hamlets of people no doubt tucked into their beds and deep asleep. He pictured the small towns those lights represented. Over the years, Odysseus had passed through enough towns like these that Terry could visualize now what he would find if he walked into one. Main Street would hold a collection of small, cute shops, perhaps clothing, or housewares and collectibles. A hardware shop would carry all the electrical, plumbing, tool, paint and other necessities for repairing and updating the old homes that would fill the side streets. A diner and general store would round out the picture.

By day, these small towns would ooze cheeriness as neighbor and friend greeted each other and chatted about whose kids accomplished what highlights in sports or other school activities, who was recently engaged or divorced, hospitalized, or recovering from various ailments.

Now, at night, those pockets of light represented warmth and security, and a coziness so far removed from life on a tour bus Terry felt a deep ache inside, an intense longing to somehow, someday, live that kind of life with Renee. He thought of Steve and Sascha, and Steve's revelation that they'd hit major problems, and wondered if his dreams of life with Renee would come true, as Rick and Laurel's had, or if he was destined for trouble like Steve, and Dave, and so many other musicians he knew.

Eight

Brothers standing together against a world neither can survive alone

—Sinéad Tyrone, *Two Guitars*

The last show of the tour was upon them. Odysseus played hard, pouring every scrap of energy and passion they had into every note, every riff, every song. After tonight they could catch all the rest they wanted; tonight they left everything in them on the Atlanta stage for their adoring fans.

Afterwards, as they gathered their gear together for the last time that tour, Terry pulled Rusty aside. "Here, I have something for you."

Rusty took the small box Terry held out to him but didn't open it right away. "What is this for?"

Terry shrugged. "I was going to give it to you for your birthday, but that's months away and I can't wait that long."

Rusty lifted the lid off the box, slid away the top layer of tissue paper, and found an antique pocket watch, the kind that hung off a chain and slid into a watch pocket in old fashioned vests.

"How did you remember I collect these?"

"You showed me once, years ago."

The top case was silver, with an intricate scroll design carved into it.

Rusty ran his hand over the top, pleased with how smooth the cold metal felt.

"Open it up," Terry instructed, impatient.

The thin latch at the front clicked easily and revealed an old face, in excellent condition. Garnet or ruby chips, Rusty couldn't tell which, indicated each of the hour positions. Black metal molded into intricate scrolled, pointed pieces formed the minute and hour hands. From his knowledge gained while researching and collecting pocket watches, Rusty estimated this one to be at least eighty years old.

Inside the top lid Terry had had engraved an inscription reading, "Brothers To The End. God bless. Terry"

Brothers. Rusty thought of the two he had back home, the two he never saw, and the sister with them. The ones who had long ago disowned him, as had the parents they shared, just as Terry's family had turned their backs on Terry. Christmas once again flashed through Rusty's mind, one more holiday he would spend without flesh and blood relatives around him. It didn't matter, he thought. His brothers, his family, were his band members and his metal friends at large. The bond they shared drew them closer than their blood families ever could have been.

"It's beautiful," Rusty managed to say without losing composure. "It's the best gift anyone has ever given me. Thanks. I have a Christmas gift for you, but I was planning on bringing it to your house with me. I'll mail it instead."

"You'll bring it," Terry insisted. "I told you you're still coming to my place for the holidays."

"Sure," Rusty answered, knowing full well he would not join Terry and Renee, but realizing debating it right now was futile. He'd bow out at the last minute when Terry couldn't force him to change plans.

They hugged, the kind of hug brothers share, strong and quick. Rusty slipped the watch into the inner pocket of his leather jacket. Until he could work out a proper way to secure the chain, it would be safe there.

"See me before you leave," Steve told Rusty after the show had ended. The packing and disbanding phase had begun, always a madhouse after the end of a tour, each of the Odysseus members anxious to get as far away from each other as they could, at least for a few days. That feeling never lasted beyond a week; four or five days after they were home found each of them calling or texting each other.

Steve and Rusty were the last ones to leave. Even though they'd cleared the air between them the night Tim had died a layer of uncertainty remained, each of them feeling each other out, testing the waters of their friendship now. Steve guessed Rusty was putting off meeting with him, unsure of what he wanted.

Steve sat on a folding metal chair and motioned for Rusty to take the one next to him. "I have something for you." For a minute he couldn't find the right words to start; then he remembered, start with the truth.

"The other day, when I told you about Sascha filing for divorce, that was true but it's not the only reason I've taken so much out on you. The truth is I'm jealous of you."

Rusty stared at him as if Steve had lost what little was left of his mind. "Why would you ever be jealous of me?"

Steve stared at the cement floor, dirty with years of dollies, cases and feet crossing it. He thought the floor must feel as helpless as he did. "I used to be the band's leader. Now they all look to you instead of me."

"We don't have an official leader," Rusty reminded him. "We're all equal. If they're turning to me, though, maybe it's because you're not hearing them. You're pushing too hard." Rusty held up a hand to stop Steve's protest. "Oh, we know it's the men in suits, the label team, pushing you, pushing us all. If we had a united front we'd at least stand a chance to slow their demands down long enough to give us a few months home here and there. That's all the guys want. You never take their side on that. If you did, they'd be right back on your side again."

As hard as they were to hear, Steve accepted Rusty's words. "You're right. I'll try to change."

"I'm no one to be jealous of," Rusty told him. "Just go back to who you were at the start, the dreamer who wanted to reach the stars and take us along for the ride of our lives."

"It has been quite a ride, hasn't it?"

Rusty nodded. "The best."

"I have something for you." Steve held out a small box. Rusty hesitated, then pulled something out of his jacket pocket.

"I have something for you too."

They exchanged the first smile between them in weeks.

"You go first," Steve suggested.

Rusty unwrapped the tissue papered object Steve had handed him. Inside was a cross, large and heavy, the kind Rusty had always admired. Three silver metal strands intertwined in an iron lace fashion, each of the four ends had been molded into an intricate design. Turning it over, Rusty discovered initials carved into the arms of the cross, Steve's on one end, his own on the other. Rusty looked at Steve, surprised. "This is great."

"I saw this months ago at a shop in New York," Steve told him. "You've always admired the ones some of our friends wear. After the way this tour has gone, maybe it means more now."

Rusty admired the cross again, and the sentiment behind it, agreeing that after all the rough moments he and Steve had experienced during this tour, the cross had a special significance. Then he handed his gift over to Steve. "Before you open it, I want to explain."

Why is it, Rusty wondered, he knew just what he wanted to say when he was alone, but the minute he was with the person the words were meant for his mind flew down a dark hole? He dug around that abyss until he found what he'd wanted to say.

"This has been a hard tour. Our hardest. Right from the start. Each night, there's been one point in the show that has gotten me through. One moment, every night. Always the same moment."

Rusty let Steve think on that for a minute, wondering if Steve would guess which moment he meant, pretty sure Steve had no clue. Then Rusty told him, "It was during our song Whispers In The Dark."

One of Odysseus' slower songs, it was Rusty's favorite this year, with words that cut right to the heart of the blind alleys life takes us down, and the way out. While Steve sang most of the band's songs, this one was Rusty's. Behind the vocals, keyboard and drums held a muted line at first, building power when Rick's bass and Rusty's guitar entered. It was a hard song for Rusty to perform; for some reason his emotions threatened to overflow each time he sang it.

"That one part," Rusty told Steve, "when your guitar joins mine. The beauty of our notes together just hits home to me. It's like you're lifting me up, lending all the support you can through the one way we both know best, our music. Like I'm not out there alone." He took a deep breath. "That one moment got me through every night. I just wanted to get you something to thank you."

The impact of Rusty's words hit Steve with full force. For all that he'd been at Rusty's throat the past several weeks, to think Rusty still felt the brotherhood they'd always shared caused a fresh wave of shame to sweep over him as he thought of how he'd treated Rusty. He was stunned that Rusty's favorite moment of the show each night was his own as well. It was like some invisible thread of brotherhood still remained, a confirmation that they could still salvage what they'd once had.

Steve opened the box Rusty had given him. Inside was a heavy chain bracelet. Central to it were two hands clasped together, like a heavy metal version of the Irish claddagh minus the heart.

"Wow." For a minute Steve didn't know what else to say. He was blown away by Rusty's gift. Then he confessed that song was his favorite part of the show as well.

He fastened the bracelet around his wrist. Its weight felt like a safe anchor holding him to a secure place while all the storms in and around him raged on.

Rusty looked as worn down as Steve felt. The past few weeks had eroded so much inside each of them. Their gift exchange had ignited a spark of hope in Steve, though. "Do you think we can get past all the shit and turn things around?"

Rusty nodded. "I still believe we have something worth saving."

"Next month there's a metal show in Cleveland. Want to go with me?"

"Terry and I were talking about that last night. Mind if he joins us?"

It felt so good to Steve, making plans that didn't revolve around work, a fun night out with friends without any pressures. "That's fine," he told Rusty. "I'll order tickets for the three of us tonight."

Nine

Will our love story shine like diamonds against life's background
         —Sinéad Tyrone, *Of Partings And Returns*

All during the plane ride home, Terry ran plan after plan through his mind, examining each for merits or flaws, which would work best, which didn't seem to fit. The scene had to be perfect. Dinner Christmas Eve, he thought at first. He would take Renee to their favorite Italian restaurant, where low lights and classical music would create the perfect atmosphere. Then he remembered that restaurant had closed Christmas Eve the year before, and would no doubt be closed again. He could take her to a movie, he thought; their first date had been a movie with dessert after, he could re-create that scene. No, that wouldn't work either, in fact Christmas Eve might not work at all. Her family had a solid, tight schedule of Christmas Eve traditions, from visiting the nearby botanical garden in the afternoon to see its poinsettia display, to a huge family dinner and trivia game afterward, capped off by a late night church service. No, there would be very little time for them to be alone, the evening would feel rushed at best. Better to concentrate on Christmas Day itself.

Renee's family had already invited him for brunch. Even though their tradition was to open presents before they sat down to a table laden with egg and sausage casserole, French toast, fruit salad, assorted pastries, and cheesy potatoes, he would find a way to steal her away for a bit. As he turned this plan over in his mind, he took it one step further and knew the exact location he would take her. The more he worked his plans out the more excited he became, and could not wait for Christmas to arrive.

As tired as he was when his plane landed, he couldn't wait to see Renee and confirm Christmas Day plans with her. He grabbed a cab back to his apartment, threw his travel bags into the bedroom, changed into fresh jeans and a sweater and ran a brush through his hair, then drove to the library.

He wasn't surprised that Renee was not in her office when he arrived. She was often hunting down books or magazines for patrons, across the street picking up coffee or grabbing lunch from the café down the street, or even transporting books to a nearby library if someone had an urgent enough need. After looking down the aisles of books and not finding her, he knocked on the half open door to Mrs. Clarke's office.

"Any idea when Renee will be back?"

Shocked, Mrs. Clarke shook her head. "She's no longer here. Didn't she tell you? She's transferred to a different branch."

"She never said," Terry replied. Or had she? The last couple of weeks he'd been so preoccupied by the growing conflict between Steve and Rusty he hadn't paid full attention to Renee. He'd blown by many of her texts and e-mails, and admitted to himself now that even in phone calls he'd had half of his focus on what she was saying, but the other half on everything else going on around him. But no, he was sure now that if she'd told him about any kind of job change he would have noticed and responded to that.

"She probably didn't want to bother me with something this big while I was on tour," he told Mrs. Clarke. "Do you have the address where she is now? I'll drive over there and see her."

Mrs. Clarke hesitated. If Renee hadn't told her beau where she was transferring to, perhaps there was a good reason, perhaps despite his kind exterior he was mean to her, perhaps he'd hurt her or they'd broken up for some other reason. Still, in all the times she'd seen Terry with Renee they'd been so obviously in love she was sure they had a future together, and she wouldn't thwart their path to happiness now. She gave Terry the address and phone number; when he'd left, she called Renee.

"Your young man was just here looking for you. Didn't you tell him you had a new job?"

Renee felt her heart stop cold and then race ahead of itself. "He's been so busy with his work I didn't want to trouble him with anything I was going through. I planned to tell him when he got home. I didn't think he'd go straight to the library before I had a chance to catch him."

"He was very surprised you weren't here. I've given him your new address. He's on his way now."

On his way? Renee glanced down at the black skirt and royal blue sweater she wore. They were fine for work; but all wrong to greet Terry in when they'd been apart for so long. She had no time to rush to her apartment and change. This would have to do. She calculated the short amount of time since she knew his plane had been scheduled to land, and wondered what he could be in such a hurry to see her for that he hadn't even taken time to rest as he always did upon first returning home from a tour.

Taking no time to reflect on how clean and modern Renee's new library appeared, Terry strode in and spotted Renee by the electronic book search keyboard terminal.

"Why didn't you tell me?" He demanded of her when they stepped into her new office, away from sight and sound of the rest of her new staff and patrons. "And don't say it's because I was too busy! Whatever's important in your life is important to me."

"Important to you?" Renee hadn't meant to snap, but found she couldn't stop, all the frustrations of the past couple of weeks unleashed. "You've hardly asked me anything about my life in our last few phone calls! All I've heard is how Rusty and Steve are at each other's throats, how you don't know how to keep peace between them, how hard your life on the road has been this time around. You've hardly given me a thought!"

"Not given you a thought?" He bristled at the accusation. "If I had no thought for you would I have rushed over here the minute I got home?"

Renee had to concede that point to him. "Why did you come over?" She asked, her heart rising and falling with as much fear as when she'd accompanied Terry on the dreaded steep roller coaster he'd begged her to ride in May. Had he come to break up with her, hurrying to get it over with so he could enjoy the holidays ahead unfettered?

"I came here because I missed you!" He laughed and wrapped her in a huge hug. "Why did you think?"

Renee didn't answer, and Terry's conscience kicked him. "I know I've been preoccupied lately. I'm sorry. I hurried over to see you because I know I've been rotten and I want to make it up to you. Can I pick you up Christmas morning, early, before you and your family open presents? There's someplace special I want to take you."

Steve paid the cab driver, then turned and stared at his sister's house. She'd been quite gracious, considering his last minute call the day before begging accommodation at least for a few days. He'd half expected her to say no; Christmas was just around the corner and she would have her usual overloaded schedule of holiday activities and errands, and they hadn't been on the best of terms with each other the past few years, ever since he'd failed to cut the band's recording schedule short when their father was hospitalized for a heart attack. It wasn't her fault he'd put off sorting out a place to stay. The truth was he'd hoped right until the last minute that he'd be able to work something out with Sascha. He should have known she wouldn't be swayed by promises over the phone, that a more personal touch would be needed. He chalked his sister's good will up to holiday spirit and hoped it would last until the new year.

The front door to his sister's house opened, and she ran down the steps and front walk to greet him. "There you are!" She hugged him, then grabbed his arm. "Come on in! It's cold out here. We have so much catching up to do."

Steve followed her into the house, his mind struggling to reconcile the cheerful, excited Sandy in front of him with the one who'd hung up on him after their last attempt at a phone conversation four months ago. Stepping into her living room, he set his luggage down and ignored her outstretched hand waiting to receive his coat.

"Sandy, I appreciate you letting me stay here. I know things have been a little rough between us. I promise I'll find an apartment or something as soon as possible."

"You're family," Sandy told him. "We have our issues from time to time, all families do. My kids will be glad to have their uncle here." She hesitated before adding, "And I need to reconnect with my brother. Stay through New Year's. We'll figure things out after that."

Once settled into the spare room Sandy had directed him to, Steve tried Sascha's number again, expecting it to go to voicemail like every other recent call he'd placed to her. Shocked to hear her answer, for a second he forgot what he'd wanted to say.

"Sasch, I just wanted to work out a visit with Kody for Christmas. You're not going to stop me from seeing him are you?"

Sascha had already discussed with her lawyer how to handle the holiday. "No, I won't stop you. You're his father, you have a right to see him.

We're having dinner at one. You can pick him up at two, but I'll need him home by seven-thirty."

Five hours? That's all he'd get? Steve opened his mouth to protest, then realized if he fought her on this she could close the door to his seeing Kody altogether. "That's fine. I'll pick him up at two."

Rusty studied the Christmas tree he'd set in the bay window of his living room, gauging now which sections needed a few more ornaments, which had too many red or not enough blue. He adjusted a few ornament placements, added a few more overall, then packed Christmas decoration boxes away in his attic. The tree was a concession at best to neighbors who expected him to have some kind of holiday lights and decorations, show some kind of spirit, and who, if he didn't at least do that much, would come over and hang lights and garland for him.

The tree served as a deterrent, as well, to the depression he fought against every Christmas and New Year. Even before Eliza had entered and then so quickly departed his life, Rusty had struggled through the holiday season, all of the family oriented, romance laced trappings that filled every storefront, every television program, and every other atmosphere he entered so not representative of his own life situation. Even spending the season with Terry the past few years hadn't fully defeated the depression demons, although he would never tell Terry that. Terry tried so hard every year to see that Rusty was happy.

"I'm heading off to Cancun with my buddies," he'd lied in his phone call to Terry the day before. "You and Renee will have to celebrate Christmas without me."

"You're really not going to spend the holiday with us?" Terry had sounded so disappointed Rusty almost caved and admitted the truth.

"You and Renee won't even notice I'm not there!"

Rusty felt bad for his lies but knew he was doing the right thing no matter how much Terry protested. Imagining Terry and Renee's special moment would be the one bright spot in Rusty's Christmas.

He stared at the tree now, as Christmas Eve descended. He had long since given up attempting midnight mass, finding a church full of warm, loving families celebrating a God he struggled to believe in too painful to suffer through. Instead, he'd baked his best lasagna, opened his favorite wine, and binge watched all of the crime scene television shows he'd missed while on the road.

Still, as night settled in he felt hollow inside. That damn sparkling tree with all its shiny ornaments and twinkling lights, symbols of a season whose joy so eluded him, no matter how cheery it looked from outside, dragged him down.

"Get a grip, Morgan," he ordered himself. "Find something to occupy your mind before you drive yourself insane!"

He spotted the sketchbook he'd kept during Odysseus' tour. An idea flashed through his mind; he opened the sketchbook and scanned the designs captured on pages within, building on the thought in his mind until he'd formulated the series of images that fit his idea.

Pulling out a clean sheet of paper, he sketched a box, large enough to hold photos and other keepsakes, with a hinged lid upon which he would carve dual Celtic style intertwined hearts, and a simple Celtic border along the top edges. He would repeat that border along the sides of the box. Inside the lid, once it had been announced, he would carve Terry's and Renee's initials and their wedding date.

Energized, Rusty threw boots and coat on and hurried out to his workshop. He worked deep into the night building the box bottom and top. Christmas Day he drew and then carved the designs, his thoughts on Terry and Renee and the beauty and depth of the love they shared as he worked.

Christmas carols played in the background, multicolored lights twinkled on the tall tinsel decked tree in front of their family room French doors, the aroma of ham baking in the oven spilled over from the kitchen and filled the room where Rick relaxed on the sofa, Laurel curled up next to him, Ryan and Christine glued to their favorite Christmas presents, a reading and game tablet for him, an electronic learning center for her.

"You picked perfect gifts for them." Rick squeezed Laurel's shoulder as a show of support, remembering her anxiety the night before over whether she'd bought the right gifts. "You always worry so much, and things work out just right in the end."

"They are happy with what they got," Laurel agreed, buoyed by their kids' obvious excitement and Rick's presence next to her. All the lonely days and nights of the previous months melted from memory as she soaked up the strength of his arm around her shoulder and the comfort of having him home. She remained curled up next to him on their sofa until the oven timer buzzed signaling time to put her potato casserole in.

Rick watched Laurel move about the kitchen, admiring how smooth and easy her movements were, pulling dishes and utensils out, cutting cabbage and apples for coleslaw, blending in dressing, setting places at their lengthened dining room table, each action flowing out of the previous one, connecting with the next, like a dance, a ballet performed on tile and hardwood. She hummed while she worked, he remembered, and listened now as she accompanied the carols playing in the background. He should help her, he thought, but he was mesmerized by her presence, by her skillful ways, by how her face glowed as she worked and the bounce of her long auburn hair. By the time he forced himself off the sofa to help, her work was done.

Seated at the head of their dining room table, with his parents, Laurel's parents, her sister Eileen and Eileen's boyfriend Sam, with Christine sitting next to Laurel and Ryan in the chair next to him, Rick listened to the conversations swirling around him, joining in on occasion but more content to observe rather than participate.

"Haven't recovered from the tour yet, have you?" Mr. Walkowicz asked after Rick had been silent too long. "You still look tired."

Rick smiled to himself. He could never put anything over his father. "Yeah, I guess I am. Seems to take me a little longer to recover from each tour."

"You boys have been working too hard. I hope you're home for a while now."

"I don't know, Dad. Steve wants to hit the studio again sometime in January."

The elder Walkowicz studied his son, noting the deep lines still visible around Rick's eyes, how Rick's shoulders still sagged, how even simple movements Rick carried out like raising a glass of wine or cutting through the ham on his plate seemed less energetic than usual.

"Strike while the iron's hot, right?" He repeated the words his son had used so many times when questioned about Odysseus' hectic schedule.

Rick had to smile even though he knew what his father meant. "You know it, Dad. It's a crazy business. Who knows? The bottom could fall out tomorrow."

Mr. Walkowicz knew from years of experience he could not tell his son what to do. Rick was way past old enough to make his own choices in life. All he could do was support his son and hope Rick's schedule would lighten up soon.

"Well, enjoy what time you have at home now. Would you like your mother and me to take the kids for a night or two, give you and Laurel a chance to spend some quality time together?"

Rick laughed. "Dad, you're something else! Laurel and I are fine, and I like being with my kids, I don't want to lose any time with them. I appreciate the offer though."

The conversation with his father brought Odysseus back to his mind; Rick now found himself wondering what his band brothers were up to, how they were spending Christmas. They remained on his mind through the rest of dinner, through coffee and dessert, through the families' traditional post-Christmas dinner movie marathon. Rick found himself divided, relishing having his wife and children near, enjoying all of the aspects of the Christmas holiday at home, yet wishing he was with Steve and Dave and the rest of the band at the same time.

After their company had departed, before ushering Ryan and Christine up to get ready for bed Laurel told Rick, "Why don't you give them a call?"

"Who?"

"Your second family, you goof! Go call your brothers. You know you want to."

"How did you know?" Rick was sure he'd hidden his divided state from her.

Laurel offered the same knowing smile she used whenever she'd seen through her husband. "You go through this after every tour. You have two families. No matter which one you're with, you miss the other."

Rick pulled Laurel to him and hugged her tight. "I'm the luckiest man in the world. I have the smartest, most beautiful wife any man could want."

Laurel playfully pushed him away. "At least you recognize that! Go make your calls, then find some wine for us, and maybe a bit more of your mother's apple pie. I'll be down in just a bit."

Between the sun's penetrating rays above, the warmth of the sand underneath, and the Pacific's waves swooshing in and out in an endless circuit, Dave found himself drifting in and out of sleep throughout his third day at the Laguna Beach home his friend Sam opened up to Dave and Jerry every Christmas since their divorces. "You don't need to be rattling around your empty places alone when I have all kinds of space here," Sam had said the first year he'd bought his house. Reflecting on it now, Dave was glad Sam had made the offer. Since arriving, he'd done nothing but relax and let go of all thoughts of home. He'd even lost track of time, and only remembered it was Christmas when a Santa suited surfer rode the waves in front of him.

At the thought of Christmas, his daughter rose to his mind. He thought of the special gift he'd worked hard to have delivered to her, surprised she hadn't called or texted him full of excitement at having received it. "I wonder if she got it," he thought, fearing a delivery problem had ruined his plans. He calculated the time difference, then called her, hoping she wouldn't refuse his call.

"Merry Christmas, Jessica," he forced himself to sound cheerful when she answered. "Have you had a good day so far?"

Jessica's voice held the same angry edge he'd grown accustomed to. "Yep."

He'd also become used to her monosyllabic answers, and knew to press ahead despite her curt communication. "Did you get the present I sent?"

"Yep."

Damn her! Couldn't she just this once break out of her mood? "I was hoping for a little more enthusiasm from you."

"I told Mom to send your present back. I don't want it."

Dave pictured the blue sports car he'd picked out for her. Any other girl her age would be screaming and carrying on, unable to contain their excitement. He could understand Jessica's anger towards him, but to turn down a free new car? How much must she hate him to turn down the exact model and color he'd learned from talking with Stacey that Jessica most wanted. Fine! He wouldn't force the gift on her. "Tell your mom to call me tomorrow so I can work out a return."

Instead of speaking, Jessica hung up. Dave stared at the phone several minutes. He'd failed at anything he hoped his gift would accomplish. If a new car didn't turn her heart towards him, he had no clue what else would work.

Jerry called out from the deck that stretched across the back of Sam's house high enough off the shore to provide a fair amount of privacy, "Steaks are on the grill! Grab more beers and get up here!"

Dave spent the rest of the day pushing Christmas back into the deep corners of his mind, focusing instead on the warmth of the sun and then, when night set in, the myriad stars overhead, the soothing sounds of the ocean below, and the comfort of friends whose lives had followed the same divorce trajectory and understood the challenges and emotions every holiday brought about.

Steve, Sandy, and Sandy's husband Ian picked at the remnants of the cookie tray between them on the kitchen table that looked out over the family room. From his vantage point, Steve watched Kody playing with his cousins Dani and Trevor. Nine year old Dani tried to teach Kody how to read words in a new book he'd received, while six year old Trevor was more interested in playing with the toy fire trucks he and Kody had been given. The fire trucks won out as Kody and Trevor hurried to put out imaginary fires, and Dani settled on the sofa with one of her own new books.

"Thank you again for letting us share Christmas with you," Steve told Sandy and Ian. "I'm not sure how I would have handled it alone."

Sandy handed Steve a fresh cup of coffee. "We loved having you be a part of it all. I'm so glad you called and we could reconnect."

"I am too." Steve's eyes met Sandy's. "I know our last falling out was my fault. I'm sorry."

Sandy waved invisible problems away with her hand. "All behind us now. Next week we're into a new year and a new start."

"I know I need to sort out a place to stay, but do you mind if I keep your room for another week or two?"

"Stay as long as you want," Ian told him. "Sandy's so busy catching up with you she hasn't had time to nag me about anything!"

Sandy gave Ian's arm a playful slap. "Just for that, I'm pulling out my list of things you promised you'd take care of while you're off next week!"

Steve laughed. "Don't worry, buddy! In exchange for my stay I'll help you out with the chores." He reached for another cookie, a frosted cut out shaped like a wreath, with red candies for holly berries and a frosted red bow. "Hey, this looks like the cookies we had when we were growing up."

Sandy pulled a plastic container of cut out cookies from the counter behind her. "Mom gave me her cookie cutters when she stopped baking last year. Recognize any more of these?"

"The star, the Christmas tree, oh, and the stocking!" Steve pulled out one of each. "Did you make her frosting too? It tastes the same."

"I did. Remember how much fun we used to have decorating cookies?"

"We had sprinkles and candies and frosting all over the kitchen didn't we?" Steve glanced at Kody. "Maybe someday Kody could come over and decorate cookies with your kids?"

Sandy gave her brother a hug. "Count on it."

Steve had promised Sascha he'd have Kody home by seven-thirty. Even though he'd be a few minutes late, he drove slowly, chatting with the little boy in the back seat whose eyes had started to grow heavy. "Did you have fun playing trucks with Trevor? Do you like the books Santa brought you? Do you like the tiger hat and mittens Aunt Sandy made?" Kody's answers were short, barely audible as sleep started to set in.

Pulling into the driveway of the house he and Sascha had owned together, Steve shut off the car's engine and sat a minute, staring at what he stood to lose, what he had already lost. He knew in his heart he'd blown his chances, he would not win her back. Splitting time with Kody over holidays, over vacations, and any other times he was home, would be the way of the future. That thought erased all the joy the day had brought.

Sascha appeared in the front doorway, waiting for Steve to deliver their child back to her. He could not delay the inevitable any longer. Before unlatching the car seat Steve told his son, "I had fun with you today. I love you."

"Love you too." Kody mumbled, a rote answer Steve knew, nothing that came from the boy's heart, just a response he'd grown accustomed to offering.

Steve picked his son up, grabbed the bag of presents and treats Kody had been sent home with, and hugged the boy tight before carrying him up to his mother.

"Thank you for letting me have him today." Steve set the bag inside the doorway as Sascha took Kody into her arms.

Sascha held the boy tight. "You had the right to see him. It wasn't my choice, it's what our lawyers worked out."

A slap across the face would not have stung more. Steve held back the harsh response his anger fed him; instead, still hoping to at least settle things amicably with Sascha, Steve answered, "I appreciate that you went along with their decision. Kody had a lot of fun, and he was so good. You've done a wonderful job raising him."

With that he turned, returned to his car, and drove around the corner before pulling off to the side, shutting his car's engine off again, and taking several minutes to clear his eyes of the blurring they had suddenly taken on.

"I thought you said we were going to your place for Christmas morning before my family's brunch." Renee watched as Terry bypassed the turnoff for his apartment, and headed instead for the expressway.

"I lied," Terry admitted. "I wanted to surprise you."

Renee read overhead signs as they advanced along the highway. "Terry, we're not going out to the shore are we? Are you sure we'll make it back to my parents' house in time for brunch?"

Terry glanced at her. "We might be a little late. I promise you, it will be worth it."

As he drove Terry prayed his plan would work, that he was taking the right step at the right time. Renee's decision to relocate to another library had thrown him, her explanation to him that the head librarian position was too tempting to pass up unsatisfactory, incomplete. He decided to dig deeper now. "Renee, why did you really take that new job?"

"I told you. It was a good opportunity."

"No, I think there's something more. You never mentioned it to me." He raised a hand to prevent the protest she was about to launch. "I know, you told me I was busy and you're right, but I thought we were working towards a future together, and something as important as a job change would be a matter we would discuss together unless you had other reasons to keep it from me."

Renee knew she had to admit her fears. She tested a few different ways to answer, settling in the end on, "I wasn't sure we had a future."

"Are you serious? All this time we've spent together and you didn't think it was heading anywhere?"

"Terry, I told you the other day at the library, you were so consumed with your problems you lost all sight of me. I understood, I knew you were dealing with some difficult things, but if we had a future together you would look beyond your issues to ask about my world once in a while, especially when you're on the road and you can't see up close anything I may be dealing with. I don't want a future with someone who so easily disregards me."

He could challenge her, Terry thought, make her see all over again the difficulties specific to touring life, the challenges of living in two worlds, his and hers, at the same time, how hard it was to stay connected to home when one was hundreds of miles away; but what good would that do? In the end she was right, and he wondered all over again if he was on the right track now.

They'd reached their destination. He pulled into a gravel parking spot by the strip of grass that separated the road from the ocean. He walked around to her side of the car, opened her door, took her hand and led her to where the ground had widened, where the view of the ocean and curved stretch of rocky beach below were most spectacular, which he pointed out to Renee now. "Isn't that the most beautiful sight in the world?"

She could list a dozen sights equal in splendor across the world, but the pure amazement on Terry's face stopped her. She knew he was crazy about the sea. They could see this sight any time, she thought, it wasn't worth upsetting her family's Christmas morning routine; but if it was this important to him she wouldn't dampen his joy. "It is lovely," she agreed. "Look how the light through clouds creates shadow patches across the water."

Mesmerized, Terry stared at the waves for several minutes. When he spoke at last, it was in the most hushed, reverent tone Renee had ever heard him use. "The ocean and the shore, that's my favorite love story. Do you see how the water leaves and returns, leaves and returns, always coming back, and how the shore always takes the water back in? They never disagree, she never bars his return, he never stays away any longer than necessary."

"You're wrong," Renee corrected. "They do fight, what do you think all the angry storms are for?"

Terry smiled, surprised. "I never thought of that. You're right. But even in their anger, they always come together in the end."

"They do," she agreed, still not sure why they needed to see this sight this particular morning.

Terry dropped to one knee before her, and took her left hand in his. "I know I can be a challenge, and I know the last few weeks left you unsure of us, but Renee, I love you as much as the ocean loves the shore. Maybe more. Would you marry me? Could we be like them, always coming together no matter what we face in life?"

Renee's heart leapt into her throat, and for a full minute she didn't know what to say. Terry had so fully caught her by surprise she hadn't seen this coming at all.

Terry read her hesitation as rejection, and his heart sank as he thought she would turn him down. He glanced to the ground he knelt on, and thought of how uncomfortable the long ride home would be with a new wall between them.

"Yes."

Terry looked up at Renee, not sure he'd heard right.

She wore a wide smile, even as tears glistened in her eyes. "Yes, you crazy fool! I'll marry you!"

Ten

If I had known the last time I saw you would be the last time
—Sinéad Tyrone, *If I Had Known*

"Thank God we made it here before the storm blew in!" Rusty zipped his leather jacket and turned its collar up to shield him from the strengthening winds blowing in off Lake Erie through Cleveland's downtown streets. "If we get as much snow as they're predicting, I might have a rough drive back home tomorrow."

Steve studied the heavy gray clouds to the west of where they stood. "Hope my morning flight isn't cancelled."

"You and I might be sharing the same airport bench if that happens!" Terry told Steve. "Maybe we should extend our hotel rooms another night just in case."

"Not a bad idea. We can decide after we eat." Steve studied options on his phone. "Steak? Italian? Or seafood?"

"You choose." All of the options sounded fine to Rusty. Since the end of the tour he had only texted Steve to wish him a Merry Christmas and Happy New Year, and to confirm arrangements for meeting in Cleveland. Even though they'd ended the tour on good terms, he'd defer to Steve's tastes now rather than risk upsetting moods.

Steve chose a steakhouse near the venue where the concert would be held. "That's closest to the show and our hotel. If the roads are bad after we could walk back instead of taking a cab."

They ordered beers and steaks, then Terry dove into the topic he guessed Steve would most want to get off his chest. "What's the latest with you and Sascha?"

Rusty cringed inside. Here he was being careful to not rock the boat with Steve, and Terry just split the evening wide open.

If Steve minded the question, he gave no indication. His eyes engaged both Rusty and Terry as he told them, "We're talking through lawyers. She's hell bent on going ahead with the divorce no matter what I say. All I want to contest is time with Kody. He's all I care about now." It was a half truth; every time he saw Sascha or heard her voice on the phone a fresh wound cut open in his heart, but there was no use saying that. Any hope he had of winning her back was lost.

"What is Kody, four now?" Rusty tried to remember how many years it had been since Steve announced the birth of his son. Years all seemed to blur together anymore. What he did remember was how over the moon Steve had been, showing baby pictures to anyone and everyone who passed by, plastering photos and announcements all over social media, calling each of the guys three or four times a day in the first few months with news of how long Kody was sleeping or not, how many times he opened his eyes when Steve held him, and just how enthralled he was with this new little creation he had helped make. "It seems like you just had him!"

"He'll be five in a few months." Steve blocked from his mind how much it would hurt to not be part of Kody's birthday.

After the waitress delivered their first round of drinks Terry asked, "What made Sascha want a divorce? You've been married so long, why would she all of a sudden decide to throw in the towel?"

"It wasn't so sudden," Steve told him. "She's been trying for the past year to tell me she wasn't happy, that things needed to change, that I needed to be home more. I just didn't want to listen."

Steve looked at Rusty and Terry, both of their faces looking way too sad for the fun night ahead of them. "That's enough about me. Tell me what you've both been up to. Rusty, did you get together with friends like you hoped?"

Rusty shook his head. "No, I stayed home."

"What?" Terry's voice carried louder than he intended. As diners from nearby tables turned to him, he lowered his voice. "You told me you were meeting friends in Cancun."

"I lied." Rusty felt guilty and told Terry, "I'll never lie to you again. But honest, didn't you and Renee have a better holiday without me preying on your mind?"

"We did, but if you ever lie again I'll have your head!"

Rusty waved Terry's warning off with a laugh. "Yeah, right, whatever! How did things go with Renee?"

Steve caught the conspiratorial glance between Rusty and Terry and asked, "What was going on with Renee?"

With a grin large enough to swallow his steak whole and bright enough to light the interior of the entire restaurant Terry announced, "I asked Renee to marry me."

"Good God! I hope she had sense enough to turn you down!"

Terry flashed Steve a superior look. "She not only said yes, she's pushing for a wedding as fast as we can schedule one! We're thinking Valentine's Day!"

"You're an incurable romantic!"

Rusty laughed at them both, happy to see Steve's mood had lightened. "Terry, did you take her to the place you wanted to propose?"

"I did." More for Steve's benefit since Rusty already knew the plan, Terry described the scene. "I took her to my favorite place along the ocean. The weather was perfect that day, like God knew I was going to do something special and sent the best conditions ever our way. The day before was stormy, and the day after was windy, but that day the sun peeked in and out of the clouds and there was just a light breeze.

"So I took Renee out to my favorite spot, showed her again how stunning the view was, how you could see around the curve all the way out to the lighthouse on the point, how the waves kept coming to shore, kissing the sand, rolling out, then coming back in again. I told her the ocean was the ultimate love story, always returning, always faithful, never ending."

Terry broke his story off then, replaying the scene in his mind, picturing once again the waves, how blue the ocean and sky were that day, how the light breeze played with Renee's blonde hair, sending tendrils of it flying away from her face.

"Are you saving the rest of the story for after the show?" Rusty teased, breaking into Terry's reverie.

"Sorry!" Terry returned to his story, "I told Renee that while the ocean was nature's ultimate love story, she was mine. I asked her if she would marry me, and yes, I got down on one knee, and yes, she cried, and she's got my ring, and my heart, and by God I'll do everything I can to make that Valentine's Day wedding happen for her!"

Steve was the first to extend a hand out to Terry. "Congratulations! I hope you and Renee will be very happy."

Terry caught an undertone in Steve's voice and realized how his story, happy as it was, must have hurt the guitarist whose own marriage was failing. "I'm sorry, Steve. Here I am going on about my love life when your own is hitting such a rough spot."

"That's okay. You're entitled to your happiness." Steve rose and excused himself. "I'll be right back."

Terry watched Steve step outside, then turned to Rusty. "Do you think he's okay? I hope I didn't upset him."

"He'll be fine. Just give him a few minutes." Rusty returned to Terry's news. "I'm so excited for you. Renee's a beautiful girl, inside and out. You two are a good match for each other."

"Do you really think so?"

"Even if I didn't, it's a little late now don't you think?"

The panicked look on Terry's face made Rusty burst out laughing. "Do you think I'm making a mistake?"

"Good God, no I don't! You're going to be fine. You already know you're right for each other or you wouldn't have proposed to her. I can just see you ten years from now, living in a house by the ocean with a dozen kids, two cats and a dog running roughshod over the countryside!"

Terry pictured the scene and grinned. "That would be fun! And each kid playing an instrument. We better have a house with no neighbors for all the noise we'll be making!"

"And parties you'll be having," Rusty threw in. "I expect a beer blast every other month out at your place."

"And your place on the alternate months!"

While Terry and Rusty planned for fun ahead, Steve had stepped outside to a sheltered corner in front of the steakhouse. The cold air felt good, although the wind had increased and light snowflakes had started to fall.

He was happy for Terry. Whenever he'd seen Terry and Renee together over the past couple of years they'd looked like they belonged together, they were natural and at ease with each other. He wasn't surprised that they were planning to marry; but he hadn't expected the news to hurt as much as it did. All he could think of was how happy, how much in love, he and Sascha had been at the beginning. She had been so beautiful back then, still was, with long hair the color of sunshine and her huge, emerald green eyes. She was tall and thin, and could have been a model if they hadn't fallen for each other and married.

It couldn't be over, he thought. All that love didn't just die. It just needed a spark to rekindle the flame that had once burned within them. He would try once more to restore their marriage. Pulling closer to the building to shield himself, he called Sascha. When his first call went through to voicemail he hung up and tried again, and a third time until she answered.

"You should be calling my lawyer, not me."

Her gruff tone didn't put Steve off. "Sasch, please, just give me a minute."

She checked her watch. "Okay, one minute, starting now."

"Sascha, I know I've done a lot of things wrong, and I haven't listened when you've tried to tell me things. But please, isn't there any way we can start again? I swear to God I'll change, I'll do whatever you want me to do. I just don't want to lose you and Kody. What we had when we started out was so strong; can't we get that back?"

Relieved when she didn't say no right away, Steve held his breath, hoping she would give in to his request for one more try. Instead, after a long moment she told him, "I don't think so, Steve. I just don't have it in me anymore to wait on you to make the changes that will keep us together. I'm sorry."

With that, she hung up.

Steve exhaled deep several times to release his disappointment, then returned to the table where Terry and Rusty sat waiting. "Sorry," he apologized, "I had a phone call to make. Snow's starting to move in, we should probably head out to the show now."

Three bands were scheduled for the show that night; members of all three were friends with Odysseus and had shared the stage with them at one point or another over the years. Steve, Terry and Rusty enjoyed watching their friends, catching exchanged looks and in between antics general audience members may have missed, admiring the dexterity with which their friends played, the power and drive of new songs they had not previously heard, and how good it felt to relax in each other's company with no conflicts or pressures pulling them apart. The night was over before they knew it.

They took a few minutes to run backstage and meet up with their friends, but storm warnings flashed on each of their phones and they cut their backstage time short. When they stepped outside of the venue they found the snow was already inches deep and roads were slick. They abandoned their idea of walking back to the hotel as winds raged over forty miles an hour, and instead grabbed the first free cab they could catch.

Terry sat in front, next to the driver. Steve took the back seat side behind the driver; Rusty sat behind Terry. The hotel was only a couple miles away; even on that short ride the cab slipped and slid, struggling to pick up enough traction to make progress for very long.

Steve saw the car rushing towards them, but had no time to react. Everything happened so fast. The driver of the car slammed on his brakes, the car fishtailed and swerved, but could not stop in time.

Terry was turned to face the cab driver, and had no idea what was coming his way.

Rusty saw the look on Steve's face, and turned to face the oncoming car. He felt the jolt as the car slammed into their cab, heard the squeal of tires, the grind of metal on metal, and the shattering of glass. He felt the impact of the cab door and the car shoving into his right side, and an excruciating pain as something pierced his chest.

Then the world around him went black.

Eleven

If only fills my mind like an oven timer whose buzzing cannot be stopped

—Sinéad Tyrone, *If Only*

The force of the car sliding into their cab had shoved the cab into a light pole with enough violence that the front of the cab was now a twisted, mangled mass of metal. From outside, Steve could hear screams and shouts, and soon the wail of sirens as police and emergency vehicles headed towards the accident scene. Inside the cab, though, all Steve heard was a deathly silence.

From his seat behind the cab driver, he could not see if the driver was alive. He doubted it; their vehicle had been shoved too far into the pole, the front end crumpled like a wad of paper of a badly written song being tossed in the trash. Steve doubted anyone could survive that much damage.

He wished he couldn't see Terry, whose body now lie crushed under the portion of light pole that had fallen across the cab, wedged into place by the car that had struck them. Terry made no movement or sound, his eyes were frozen open, unblinking, and blood covered his face, arms, and clothes.

There was no doubt. Terry was dead.

Even if he hadn't been Steve could not have reached him, pinned as he was to his back seat position by the twisted wreck of the cab and Rusty's body slumped against him.

Rusty was all he could think about now.

Blood was everywhere, along with shards of metal and glass. One jagged piece of metal was stuck in Rusty's chest. Steve pulled it out, a natural reaction he thought would minimize some of Rusty's pain; instead it sped the flow of blood oozing from the wound. He managed to slip his leather jacket off and cover the wound with it, pressing as hard as he could to stop the bleeding although the flow still continued at an alarming rate.

"Don't die," he ordered Rusty, not sure if the unconscious guitarist could hear. "Don't you leave me. I promise I'll stay with you. Just don't leave me."

Paramedics arrived, their actions swift, orderly, as if the accident was a common routine. "This one's gone," the first paramedic to reach the cab driver confirmed to his partner.

His partner checked Terry's eyes, checked his wrist for a pulse, placed his fingers along Terry's neck to try and locate a pulse there, then, finding nothing, shook his head.

Steve tried to not watch as Terry's body was removed and a white sheet secured over it. His own breath came in short, ragged gasps as the truth was confirmed. There was nothing he could do to save Terry. He struggled to focus on images of Terry drumming, or laughing as they watched sports on the bus, and not on the ghastly scene in front of him.

"I don't think I'm hurt," he told the paramedic who reached him first. "My friend here, he's pretty bad off."

The paramedics maneuvered Rusty through the cab's wreckage, secured him on a stretcher and transported him into an ambulance, allowing Steve to ride with them. They slipped an oxygen mask over Rusty's face, started an IV to replace the blood he'd lost, injected something else into his arm and treated his open chest wound as best they could while racing to the hospital. Steve listened hard to catch the few words they exchanged, shock, critical, thready, and tried to not read anything into them, forcing himself to believe Rusty would be okay. All while they worked, Rusty showed no signs of coming around; he looked so pale and still Steve was terrified he had already been lost.

As they sped towards the hospital, all Steve could do was pray, something he hadn't done in so long the words felt clumsy, foreign, and he wondered if anyone in the spiritual realm heard him at all. Probably not, he guessed, but he prayed anyway, fearing Rusty would not survive if he stopped.

Steve hurried to keep pace with the paramedics as they wheeled Rusty into the emergency room. Stopped at the doors to the treatment area, he pled with the guard, "I have to stay with my friend."

"I'm sorry, you have to wait in the lounge area."

No amount of protests would sway the guard; all Steve could do was take a seat as close to the doors as he could and watch for any possible glimpse of activity when the doors swung open, any sign of a doctor coming his way with an update.

While he waited he placed phone calls, first to Larry their manager. "We were in a car accident," he explained. "I'm okay, Rusty's hurt pretty bad, they're working on him now. Terry," he stopped, unable at first to force the words out. "Terry's dead."

In his phone calls to Dave and Rick, Steve told them, "Terry's dead. Rusty, I don't know, he's hurt bad. I don't know if he'll make it. Yeah, sure," he agreed when they both insisted on joining him in Cleveland, "you can if you want, unless you want to wait to see if he pulls through." At the thought that Rusty might not, Steve wanted to scream inside. Dave and Rick both promised to find a way to Cleveland as soon as they could.

Steve wished he hadn't quit smoking. He was desperate for a cigarette, or a shot of whiskey, or a hit of whatever drug might bolster him through the hell he was in right now. He wanted out of this nightmare. He wanted to find out it was just that, a nightmare, and that he'd wake any moment to find his world once again intact. He knew it was real, though, by the blood that splattered across his shirt and jeans, the minor cuts across his own hands, arms, and face, and the bruises he felt already forming across his arms, legs, and back.

Dave stared at the phone in his hand. Terry? Dead? It couldn't be. He'd just talked to both Terry and Rusty two days earlier, wished them well on their Cleveland trip and reminded them he'd see them in the studio in a couple of weeks. The idea that he'd never see Terry, and possibly Rusty, again strangled his heart and his throat. He found breathing almost impossible, his mind a jumble of thoughts and memories flying at him like hail striking, hitting hard but not sticking. His hands shook as he searched his computer for flights to Cleveland and texted Steve, Rick and Larry with his travel plans.

"That was Steve." Rick turned to Laurel, seated across from him at the kitchen table, his scrambled eggs and toast now forgotten. "They were in a car accident. Rusty's hurt. Terry . . ." He broke off, unable to connect the words in his brain with the muscles needed to say them. "Oh God, Laurel, Terry's been killed."

Laurel rushed to his side and wrapped her arms around him; Rick buried his face in her chest and cried. Then he forced himself to stop, to face what he needed to do next. "I have to get to Cleveland, to be with Steve and Rusty."

"Let me go with you," Laurel begged. "My mom can watch the kids."

"No. Thanks, but I don't know how long I'll be gone. You better stay here."

Morning lightened the skies outside the waiting room window. Snow still fell, but the wind had died down and the world outside didn't look as angry as it had the night before. The bruises along Steve's body had started to throb, helped, he was sure, by hours of sitting in the same position. He was tired, he wanted to fall into any bed he could find and sleep for hours, for days. He wanted to escape to the dream world Morpheus controlled, and prayed the god of dreams would be kind and grant him mindless rest.

He wanted to turn back time and change the outcome to the night before, to not get in the cab, to not go to Cleveland at all.

"Mr. Marner?"

Steve turned to the voice, found a doctor walking his way, and stood up.

"You came in with Mr. Morgan, correct?"

"I did." Steve tried to read the doctor's face for any positive signals but found none.

"If you'll come with me I can update you on his condition."

"Can I see him?"

"Not yet." As they stepped into a small office, he introduced himself. "I'm Dr. Bales. I performed surgery on Mr. Morgan."

"Please, call him Rusty and call me Steve." Formality sounded so foreign to Steve it grated on his already frayed nerves. "How is he? When can I see him?"

"He has a punctured lung from the wound to his chest, a couple of broken ribs, he had some internal bleeding which we've taken care of, and a bruised liver and kidney. He should recover okay, but it's going to take some time."

"I need to see him."

"They're getting him settled into intensive care right now," Dr. Bales explained. "Visiting rules there are stringent. Family only, and for limited periods of time."

Steve wouldn't be denied. "I'm his brother. And I'm staying with him."

"Do you have any way of contacting Rusty's family?"

Steve thought of the few times Rusty had mentioned the family that had abandoned him so many years earlier. Even if he had a way of contacting them now, he was sure Rusty would want nothing to do with them anymore. He shook his head. "I'm all the family he has."

Dr. Bales dropped his business façade and nodded. "As a physician I can't allow personal feelings to intrude when I'm treating someone. I'm a huge Odysseus fan, though. I know who you and Rusty are. I'm going to list you as a brother on the forms so you can see him when the intensive care nurses allow."

"I'm staying with him."

"I'm afraid that's not allowed."

Steve would not budge. "I know you have rules, but I'm not leaving him."

Dr. Bales weighed the man standing before him against the hospital's protocol. Sometimes rules were meant to be broken. In this case, he reasoned Steve occupying a quiet corner in Rusty's room would be far less disruptive than any chaos he might cause if denied what he pushed so hard for. "Alright. You can stay in the room as long as you don't get in the way of anything the nurses or doctors have to do."

The intensive care room Dr. Bales led Steve to had low lights, except for a slightly brighter panel of lights over the bed, a window that looked out over downtown buildings, and a panel of monitors hung on a wall by the bed, each of which beeped out in a steady rhythm indicating blood pressure, heartbeat, and other statistics. Steve ignored all of them and focused on the bed where Rusty was sleeping.

"He'll most likely sleep for several hours," Dr. Bales told Steve. "You should get some rest. You've been through a hard night."

Steve shook his head, pulled the lone chair in the room closer to the bed, and sat down, his eyes fixed on Rusty. "Thanks, but I'll stay right here."

Sascha was making breakfast, mini pancakes with blueberries, for Kody when she heard the news on the radio: three members of the rock band Odysseus in a car accident overnight, details at the top of the hour.

She dropped the spatula, turned the oven burner off, and called Kit. "Did you hear? The station didn't say which three. Oh my God, what if something's happened to Steve?"

"The news is on in five minutes. We'll know then."

"Would you come over? I don't want to hear this alone."

Kit abandoned the omelette she had been cooking and rushed over, arriving just in time for the eight a.m. news.

Sascha held her breath as the radio newscaster announced Steve Marner and Rusty Morgan injured, Rusty in critical condition. As she released a long, relieved sigh, the announcer continued, informing listeners Terry Delaney had been killed in the accident.

Sascha felt dizzy and nauseous as she thought of Terry gone and the nightmare Steve was going through now. "I have to call him," she told Kit. "Will you keep an eye on Kody for me?"

Without waiting for an answer, she ran upstairs and placed her call. "Steve, oh my God! I just heard the news. Are you okay?"

Surprised that she had called at all, Steve turned his attention away from Rusty to Sascha. "I'm fine," he told her, not feeling fine at all, feeling scared and shaken and broken inside. "Terry . . ." He stopped. He was able to say the words earlier, in talking to Larry, because they had to be said. Larry had to know. Now though, sitting beside Rusty with the accident's aftermath all too real, with no sleep and emotions closer to the surface, he couldn't force the words out.

"I know." Sascha's voice was gentle, understanding. "Who's with you? You're not alone are you?"

"Rick and Dave will be here soon."

"Good. Steve, is there anything I can do for you?"

Where do I even start, Steve thought. You could drop the divorce, let me come home, help me build a proper family. You could bring Kody here, let me hug and hold him, pretty sure he's the best medicine for me right now. You could wake Rusty up, bring Terry back, erase this whole event and let us start last night over.

She couldn't do any of those things, though. Instead he answered, "Just give Kody a hug for me."

"I will," Sascha promised. "And Steve, please keep in touch, let me know how you and Rusty are doing. You can call me any time."

Renee was on her way to work, her early morning playlist accompanying her, soothing nature sounds enhanced by soft violin, light piano, and an occasional flute filling the space inside her car and her mind. Sunlight caught her diamond ring as she eased her steering wheel into the next turn; its bright sparkle catching her eye, making her smile as she always did when she looked at her left hand and relived Terry's proposal. She still couldn't believe they were engaged, discussing where they would hold their wedding and reception, where they would live, planning a future together.

She turned into the coffee shop drive through lane, ordered a mocha latte with extra whipped cream, received her order, and had turned onto the side street that led to her library's rear parking lot when her phone rang.

The number didn't look familiar, but she'd listed her cellphone number with so many wedding planning businesses that didn't surprise her. "Hello, Renee here," she answered, expecting the caller to be the wedding cake baker, photographer, or hotel front desk receptionist.

"Renee, it's Larry, Terry's manager."

She remembered meeting Larry at some of the Odysseus shows. Why was he calling her and not Terry, she wondered. "Oh, hi. What can I do for you?"

She sounds cheery, he thought. He'd half hoped she would have heard about Terry through news broadcasts, social media, or others around her. He hated having to deliver the message himself. He ran his mind through the words he'd chosen, and steeled himself for the job he'd been forced to handle. "Am I calling at a bad time?"

"Not at all. I just pulled into a parking spot at work."

"Okay, I have some hard news for you. You know Terry went to Cleveland yesterday, right?"

Something in Larry's tone scared Renee. She set her coffee back into her car's cup holder and turned the engine off, dread rising in her. "Yes, I know."

"He was with Steve and Rusty," Larry continued, speaking a little faster now, anxious to finish his task. "They were in a car accident, the weather in Cleveland was bad, roads slick, a car crashed into their cab."

Renee felt pieces of her world start to crack and crumble. "Larry, was Terry hurt?"

"Renee, I'm so sorry. He was killed."

She didn't hear the rest of his words. Her phone slid onto the car's floor, where it remained until a coworker came out twenty minutes later, found Renee staring ahead as if in some kind of trance, and escorted her inside. It took a full ten minutes before the library staff could pry what had happened out of Renee, and another hour before her mother could pick her up and take her home.

Luke heard some of the guys talking before his biology class started.

"Odysseus members in a car accident."

"One killed."

"Which one?"

"I don't remember."

"Steve Marner, Rusty Morgan, Terry Delaney. One of those three."

Luke felt the room start to spin as class started. He could not hear the teacher's words through the buzz in his ears, her writing on the chalkboard swam before his eyes. He excused himself, hurried to the restroom, and threw up. Then he ran out the double doors at the end of the hall.

"Dad! Uncle Rusty's been in an accident!" he shouted into his cellphone, his panicked words running together in a jumbled heap. "You have to find out what happened! He might be dead!"

"Aren't you supposed to be in class?"

Luke could not be calmed by his father's cold reaction. "Turn the news on, Dad! Find out if he's alive!"

"If I do will you go back to class?"

"Yes."

Harold checked the internet and informed Luke, "He's in the hospital, he'll be okay. Now get back to school and let's have no more interruptions."

By the time school ended, Luke had gathered enough information from listening in on other kids' conversations to know about Terry and that Rusty Morgan was in critical condition. Dashing into the house after his school bus dropped him off, he ran up to his room and searched the internet for any updates on Rusty's condition. As soon as his father walked through the front door Luke begged, "Please Dad, can we go to Cleveland? I know what hospital Uncle Rusty's in. We have to go see him."

With slow, deliberate actions, Harold hung his coat in the front closet, left his boots in the boot tray by the front door, and entered his study where he set his brief case on his desk where he would return after dinner. "You have midterms next week to study for. You're going nowhere."

Defiant, Luke shouted, "If you don't take me I'll go myself! I'll take a bus or a train, whatever I have to do!"

Harold leveled his sternest look on his son. "I told you you're to stay away from your uncle. No phone calls. No cards. No visits or reaching out of any kind. If you disobey me, you'll be grounded for a year. Understand?"

Luke never hated anyone as much as he hated his father at that moment. "Understood," he agreed through clenched teeth, vowing in his heart that someday he'd connect with his uncle. In the meantime he would pray every prayer he could think of, and light as many candles at church as he could. His father could not stop him from doing that much.

Rick picked Dave up at the airport, then they joined Steve at the hospital. Their meetings had always been exciting, as if they hadn't seen each other in years instead of months. This time when their eyes met pain reflected back at each other instead of smiles.

"I can't believe it." Rick still couldn't wrap his mind around the news. "I can't believe he's gone."

Dave shook his head and fought to quell the emotions so close to spilling over inside him. "Me either. It feels like it can't be real, but I know it is."

"Have you had any updates on Rusty?"

"No. God, I hope he pulls through. Losing Terry is hard enough. We can't lose them both."

Even as he said the words, the truth of them hit Dave like a sledgehammer. As he and Rick drove to the hospital, he prayed Rusty would make it, his words to God desperate, pleading.

The hospital's visiting policy allowed only one of them at a time to join Steve. "You go first." Dave insisted, not sure, no matter how much he cared, if he was ready for what he'd find in the intensive care room.

Rick stepped into the hospital room, took in Rusty's body lying motionless underneath a thin white sheet and blanket, thought his face held about as much color as the sheet, and turned to Steve. "How are you? How is Rusty?"

Relieved to see his brother, Steve rose and gave him a quick hug. "God, I'm glad to see you. Is Dave here?"

"Yeah, he's downstairs. He'll come up on the next shift."

"Okay."

"How are you?" Rick repeated. "How is Rusty?"

"I'm fine. Rusty not so much, he's hurt pretty bad."

Rick ran a hand along Rusty's arm. "Has he woken up at all yet?"

"No." Steve remembered what Dr. Bales had told him. "He might not for a while, he's been through a lot."

"You both have."

Steve didn't deny that. He'd spent the hours since taking his place in Rusty's room focusing on the friend before him, shutting his mind to what he himself had gone through. Now, with Rick's questions, his mind replayed the accident over again. Even after Rick had returned to the waiting room, Steve visualized the scene and its horrible aftermath. He felt himself shake, felt his fears build to the point of almost strangling him. He forced himself to shut his fears off, to not think beyond the moment, to focus on what was immediately before him and not what was past or what might lie ahead. He placed his hand over Rusty's which was resting on top of the sheet. "I promised I'd stay with you," he spoke as close to Rusty's ear as he could, hoping his friend could hear. "I'm not going to leave you. Don't you leave me."

Nurses and doctors shuffled in, checked on Rusty, made notes on a chart, replaced IV bags, and retreated. Dave and Rick took turns stopping in, looking after both Rusty and Steve. As word of Terry's passing and Rusty's critical condition spread, other friends texted or called. Some messages Steve responded to, giving the briefest answers he could. Others he let slide, knowing Larry would send word out to the public at large.

With nothing else to occupy his mind, memories of Terry flooded in. The huge stuffed giraffe Terry brought to their house when Kody was born, the damn thing bigger than Terry himself, hiding him as he carried it down the street so it looked like the giraffe was walking on its own. His relentless competitiveness when they played poker or, more recently, took on group fitness challenges. The little inspirational notes he would slip onto Dave's keyboards or any of their guitars on occasion, cheering them on when he sensed they were struggling with some issue or other. The way he always believed in the good of every person he knew, or of life in general. Steve realized he'd taken so many of Terry's unique qualities for granted. Now it was too late.

Hours passed, blended from daylight to night, marked by darkness outside Rusty's window. Lightness returned, Rick and Dave brought Steve coffee and sandwiches on their alternating visits; in the quiet stretches between their stops he spoke softly to Rusty, "You keep fighting, little brother. We're all right here. You stay with us."

"No change in his condition?" Dave asked on his next trip up to the room.

Steve shook his head. "No, he hasn't shown any signs of coming around yet."

"You haven't left him at all have you?"

"Only when I've needed the restroom." Steve looked from Dave back to Rusty. "I can't leave him. I promised him I'd be here."

Steve needed a shave, Dave noticed. He could use a change of clothes as well, and probably a good meal on top of that. He told Steve, "There's no telling how long he'll sleep. Why don't you go get some fresh air and give yourself a break?"

"No. Thanks, but I'm fine right here."

He gave the same answer the next hour, when Rick joined him in his vigil.

"Dave and I have two hotel rooms reserved across the street. You should go get some rest. You haven't slept since the accident."

He was exhausted, Steve admitted to himself. Rusty was still asleep; each time Steve asked the doctor he was told it was not uncommon and they weren't worried yet, all of Rusty's vital signs were holding steady and he was doing as well as they expected. It couldn't hurt for him to just take a few hours away, as long as Rick or Dave maintained the vigil in his absence.

"Alright, I'll go across the street and get some sleep." he agreed. "If anything happens though, call me right away."

He took a hot shower, shaved using the razor and shaving cream Rick had supplied, and stretched out on the bed, which felt like heaven. Within minutes he was in a deep sleep. He woke two hours later, though, worry about Rusty penetrating through the dream world he had entered. He rose in a hurry and pulled on clean clothes Rick and Dave had bought, moving as fast as he could, desperate to return to the friend he'd left behind.

"How is he?" He demanded of Dave as soon as he entered the room.

"No change." Dave was disappointed to see Steve back so soon. "I thought you'd sleep longer."

"I thought I would too. I couldn't stay away." Steve studied the monitors on the wall. "His blood pressure's down a bit," Steve noted, panic rising in his voice. "Has the doctor been in?"

Dave answered, "Not yet. The nurse was in about a half hour ago, she didn't seem worried."

Steve took the chair by the bed Dave gave up. "I'm back," he told Rusty, not convinced at all his friend could hear him, acting solely on hope. "I'm not going anywhere, but I need you to wake up. I'm getting bored just talking to myself." He watched Rusty breathing and studied the monitor numbers again, thinking Rusty's color was a bit off, begging God to heal his friend.

All of a sudden, monitors screamed out in alarm and Rusty's heartbeat showed a flat line.

Nurses rushed in, and Steve was forced to step outside to the hallway just as Rick turned the corner with food and coffee in hand. He rushed to join Steve. "What's wrong?"

"I don't know. His heart stopped." He turned terrified eyes to Rick. "I think we've lost him."

Rick's heart dropped to the bottom of his stomach. "Oh my God! Steve, we can't!"

They waited, panicked, breathing silent prayers begging God to save Rusty. After what seemed forever, nurses filed out of Rusty's room; Steve could not tell from their faces whether Rusty was okay or the unimaginable had happened. Fearing the worst, he peered around the doorway into the room.

"It's okay, you can come back in." Dr. Bales motioned for them both to join him.

Both friends were relieved to see that, even though Rusty had not regained consciousness, his monitor readings were back to a normal range.

Dr. Bales informed them both, "Rusty's okay. He's developed a secondary infection; I believe that's what caused his cardiac episode. We've changed his medications. He should be fine now."

"He still hasn't come around," Steve pressed Dr. Bales, "shouldn't he have by now?"

"The infection may have delayed that, coupled with the severity of the trauma he suffered." Dr. Bales explained. "I'm not worried yet."

Relieved but still shaken, Steve returned to his place by the bed.

Rusty hadn't seen the car that slid full speed into his side of the cab. He'd heard the grinding steel and shattering glass, felt the impact of being struck, and something cutting into his chest. He felt pressure on his chest, and heard Steve speaking although he couldn't make out the words. The world around him became fuzzy. He felt something draining out of him, life, he thought, as everything around and inside him became thin, watery, fading at last into black.

He hovered, not horizontally midair, but in his spirit, as if he were trapped in a sort of mid-world, not part of the physical one he'd belonged to nor of the spiritual world that called to him now. He wasn't sure how long he remained in this state. On occasion a sound would break through, a rhythmic tone like a car alarm repeatedly ringing, only not so jarring, or a voice, a series of voices, some familiar although unidentifiable, one constant voice always whispering to him, a voice he knew well but could not at the moment place. Breathing was hard, pain lingered on the periphery, nothing was clear.

Then the voices and alarm sound vanished, as did the pain. He felt himself drawn upward, surrounded by lights, some soft, other sources of light brighter, small orbs of light, and occasional odd glowing shapes. Voices he recognized called out to him, his grandfather, his favorite aunt, a school friend, a musician he'd once worked with, and Terry, somehow Terry's voice was in the mix. He felt more peace than he'd ever experienced in his life, and he wanted with everything in him to see where the light led.

Then he felt himself drawn down, back to the middle world he'd been in, a state of limbo that was neither light nor dark.

Then he was drawn down further. The beeping sound became clearer, voices as well. He recognized Steve's voice, urgent, pleading, and opened his eyes.

"Man, it's about time you woke up!"

Rusty scanned his surroundings then turned to Steve. "Where are we?"

"Still in Cleveland. Do you remember what happened?"

"Something hit our car." Rusty tried to focus on the fragments of memory that drifted in and out of his mind. "It was snowing. We'd gone to a concert. Terry with us." His heart raced at thoughts of Terry. "Where is he?"

Steve ignored the question. "Do you know how long you've been in the hospital?" He wasn't surprised when Rusty shook his head. "You're on your fourth day."

Rusty was stunned. "Four? Are you kidding?"

"No. Dave and Rick have been here with me on and off. You gave us one hell of a scare."

Rusty could not fight the sleep that overtook him. When he woke up next, the view outside the window was dark, Rick sat by the bed and Steve was in a chair by the corner, asleep.

"Hey brother, am I glad to see you."

Rusty nodded towards Steve. "He doesn't look like much company for you."

Rick shook his head. "Dave and I tried to get him to go to the room we have at the hotel across the street. He wouldn't budge. This is the fourth day since the accident. He's hardly left your side in all that time."

"Really?"

"Yep. Said he promised you he'd be here. You had him pretty scared." Rick was quiet a minute. "You had all of us scared."

Rusty studied Rick's face, the worry lines etched deep around his eyes, the shadow of a beard as if he hadn't shaved since yesterday. "Are you getting any more sleep than Steve?"

"A little. Dave and I take turns. This is the first real sleep Steve's had, though."

Rusty let Rick's words sink in, gave himself time to digest all he'd learned from Steve and now Rick, before asking, "Where's Terry?"

Rick hesitated. He didn't want to set Rusty back. We have to ease him into the news, Rick thought. He told Rusty, "Terry was hurt bad, worse than you."

Rusty was sure Rick knew more than what he was saying, but chose not to push further, afraid of what the truth was. He closed his eyes and let sleep carry him away one more night.

Morning came, and Rusty's mind was clearer than ever. "Last time I woke up you were asleep," he told Steve, who had returned to his customary place by the bed. "You look better now."

Steve smiled. "So do you."

With Steve's help, Rusty raised his bed so he was in more of an upright position. He wanted to be fully alert for his next question. "Tell me about the accident. I don't remember much."

Steve closed his eyes a moment to focus once again on memories he knew he'd never forget, and to steel himself for the telling of it all. "It happened so fast," he told Rusty, eyes open again, watching, gauging Rusty's reactions so he could pull back if it all became too intense. "The roads were slick, we were in a cab going back to our hotel. Terry was in front, you and I were in the back seat. A car going too fast to begin with slid on the greasy roads and hit our cab."

Steve paused, both because he didn't want to say the next words and because he didn't want to break the truth to Rusty. There was no way around it though. The words had to be said.

"Terry was killed on impact. I couldn't do anything for him. I could do something for you, though. You were bleeding a lot, there was blood everywhere. I didn't know how to make it stop. I used my jacket to try to stop it, I put as much pressure on it as I could. I begged you to not die. We'd already lost Terry. We couldn't lose you too."

"That's why I heard him."

Rusty didn't think he'd spoken that out loud, and was surprised when Steve asked "What?"

He didn't know how to describe his experience; he didn't really understand it himself. He just told Steve, "I heard some voices, people I knew who had passed away. I heard Terry's voice and didn't know why. Now I do."

He changed the subject. "Rick said you never left my side while I was sleeping."

Steve recalled again his repeated promises to his friend. "I couldn't. I promised you I'd be here. I couldn't take a chance you'd wake up and find I'd let you down."

Reality set in, Steve and Rusty both replaying the accident in their minds, trying to come to terms with their loss, and the harrowing experience of it all. When they did speak the rest of that day it was only about weather, or what they wanted for lunch or dinner, or what sports game they could find on TV. Dave came in for a while, then Rick. Steve stepped away for an hour, but returned, saying he wasn't quite ready yet to be gone longer than that. Between the four of them they kept conversation short and light, none of them willing or ready to tackle what had shattered their hearts.

Twelve

I never expected this break, never wanted this pause
—Sinéad Tyrone, *The Space Between Notes*

"Rusty how are you doing?" Larry stepped into the hospital room where Steve and Dave continued to keep vigil over him. "I see you've been upgraded from critical to stable condition."

Rusty eyed Larry. How was he? He could catalog the pain he felt from his multiple injuries, but guessed Larry didn't want to hear that any more than he wanted to dwell on it. He could say he was tired of the hospital and wanted to go home, but knew the doctor had cautioned him he had several more days of recovery ahead before they'd release him.

He could say he was shattered inside, broken into a million pieces that no one, not even Larry, could glue back together, but he was sure Larry already knew that.

He gave no reply. One wasn't needed. Larry was already launching into his next announcement. "I've heard from Terry's parents. They're holding his funeral the day after tomorrow."

Larry's words hit Rusty with a sharper pain than any shard of metal cutting into his chest could inflict. "His parents?" Rusty spat the words out as if they were poison. "They never wanted anything to do with his life, they have no right to be a part of his. . . ." Rusty stopped, unable to say the next words. He glared at Larry. "He told me once he wanted to be cremated and his ashes scattered over the ocean; I'll bet his parents don't even know that."

Larry thought back to his brief conversation with Terry's mother. She'd been direct, businesslike, not at all the grief stricken mother mourning her loss that he'd expected. He recalled conversations he'd had with Terry over the years about his parents shutting him out of their lives, and how deep that had hurt him, a wound he'd never fully recovered from.

"Rusty, you and I both know no matter what we say, his parents will do as they wish."

"You're right." Rusty admitted, furious that Terry's parents could show so little regard for him but helpless to change them.

Larry looked around the all too quiet room. "Rusty, I know you won't be able to attend the funeral. Does anyone else want to go with me?"

Steve declined, "I'm staying here."

"You don't have to." Rusty didn't want or need guilt added to so many others issues he could not contend with. "You should go. Terry would want you there."

Steve's mind was made up. No force on earth would pull him away.

Dave and Rick both agreed they would accompany Larry to Terry's hometown outside of Raleigh. The funeral home they entered was crowded with well dressed, middle aged people they were sure were friends and business acquaintances of Terry's parents. Sprays of flowers lined both walls of the large room. At the far end of the room, a partially opened dark mahogany casket drew their attention.

Dave caught sight of Mrs. Delaney eyeing them as they entered the room. She whispered something to her husband, then fixed a steely eye on the trio as Mr. Delaney approached them.

Ignoring Rick and Dave, Mr. Delaney extended a hand to Larry. "Mr. Hoffman? Thank you for all you did for Terry."

"Terry was a joy to work with." Larry motioned to include Dave and Rick in the conversation. "We're all so sorry for your loss."

Mr. Delaney nodded towards the casket. "I'm sure you'll want to pay your respects and then get some rest back at your hotel after your travels. Terry's mother and I will see you tomorrow." With that he returned to his wife.

"Did he just dismiss us?" David asked, stunned.

"Dismiss us, hell! He's kicking us out!" Rick seethed inside. "Let's pay our respects to Terry and then stick around for a while to see what he does."

Larry shut Rick's idea down before it could take hold. "We don't want to make things worse, not today. Let's just handle this all in a way that will make Terry proud."

None of them were prepared for the sight of Terry, his spirit departed, just the remains of the body he'd worn in life lying so still, so cold, in the satin lined box that held him now. One by one they knelt beside the casket and whispered prayers, still struggling to accept the fact that Terry was gone.

The next morning they took a cab to the church, arriving later than they'd planned. Dave and Rick stood outside the gray stone building, its hard cold façade so unwelcoming they almost called the cab back.

Larry finished paying the driver and joined them. "Are you ready to go in?"

"No." Dave was blunt, knowing their manager would understand. "I can't believe we're here. I can't believe we're saying goodbye to Terry."

"They're not going to want to see us." Rick turned to Larry. "You saw how they reacted to us yesterday. Why are we even here?"

Larry ached inside for the musicians he'd managed the past dozen years. He'd seen them through failed relationships, alcohol and drug issues, all the ups and downs of the cutthroat industry they worked in, but never anything as painful as what they were facing now.

"We're here for Terry, not them," he reminded Dave and Rick. "Focus on that."

Stepping inside, Dave and Rick scanned the packed sanctuary and slid into a back pew.

Larry spotted a few empty places closer to the front. "You were Terry's best friends. You shouldn't be back here. Let's move up."

Rick stayed where he was. "And face his parents' wrath again? No thank you. I'll stay where I am."

The altar area was filled with sprays of flowers brought in from the funeral home, the most ostentatious carrying red banners with script spelling out "beloved son" or "beloved brother". On top of the dark wood casket with shining brass handles was a photo of Terry as a young boy in a team baseball uniform, hat on head, bat in hand.

"Couldn't they at least ask you for a more recent photo," he whispered to Larry, "or find one on the computer? God knows there are plenty of good ones they could have printed out."

"Let it go," Larry advised. "They're dealing with loss the best they know how. No parent is prepared to lose a child, no matter what age."

"They lost him years ago."

Larry agreed with Rick. "They don't have the wonderful memories we do. I feel sorry for them."

Rick couldn't find within himself the same capacity for compassion Larry had shown for a family who had shunned their son. He'd shared with Terry too many times when holidays or other events surrounded them and the absence of family most keenly felt. That Mr. and Mrs. Delaney could so easily cut their "beloved" son out of their life did not move him to sympathy, it filled him with disdain.

They listened as the readings and eulogies all focused on the heartbreak of parents losing their offspring, nothing about Terry himself, what a compassionate person he was, what a brilliant musician, friend, or son. Dave was furious. Rick would have stormed out of the church if others hadn't taken seats blocking the three of them in. They were forced to sit through the whole service, seething inside while maintaining a respectful demeanor outside.

The first to depart as the service concluded, Mr. and Mrs. Delaney walked past the pew Dave, Rick and Larry were in, spotted them, and flashed such looks of hatred that Dave and Rick both glanced away. They remained where they were until the church had emptied out.

"Can you believe that?" Rick demanded, staring at the departing congregation. "What the hell did we just sit through?"

"It sure wasn't about Terry. My God, do they even miss him? This was all nothing but a play for sympathy." Dave watched Terry's parents ease into a black stretch limousine. "Thank God Rusty wasn't here, he would have had it out with them!"

At the mention of Rusty, all of their thoughts turned back to the hospital room in Cleveland. Larry pulled out his phone, and set it on speaker so they all could hear.

"Steve, just checking in with you. How are you, and how is Rusty?"

Steve watched Rusty's even, unlabored breathing, grateful the movie they were watching had lulled Rusty to sleep. "We're fine. Rusty's taking a nap. How did everything go?"

"Not easy, I'm glad it's over. We'll be back this evening. Is there anything you need?"

"No, I'm fine. Just come back safe, the three of you."

Renee watched the clock on the wall of her office as the hour hand reached eleven. "They must be just about done," she thought. The dread gnawing at her insides lessened a small degree.

She hadn't even considered going to the funeral, and she had no regrets now that it would almost be over. "They cut him out of the family when he chose the music career he wanted," she reminded her mother when her mother asked why she wouldn't attend. "They didn't even call me or anyone in Terry's band; we only found out what they'd arranged when they called Larry, the band's manager, and I'm sure they did that more to find out about insurance, royalty, and any other money owed Terry they might benefit from."

She'd considered staying home from work today, allowing herself time and space to grieve, but decided against it. She'd be better off occupying her mind with the tasks her new head librarian job entailed. For the first hour she'd been right. As ten o'clock approached, though, Renee could not concentrate, papers blurred before her eyes, all she could think of was Terry.

"I have some phone calls to make," she told her assistant. "I'm going to close my door for a while."

Renee stared at Terry's photo on the corner of her desk, the one of him dressed for an Odysseus concert, sleeveless arms exposed showing his powerful muscles, his long hair flowing down his back, warm brown eyes smiling despite his attempts to look serious, even stern, as most metal musicians did. The lighting and angle the photo was taken at caught Terry at his sexiest look and always caused Renee's heart to race five times faster than normal.

Renee stared at the photo several minutes, and felt her heart so shattered she was sure it could not be repaired. Eyes screwed shut, she allowed herself one more round of tears, then opened her eyes, wiped them dry one more time, removed the photo from her desk and stored it in a drawer.

She twisted her diamond ring around her finger several times, savoring its smooth feel, its brilliant glimmer, its elegant simplicity. Then she slipped the ring off her finger, wrapped it in a Kleenex, tucked it into an envelope and sealed it, then placed the sealed, folded envelope in her purse.

Half past noon now, she noted. The service would be concluded, and Terry's body laid to rest. It was all over.

A series of adventure movies ran on the TV that Steve thought might take Rusty's mind off the funeral being held miles away. They watched the first two, passing light conversation during commercials. By the third movie, Steve noticed Rusty's end of their conversation had grown shorter, his focus not on the TV screen but on the wall behind it, or rather on some distant point far removed in space and time from the room their physical bodies occupied.

Of all of the Odysseus brothers, Rusty was the one who held things the deepest and longest. Steve had grown accustomed to his long silent stretches; most times he left Rusty alone to work out whatever shackled his heart and mind during those periods.

After the episode with Eliza, Steve paid more attention to these silences, drawing Rusty out when he felt afraid Rusty might drown in his internal struggles.

Steve turned the TV's volume down. "Do you want to talk about Terry?"

Rusty shook his head, his eyes still glued to their focal point on the eggshell colored hospital room wall.

Steve pushed a little harder. "I wonder how the others are doing."

No response.

"Do you think any of our metal brothers went to the funeral? Terry had so many friends among them all."

Rusty pulled his eyes away from the hole they'd burned through the wall to the dry erase board where aides every day updated date and the names of who was on duty. "I wasn't thinking about the funeral," he confessed, his voice soft and careful, as if his words walked over hot coals. "I was thinking about the show the other night."

"What about it?"

"It was all my fault."

Steve knew where Rusty's thoughts were heading, and pushed him further, drawing out of Rusty what was hurting him most. "What was?"

"I pushed Terry into coming with me to Cleveland. He would have been content staying home, planning his wedding with Renee, or running out to his beloved ocean. I begged him to go to the show with me."

Steve lowered his head. "You're wrong, Rusty. I'm the one to blame. I suggested the show as a peace offering. If I'd treated you, all of you, right the past few months I might not have even brought the concert up and Terry would still be alive."

Their eyes met, mirroring back to each other the same excruciating guilt. They were both right, they knew, and both wrong although neither would concede that point yet. In time they would share their guilty feelings with Larry, Dave and Rick, and find the comfort and release they were so desperate for. Now guilt lie like an ocean surrounding each of them, two islands so close to each other yet separated with no solid bridge to close the gap.

Steve took a rare break that evening, after dinner, after Rusty had drifted off to sleep again. He would return an hour later, and would sleep overnight in the chair by the bed, as he'd grown used to doing. For an hour, though, he needed fresh air, and a break away from the hospital scene and the constant reminder of what they all were going through.

Walking felt good, a chance to loosen stiff muscles and clear his mind. He walked several blocks, found a fast food joint where he ordered a double cheeseburger and large fries, and chose a booth by a window where he could watch people pass by. He was used to eating alone, in fact sometimes preferred the solitude where he didn't have to keep his end of a conversation going, where peace and quiet could be a gift. Tonight, though, he was tired of aloneness. He wanted to interact with someone, in fact not just someone but with one particular person. He pulled out his phone, stared at his contact list for several minutes, then dialed.

"Steve, how are you?"

Sascha's voice on the other end was comforting, the balm he needed after so many days surrounded by hospital routines and fear. "I'm okay," he told her, then changed his response. "No. I don't think I am. You told me the other day I could call anytime."

"Of course you can." Sascha switched off the movie she'd been watching. "What's going on?"

Steve ran a hand through his hair, frustrated himself at his mixed moods. "I don't know. I mean, Rusty's doing better, I think he'll be okay. I'm just … I just wanted to hear … Sasch, it's just been a hard week, one of the hardest I've ever gone through. I just wanted to hear a friendly voice, have someone tell me it will all be okay."

"It will be," Sascha reassured him. "It's just going to take some time."

"Terry's funeral was today."

"Oh God, Steve. I'm so sorry. Did you go?"

"No."

"Have you taken any time away at all? Or are you still at the hospital round the clock?"

"Pretty much full time there," he admitted.

Sascha wasn't surprised. Steve never did anything in half measures. His mood swings, good or bad, were always intense. He dove into music full force, throwing all his passion and attention into the project at hand. The only thing he hadn't given everything in him to was their marriage; but this was not the time to remind him of that. Instead she cautioned him, "Steve, you know you need to give yourself more breaks. You said Rusty was improving. You need to start looking after yourself now."

"I know. I will. Hey, can I ask you something?"

"Sure."

"I'm not sure when I'll be home." Steve paused. Home wouldn't be where it had always been anymore. "I don't mean home, I'll find an apartment, of course. But when I'm back in town, can we set up a schedule for me to see Kody? We don't need the attorneys for that, do we? I mean, all these years we've been able to work things out between us. I don't mean our marriage, I know I've blown that. But Kody, we don't need to fight over him."

Sascha recognized a broken tone she'd never heard before in Steve's voice. As much as she hated the way he'd behaved the past year or so, her heart broke for him now. No matter what he'd done, she couldn't inflict any more pain on him. "No, Steve, you won't need an attorney for that. You need Kody as much as he needs you. I'm sure we can work visits out."

It was only a small gesture, a tiny glimmer of light amid so much darkness in his life, but Steve was grateful. "Thanks. I'll let you know when I get home."

Sunlight streamed through the patient lounge area at the end of the hallway beyond the room Rusty had spent the last several days in. After days of bitter cold and blowing snow, the warm bright sun was a welcome relief, just as the panoramic windows and open area were a pleasant change from the room he'd been confined in. Larry, Rick and Dave, returned from the funeral the day before, joined him in the lounge, while Steve was catching some much needed sleep at the hotel across the street.

"Tell me about the funeral." Rusty caught the concerned glance they exchanged between each other and added, "And don't pretty it up to spare me any feelings. I already have an idea how it would have gone."

"The church was packed," Rick started out. "We sat towards the back; his parents had a lot of friends."

"Lots of flowers," Dave added, "and they had a photo of Terry up by the altar."

"What photo?" Rusty wanted to know.

Rick recalled, "One of him when he was younger, in a baseball uniform."

"Oh God, he hated that picture!" He would have laughed at the idea of the image if he hadn't been so angry. "What did anyone say about Terry?"

Rick and Dave looked at each other, neither wanting to tell Rusty the truth. Larry stepped in and told him, "Terry was mostly mentioned in context of Mr. and Mrs. Delaney's losing their son and the grief they were suffering."

"Grief!" Dave spat out, unable to hold his feelings back any longer. "They hardly showed any emotion at all! It was almost like they were glad to let Terry go, he was an embarrassment to them, a thorn in their side."

Rick commented, "The whole thing was such a farce, all about comforting them, hardly a word about who Terry really was, such a gifted musician, amazing human being, so full of life, so full of energy and love. There was nothing about how much they loved him, the focus was all about what a tragic blow they'd been dealt."

"That's about what I expected of them." A question nagged at the back of Rusty's mind, as it had for days. He chose to ask it now. "I don't suppose anyone from my family has been in touch?"

"No," Dave confirmed, "none of us have heard from your family. I don't think they've called the hospital either."

"I didn't think they would." Rusty tried to sound nonchalant, as if it didn't matter to him whether they called, but they all knew different.

"Screw them!" "Rick told him. "We're your family. You don't need them."

"I know that." Inside Rusty's heart, though, it was one more hurt to move beyond. Unbidden, memories flashed through his mind like a slideshow, not recent ones, but images decades old. He saw himself as a toddler, and then a young child, following wherever his father went, listening to stories his mother read to him, of family cookouts where he and his brothers and sister played tag, threw water balloons at each other, played hide and go seek. He saw holiday dinners, Thanksgiving and Christmas, where grandparents and aunts and uncles crowded around dining room tables and he was on the receiving end of more hugs than he could count. He knew the moment all of that ended, when he chose a musical path that seemed to fly in the face of so many of his family's values, although those values were still there, more deeply ingrained in him than any of his family would have guessed.

He wondered, if he had to do it all over again would he make the same choice? Knowing how complete his family's shunning would be, would he still choose this path?

He would. He didn't have to debate within himself long. Rick was right, Odysseus was all the family he needed. Drained of energy, as much emotional as physical, he scanned the faces around him. "Alright, family, which one of you is going to guide me back to my bed?"

Physically, Rusty continued to improve, eating more, taking longer walks through the hallways, and sitting in the chair in his room more rather than reclining on the hospital bed. Before long, the doctor was ready to release him.

"Are you ready to go home?" Steve asked the morning Rusty was to check out.

Rusty knew what they all wanted to hear. A lie. Yes, he was ready. He would tell them that, make them feel better, more at ease. Inside though, the truth was he didn't care. Whether he was in the hospital or at home, in a penthouse or on the streets it didn't matter. Terry was gone. He had no idea how he'd get over that. His surroundings meant nothing to him.

"I'm ready. I'll be glad to get home."

"I'm going with you," Steve informed him. "I'll stay the first week, then Rick and Dave will take turns."

"No you won't. You've all been here long enough; it's time you went home." Rusty was sure they were all thinking of his suicide attempt after his failed engagement plans. "I'm not going to do anything, you know," he promised them now. "Once was enough. I won't go down that road again."

Steve leveled the most serious, worried look he could at Rusty. "We need you. We couldn't stand to lose you."

Rusty didn't believe that. He knew a half dozen guitarists Odysseus could call on to replace him in an instant. He chose to accept Steve's words though. They were nice to hear.

"I swear I won't do anything. It's enough that we lost Terry."

"Just the same," Dave insisted, "we're all taking turns the next few weeks."

"It's the only way we're letting you go home," Rick added.

Rusty could tell he wouldn't win this round. It didn't matter, he thought. They could be there, or not be there. He would go home; whoever wanted could stay at the house with him. None of it mattered anymore.

Thirteen

Set a steel door against my heart, enter a new day without you

—Sinéad Tyrone, *Set A Steel Door*

Dave inserted his key into the front door of his house, stepped in and locked the door behind him, and sank into the sofa by the bank of windows that looked out over the lake upon whose shores his house had been built. Overcast skies reflected steel gray on the lake, its surface was rippled by a steady breeze, trees and shrubs swayed under the hands of that same invisible force, sparrows nestled in the haven of a small pine to the left of his deck. Any other day he would have found pleasure in the comfort of his home while the wind and weather blew outside. Today, the scene mirrored the storm that churned inside him.

He'd been gone two weeks, he calculated. What a long two weeks they had been. Everything in Odysseus' world had shattered in that period of time, like his mother's fine china platter he'd dropped once breaking into a hundred pieces. It could never be glued back together, nor could his marriage when that fell apart. Now, his band was irretrievably broken.

They'd all been so focused on Rusty there had not been much time to grieve for Terry. Now, alone in his house, with no distractions to interfere, Dave allowed memories of Terry to flow across his mind, some of which he laughed over, some of which made him cry. Terry singing karaoke, exaggerating his dance steps to try to hide his lack of vocal talent. Terry skiing once when they'd had a day off in Colorado, his prowess on the bunny hill only slightly worse than his karaoke skills. Terry sitting on the edge of a stage with him one day after soundcheck, commiserating with Dave over his recent divorce.

"How could you take him, God?" Dave demanded of the air around him. "Why Terry? Why not some horrible human being instead? There are so many bastards around us, why couldn't you have spared Terry and taken one of them?"

Try as he might to understand, Terry's death made no sense to him. When the struggle to understand became too hard, when the memories became too painful and his heart and mind too exhausted, Dave rose from the sofa. He unpacked, sorted through mail that had piled up in his absence, checked the refrigerator for some kind of dinner and threw out half the food in there as it had gone bad while he was away.

He was hungrier than he thought. Nothing he had on hand appealed to him, nor did the thought of sitting alone all evening. He called Gary, but Gary had a new girlfriend and was taking her to the movies. Carl was just getting over the flu. Renaldo was heading out of town for a week, Tony had been out three nights in a row and was tired, and Marcus was working a late shift at the plant.

At odds with himself, not sure what the hell he wanted to make himself feel better, not sure anything would make him feel better for quite a while, Dave wandered from room to room in his house, not even sure what he was looking for.

He thought about how different each of the Odysseus members' lifestyles was. Rusty had a farmhouse in a small rural town in Western New York with a good bit of land around it. Terry had an apartment in

Massachusetts. Rick lived outside of Pittsburgh in a traditional colonial style house. Steve lived in a large house with modern amenities near Milwaukee. Dave, himself, had the most modern house of all, not too far from Chicago, a one floor layout with granite countertops, stainless steel appliances, hardwood laminate floors, and tall, wide windows all across the back that provided a stunning view. It had seemed like a perfect, fresh, clean start after his divorce from Stacey was finalized. Now, tonight, hurting and more alone than he wanted, the house echoed with every step he took and carried a cold, warehouse type feel.

Stacey had called the day she'd heard about Terry's death, but he had been rushing to make his flight to Cleveland so they hadn't talked long. Now, surrounded by silence and an all too sterile atmosphere, he reached out to her.

"Stacey, I'm sorry I haven't gotten back to you sooner. It's been a little crazy around here."

"Oh my God, Dave. You don't have to apologize. Are you okay?"

"Yeah. Just tired."

"How was the funeral? How is Rusty?"

"He's home. Steve's with him this week; I'll be staying with him next week." Hearing Stacey's voice brought years of memories back to him. Life looked different after the weeks he'd just gone through. He couldn't change the mistakes he'd made, the opportunities he'd blown, the wonderful things he'd had and thrown away, but he could own up to some of them and try to make amends, however small. "Stacey, there's so much between us, so much behind us. I just want you to know, it was never your fault. You were always a wonderful wife. You're a fantastic mom to Jessie. I know you're seeing someone new. I hope it works out; you deserve to be happy."

Caught off guard by his words when every other conversation between them had been testy, to say the least, it took a minute for Stacey to respond. "Thank you. That's very kind of you to say."

"I mean it. Hey, were you able to get Jessie the tickets to the concert she wanted?"

"Yes. She's thrilled."

"It's a far cry from the car I tried to give her. I know she took the tickets only because it's a show she wants to see, not because she cares about me."

More used to the ways of teenagers than Dave was, Stacey assured him, "Give her time. She'll come around when she's ready. Just keep being supportive with her and reaching out to her."

The house still felt empty after his conversation with Stacey was over, but Dave's heart seemed slightly less painful as he turned the TV on, selected the first sports channel he came to, and let a game he could have cared less about fill the space around him with dull, mind-numbing noise.

Rick arrived home in time to make dinner for his family, macaroni and cheese and hot dogs, his kids' favorite meal. All through the meal Ryan and Christine kept up a steady stream of chatter about play with friends, or what they'd seen on TV, or which toy or game they were enjoying most at the moment. Laurel tried to hush them and turn their attention to their dinner plates, while Rick was happy to let them prattle on, their child voices and silly subjects a balm to the anguish that simmered just under his surface façade.

After dinner, while Laurel bathed the kids and got them ready for bed, he washed dishes and cleaned the kitchen, relishing the mindlessness of the work, shutting his mind and heart off from any attempts to pull him back to recent events.

They all settled on the sofa then and watched TV, kids shows he enjoyed solely for the laughter they drew out of his children, that laughter sweeter than any music he played or heard.

After he'd tucked the kids into bed, he returned to the family room where Laurel was folding laundry.

"How is Rusty doing?" she asked as she set a stack of clean towels aside.

"I think he'll be okay. Are you sure you don't mind that I'll be taking a week here and there to be with him for a while?"

"Of course not. You do whatever you have to for him."

"He's going to take this harder than the rest of us. He and Terry were so close."

"Rusty's also got the most sensitive spirit of you all."

"I know. That's why we're so worried."

"What about you? How are you coping with losing Terry?"

All of the thoughts and emotions Rick had tried to hold at bay rushed forward. "It's hell," he told her. "I just can't believe he's gone."

Each of the memories that surfaced across his mind's screen left the same impression on him, how fun and funny Terry was, how his humor carried each of them through the hard days, how his playing anchored them during their shows, how steady he was, and that steadiness the most valuable of his qualities. While Odysseus' world, especially while they were on the road, was a constant roller coaster ride between creating and releasing music, approval or disapproval from critics and fans alike, and the endless sea of change they navigated through every tour, days and nights in so many cities they could never keep track of which one they were in without a chart, the fact that Terry was always the same, rarely had a bad mood or off day, was one of the few things they could all depend on.

He remembered the last conversation he and Terry had shared, as they were closing out the last tour.

"How do you manage it?" Terry had asked, eyes full of amazement. "How do you balance family life and life on the road? You're one of the few I've seen handle it well."

"It's Laurel," Rick had replied. "She does all the heavy lifting in this marriage. She manages the house and kids."

Terry had shaken his head and pressed further, "No, it's you too. You both make it work. What's the secret?"

Rick set down the suitcase he'd been carrying back to the bus, and fixed a closer eye on Terry. "You getting serious about Renee?"

Terry grinned like a Cheshire Cat, holding something back although each of his band brothers could have guessed at the secret. "I might be."

Instead of saying "go for it," Rick offered serious advice he hoped would make Terry and Renee's marriage succeed. "Laurel and I work together with the kids. You've seen me on the bus, or backstage, always communicating with her so we're on the same page with the kids and with everything else going on. Communication is the biggest key. Always be honest and open with each other. We also bend a lot, adjust our desires to what the other person needs as well. If Laurel is having a hard day, I'm less demanding and more patient. She's the same when I have a crap day. So bending, being flexible with what each other is going through, is another key."

Rick could see Terry was focused on every word, making mental notes, trying hard to remember all he said. He continued, "We're committed to each other, so we forgive a lot in order to keep that commitment. Okay, she forgives more of me, she's pretty damn near perfect herself and I have far less to forgive. You've seen me on the road. I can have a wandering eye, although I act on it far less than I used to. She's hung in there through all of my ups and downs, all of my mistakes. Love covers a multiple of stupid decisions, and Laurel and I love each other so much we find a way past all the stupid moments, keeping our commitment to each other. Love is the final key, Terry. If you and Renee always remember how much you love each other, you can find your way through all the rest."

"Thanks, Rick."

Terry's voice and eyes were deep with respect and gratitude. Rick could see how serious Terry was taking this; it wasn't just a casual conversation,

Terry did intend to move forward with Renee. He offered Terry one last thought. "If you two ever do get married, you know I'm always here for you if you hit a rough spot or ever need a bit of brotherly advice."

Rick recalled all of those words now, and could not stop his tears. Laurel set her laundry aside, and wrapped her arms around him. He buried his face in her hair and cried like a baby.

Steve sat at Rusty's kitchen table and drank from his fresh brewed cup of coffee. Outside a storm was building, winds blowing stronger and snow flakes growing thicker and more numerous. From the picture window where the kitchen table had been centered, Steve had a panoramic view of the length and breadth of Rusty's property, noting how snow, which had only been a couple of inches deep when he'd first come downstairs, now reached the top of the first crossbar of the fence along the side of the yard.

Despite the rush of wind outside, Rusty's house, especially early morning before a day got started and music or television filled the air with noise, was quiet, the soothing, easy kind of quiet that left one feeling equally peaceful inside. This morning, though, Steve did not feel that inner satisfaction. He felt bone tired and anxious for home, although he would never admit that. He'd made a promise to stay by Rusty's side, and he was determined to see it through until Dave arrived on Sunday.

Home. He'd stayed with his sister, Sandy, over Christmas, but knew that was temporary and he needed to find a more permanent arrangement. While Rusty slept upstairs, Steve searched online for apartments, condos, and houses to rent close enough to where Sascha and Kody lived that he'd be able to see Kody as often as possible. Nothing he found seemed as satisfying as the home he'd shared with Sascha; but then, nothing ever would. He'd had a phenomenal home, a beautiful wife, and an adorable son, and he'd thrown them all away. He reviewed once more the options available to him, chose a modern three bedroom condo and an older three bedroom ranch house, considered the ranch to be the better choice as it came with a fenced in yard where Kody would enjoy playing, and e-mailed the contact listed on the site. By the time Rusty came downstairs, showered and dressed in jeans and a flannel shirt, Steve had finalized the house rental, grateful that it came fully furnished and he'd be able to move right in.

"How about bacon and eggs for breakfast," he offered as Rusty brewed his first cup of coffee for the day.

"Fine, but I can cook. I'll make breakfast for us this time."

"Nope!" Steve rose and pulled a chair out for Rusty to sit on. "You'll be independent soon enough. I'm on duty this week and I'll do the cooking."

As he fried eggs, bacon, and potatoes for their breakfast, Steve told Rusty about the house he'd found. "Of course, it's nothing as big and wonderful as the place you've got here, but for what I need right now it should be okay."

Rusty surveyed the kitchen they occupied and the dining room that ran off to the left of it, and thought about all the other rooms that made up the eighty year old farmhouse he had bought several years ago. He'd put a lot of sweat equity into the house, patching old plaster walls, replacing sections of hardwood flooring that a leaky roof had destroyed, remodeling kitchen cupboards and updating kitchen fixtures. "Remember the mess this house was in when I first bought it," he reminded Steve. "It's taken years to fix up all the problems it had, and still needs a lot of work."

"Remember when we all came out to help you when you first moved in?" Steve kept an eye on the food he was frying as he conjured up memories of their repair attempts. "Remember the gallon of paint Rick spilled all over your living room floor?"

"And he stepped in it and left tracks all downstairs!"

Steve dished up breakfast for both of them as he continued to reminisce. "And Dave almost shot himself through the hand with the nail gun!"

"Let's face it, handymen we're not! Terry broke the window here trying to carry some old copper pipes outside." As he spoke, Rusty felt his throat tighten with emotion. He forced tears back and changed the subject before his feelings could get the best of him once again. "Where will you practice guitar in the new house? I'm guessing the neighbors won't be metal folks."

"I know. I'm hoping the basement will be soundproof enough for that. If not, my sister might be seeing more of me than she wants; their finished basement could withstand the noise of a small explosion!"

Despite Rusty's protests, Steve kept the driveway cleared of snow during the week's storms, insisting with a laugh he'd send Rusty back to the hospital if he dared pick up a shovel. Rusty walked laps around his first floor with Steve counting the laps, giving him high fives each time he reached the goal they'd set for the day. In turn, Rusty taught Steve some of the finer points of cooking.

"You're going to be on your own now," Rusty told him, not that Steve needed the reminder. "You can't live all your life on fried eggs and potatoes."

Under Rusty's guidance Steve made lasagna, chicken cacciatore, and roast beef with potatoes and carrots. In between meal preparation and dining, Rusty rested while Steve watched horror movies and crime shows.

One afternoon, during lunch, Steve took note of the carved wood board at the center of Rusty's dining room table.

"Did you make this?" he asked.

"Yeah, a couple of years ago."

"I've always been fascinated by your woodwork. Would you teach me someday?"

Steve had never shown an interest in any hobby or craft. Hoping it would occupy Steve while he adjusted to life without Sascha and Kody, and until, if ever, Odysseus returned to work, Rusty agreed. "I'll show you after we eat."

Steve followed Rusty out to the workshop to retrieve the tools they would need. While Rusty sorted through and selected various items, Steve picked up the box Rusty had worked on during the holidays.

"This is nice. What's it for?"

Rusty froze. With the Cleveland trip and its aftermath, he'd forgotten about the gift he'd crafted.

Sensing he'd crossed a wrong line, Steve set the box back down where he'd found it on the workbench. "I'm sorry. I shouldn't have pried."

"It's okay." Rusty picked the box up and added it to the items he would bring inside. "It's a gift I made for someone."

Back inside, Rusty spread various tools and pieces of wood across the dining room table. He demonstrated how he selected and then drew designs on the desired piece of wood, then unwrapped the knife he used the most in the carving process. He showed Steve the proper way to hold the knife, and the method of carving involved.

With Rusty's guidance, Steve outlined Kody's name on a board then cut into the letters, at first with light, tentative strokes, his movements becoming stronger and more confident as he went on. By the end of the evening, Steve had carved out two letters and felt proud of his accomplishment.

"I can see why you enjoy this so much. It's pretty relaxing."

"Yeah, you can't hurry the process, you have to take your time and focus on the project at hand." Rusty stared into the fire he'd built for the evening. "You can set a lot of worries aside while carving."

Rusty stayed downstairs long after Steve had gone to bed. He wasn't ready to face a sleepless night like the last few had been, nor the nightmares that haunted his dreams.

Working with Steve had been easy, Steve grasped the basic concepts of carving in no time and seemed to truly enjoy setting his hands to the task. The feel of wood, its smoothness, its sturdiness, the balance and weight of his carving knives in his hands, searching his mind for a design and digging into a project, they were all various parts of carving Rusty so loved.

The box, though, had thrown him. Seeing it on his workbench, and Steve asking about it. Facing what it represented, what it could no longer mean. Even as he taught Steve, that box hung on the periphery of his mind, nagging at him, chiseling its way back into his heart, dragging with it fleeting images of Terry and Renee, and Terry alone, until he thought he could no longer stand it. He was glad when Steve had set his carving work aside for the night. Perhaps he could block the box and all it represented from his mind once again.

The box and all its memories remained.

Rusty retrieved the box from his desk, ran his hands along its smooth sides, traced its intricate carvings with his fingers. He allowed his mind once more to imagine Terry and Renee and the wedding day they had planned, to imagine the future they would build, the children that would run through their home, how the love they shared would spread outward to everyone in their surroundings and how brightly the world would shine because of them.

The dream was shattered. Like the cab in Cleveland. Beyond repair. So many things had broken that night Rusty could not bear thinking on it anymore.

He placed the box in the fire, and for the next half hour watched it burn to embers which glowed bright red and orange and then, eventually, grew cold.

Alone in the house, with Laurel at work and the kids at school, Rick finished unpacking from Cleveland. He added his dirty clothes to the stack already in the laundry basket and ran a load of wash for Laurel, sorted out his toiletries and stored them in the bathroom closet, and left his empty suitcase under their bed. He would need it again in a couple of weeks.

Then he entered the music room where all his bass guitars and equipment were housed. After the tour he'd been so preoccupied with Christmas he hadn't spent much time looking over the instruments he'd sent home with their tour crew; now he checked each to ensure it had arrived home undamaged, he inspected strings and straps, then placed each one of his bass guitars in the rack he'd installed along one wall of the room. Last of all, he went through the bag of tour mementos he'd collected, from a few gifts and cards from long standing followers, to T-shirts and photo collages friends of Odysseus had presented them.

One of the photo collages in particular caught his eye, closeups of each of the band members from a tour they'd done several months ago. In each of the photos, he and his band brothers looked like they were in heaven as they played their music, their passion clear in each of their eyes.

By some eerie design fluke, Terry's photo had been placed in the center. Rick studied it now. How would they ever move on, he wondered, without the anchor that bound all of their music together? Would they even go on at all? Or had Odysseus reached its end?

"You still going to Rusty's next week?"

Dave nodded, and confirmed to his friend Mike, "Yeah, on Sunday."

"How is he doing?"

"Steve said he's getting better, moving around and eating more."

"Those are good signs." Mike was a huge Odysseus fan, as well as Dave's best friend, and had been as heartbroken as the band members themselves over Terry's death and fears for Rusty's recovery. As he and Dave spent a night out at their favorite steakhouse, he asked, "Any ideas what you'll all do next?" As a fan, he wanted reassurance that the band he loved best, whose music had been the playlist of his life for the past dozen years and whose tunes and lyrics sent their fingers deep into his heart and soul and drew out of him more emotion than anything else in the world, would go on. As a friend, he sought confirmation that Dave would be okay in the long run.

Dave turned his beer glass in circles in his hands, debating how to answer. After turning several options over in his mind he told Mike, "It's still early days, but I think in the end we'll pull things together. Terry would want us to."

They turned to other topics then, Mike's marriage which was on rocky ground, his kids, Dave's daughter, how Mike's job as a truck driver was in jeopardy as the company he worked for faced economic failure. They left the steakhouse and sought out their favorite corner bar, competed against each other for the top score on the pinball machine, consumed more vodka, beer, and whiskey than they should, and were wise enough to call for cab rides home.

The next morning, head and stomach worse for wear after the night out, Dave gave Mike's question more serious thought.

Terry's role as drummer could no doubt be filled. Dave alone knew three or four good candidates for that job. So soon after the accident, he knew no one in Odysseus was ready to even discuss the possibilities, let alone make any decisions as to Terry's replacement.

The larger question, he knew, was whether they had the heart to go on.

Picturing anyone else sitting behind Odysseus drums broke Dave's heart. He just couldn't see any other person there. Truth was, he didn't want to. That was Terry's domain; no one else on earth had the right to sit in that spot. Even if they somehow earned that right, it would never be Terry's face smiling over at him in the moments they caught during and in between songs. It would never be Terry's signature twirling of the drumsticks or the way he pointed them heavenward at the start of each show. No one else would match Terry's laugh, or his humor backstage, or his intense way of listening whenever Dave brought serious concerns over music or family or life in general to him.

Nothing would ever be the same without Terry. Dave and all the rest of Odysseus were old enough and wise enough to know that. They'd seen other bands lose members, and how those bands had struggled to find their way forward after the loss. Only two weeks had passed, Odysseus was still in the midst of the emotional upheaval, and thoughts of moving forward without Terry cut Dave so deeply he could physically not stand the pain. He did the only thing he could think of to ease it. He brought his toolbox up from the basement and fixed every loose doorknob he'd been meaning to get to. He pulled up the wall to wall carpeting in the spare room that he'd wanted to replace ever since moving into the house, and scrubbed the now exposed hardwood flooring. He replaced the dining room dimmer switch that had needed replacing the past eight months. By the time he went to bed he was too exhausted to think or feel anything, and slept the first deep sleep he'd had in two weeks' time.

Fourteen

I would give all this land and everything I own if you could return to this place
—Sinéad Tyrone, *Stream-Side Dreams*

Rusty woke early, while the eastern sky outside his bedroom window showed only the faintest hint of dawn.

In truth, he had not slept much the night before, or any night since returning home. Terry's ghost infiltrated his dreams every time he closed his eyes; each time he woke with a heart so heavy he thought the weight of pain would break it apart, or the weight would bury him deep within his grief. He'd never before experienced such a profound loss, had never before felt such unending overwhelming hurt.

Steve had gone home, and Dave was now staying with him. Careful to not wake Dave up, Rusty rose, pulled sweat pants and a sweatshirt on, and tiptoed downstairs. He slipped boots and his heavy coat on and stepped out onto the patio off his kitchen where he could watch the dawn rise.

Color in the sky to the east of Rusty's back property changed from charcoal gray to the color of fog, then to a light gray, before a ribbon of white appeared on the horizon. The white band grew wider, and the trees across his land transformed from dark shadows against the night to individual brownish gray soldiers anchored to the ground, standing guard over the clearing close to his house and the woods that extended far back to the stream that marked the boundary of his property.

Terry had spent many nights at Rusty's house. Rusty recalled now how often Terry had watched sunrises and sunsets in this same yard, how he'd always found such beauty in watching the skies. He would have loved this sunrise, Rusty thought, would have loved the first song of a sparrow to cut through the early morning silence, and the tinge of gold that appeared along the white band as the sun made its presence known.

Rusty didn't feel any sense of beauty or inspiration from the scene unfolding before him. All he felt was emptiness, stone cold as the cement floor of the patio, as barren as the fields around his land.

He turned, stepped back into the house and closed the door behind him as he tried to close the door to the memories that weighed his heart and spirit down.

Over lunch Rusty informed Dave, "Looks like another storm moving in tonight." He watched the radar projections and the storm's timing and noticed how even now, as they lunched on tomato soup and grilled cheese sandwiches, the sky had darkened a shade and fat snowflakes were drifting through the air outside his dining room window. "We should head to the store now for anything we want; the weather could change sooner than expected."

The grocery store was clogged with people panic buying milk, bread, and every other provision they thought they could not live without if snowed in for a day or two. Dave watched one woman with three gallons of milk, two loaves of bread, two packages of cookies, a bag of potato chips and a half gallon of ice cream in her cart. "All that for two days?" Dave laughed. "Isn't it crazy what people think they can't live without in a storm!"

Rusty glanced at the specialty Irish cheese, two boxes of crackers, spaghetti fixings, boneless chicken, box of rice, stew beef, vegetables, and apple pie in their cart, and cocked an eyebrow. "Isn't it, though? What are you planning for, being stuck inside a week?"

As they passed the gift shop next to the grocery store on their way back to Rusty's car, Rusty spotted a dark green and white marble chess set in the front window. He thought of all the times he'd listened to Dave and Rick play chess, and the promise he'd made to himself a dozen times over that someday he'd learn the game. He stopped Dave and pointed to the chess set. "Hey, while we're snowed in think you could teach me to play?"

They bought the set, and that evening Dave taught Rusty the names and movements each piece represented, the significance of protecting the queen and king on the board, the opening moves, and initial basic strategies. As they played, the storm increased outside, snow fell at a rate of two inches an hour and winds rattled the old windows in Rusty's house.

They broke for dinner, Dave's specialty molasses beef stew, then Dave cleared the driveway with Rusty's snowblower. "Don't even go there!" He raised a hand to stop Rusty's protests. "And don't think you're getting off free! You get to clean the kitchen while I face the frozen north!"

Rusty surveyed the pots, utensils, spice bottles and dirty dishes strewn across the kitchen counters. "I think I'm getting the bad end of that deal!"

By the time they were done, both were tired enough that they set aside chess for the evening, choosing to binge watch a mystery series neither had seen before. As they sat in front of the TV, with a fire blazing in the fireplace to ward off the cold, Dave spotted Rusty's favorite guitar, the White Rose, where Rusty had returned it to its customary stand in the family room after their last tour. He nodded towards the White Rose and asked Rusty, "How about a little music instead of this show? I can pull a keyboard up on my laptop; hell, we can pull up a whole group!"

Rusty stared hard at the guitar. All his life, from elementary school and beyond, he'd loved music. From the first time he'd held a guitar in his hand until now, on only a handful of days had he not picked up one of his guitars and spent time noodling around with notes and chords, practicing new techniques, playing songs he knew well and making other tunes up. His guitar was as vital to him as breath and heartbeat were.

Now as he stared at the White Rose his mind automatically shifted to Odysseus, his brothers, and the catalog of music they'd racked up over the years. He recalled their last shows, the feel of them all tied together by the bond of music they shared, by the brotherhood they'd forged through so many years together, the sheer heaven of them playing off each other, and the comfort and security of knowing they always had each other's backs throughout the challenges and storms that rocked their lives.

The bond had been broken with Terry's passing. Odysseus' music had been silenced. The White Rose blurred before Rusty's eyes. When he was able to speak at last all he told Dave was, "I'm not in the right mood tonight. Let's just keep watching the show."

The storm lasted three days. Dave kept up with the driveway, Rusty prepared meals, and in between they continued their chess lessons. Rusty was an eager student, fascinated by the constant flow of decisions to be made, when to defend and protect one's positions, when to attack an opponent, when to leave one's self open and vulnerable, when to retreat. He thought chess was much like the music industry, how individual players and bands as a whole were constantly forced to make choices based on the whims of the record label managers, the promoters and venue operators, various radio station and marketing team strategies, and the tastes of the public at large. At times he and each of his Odysseus brothers had felt like pawns on a life size chessboard, helpless to control the advances and retreats that dictated their lives. They each carried battle scars in their hearts, hidden from view from everyone except among themselves.

He thought again of the conversation he'd had with Terry in New

Orleans, how Terry had always compared their journey to the journeys the characters in Homer's books faced. Over the years, in addition to feeling like game board pieces moved about at the whim of various outside forces, they'd each made their share of mistakes in their long journey navigating metal world and music industry waters. Some battles along the way they had lost, Dave's divorce and Steve's pending one, each of their individual battles with drinking over the years, Dave's addiction to pills, and Rick's brief sojourn into the world of heroin, which they all, thankfully, had been able to pull him away from.

"I thought we were pretty well home safe," Rusty confessed to Dave after he'd lost another game to his teacher.

"What do you mean?" Dave asked, confused.

"I was just thinking how much like chess our lives have been, and how much like Homer's books, all the ups and downs, the shifts back and forth between winning and losing, the long road we have to travel to get to that happy place in life."

"The past few years have been good."

"They have. I just thought we'd 'arrived', that our good luck would hold, that we were finally on top of the world."

Dave leaned back into his chair and turned several responses over in his mind. A number of positive, reassuring thoughts came to him; he knew, though, none of them would help Rusty or himself. Instead he told Rusty, "I know it's hard right now. Once we know you're back on your feet we'll figure out where we go next. It's like looking too far ahead in chess. Unless you're a world class champion, you can only see so many moves at a time. We can't see very far ahead right now, but that will improve."

"I don't know. I don't know that the road will ever look clear."

"Remember when Stacey and I first split up?"

Rusty nodded, not sure what that had to do with Terry and what they were going through now.

Dave continued, "When that first happened I was sure my world had crashed and burned right before my eyes. I thought I would die." He watched Rusty carefully as he said the next words, "Like you did after Eliza betrayed you."

Rusty glanced down at his arms, where scars were still faintly visible among the various tattoos that decorated his skin.

"We didn't die, Rusty. We both wanted to, but life has moved on for each of us. It will be the same with Terry. It hurts like hell right now, but it will get better. We'll push past this somehow. For now, though, you can set that chessboard up while I make us fresh coffee. That is, unless you're afraid of losing again!"

By the time Dave left at the end of the week, Rusty had lost seventy four games of chess, won ten, and had resigned himself to the knowledge that he would never reach Dave's level of proficiency at the game. Part of him was happy Rick had arrived to replace Dave. At least he'd go to bed at night without the bruised ego he suffered after each new round of chess defeats.

Poker was Rick's game of choice; but after a couple of days they both agreed playing against each other only was not much of a challenge. Every night Rick pulled up hockey games on the TV, one of his favorite sports, and tried to teach Rusty the finer points.

"That's icing," he would say, pointing to the action on the screen. "That's offsides. And hey! That's tripping! You lousy ref! Right in front of your eyes and you couldn't see that?"

Rusty would laugh at Rick's outbursts, not understanding what the infraction was but enjoying Rick's passion all the same. As for hockey, as much as Rick tried to enlighten him he just couldn't get into the game, and spent much of the evenings letting a game he could care less about fill the spaces in his mind so his thoughts could not wander elsewhere.

Rick always rose earlier than Dave had; Rusty woke every morning to the aromas of coffee and frying bacon, and the sound of news playing on the TV. Rick created variations on pancakes no one in his right mind would think of: pistachio pancakes, shredded chicken stuffed pancakes, and sweet potato pancakes, that sometimes made Rusty shudder at the thought of eating them, but with enough butter and maple syrup each turned out delicious.

"Hey, it's been a while since I've walked the length of your land," Rick commented after breakfast his third day there. "It's not bad out today, why don't you give me the guided tour again?"

They pulled boots and coats on and headed out the back door.

The two or three inches of fresh snow that had fallen while they slept glistened like diamonds strewn at will across a clean white quilt. Clouds that had carried the snow had dissipated, and a pale blue sky spread overhead. Against the crisp white and blue, leafless trees stood out tall and dark as black pencils, their light gray shadows against the ground like brushstrokes nature's artist had painted with great care.

Snow crunched lightly as Rusty led Rick along the perimeter of his back yard and into the treed expanse that covered the last half of his property. "Look." He pointed to marks in the snow. "Fox tracks. Probably chasing after the rabbit whose tracks are over there to the side."

A little farther on he held out his hand to stop Rick from proceeding, and placed a finger to his lips indicating silence. As they listened, Rick heard a faint tapping and staccato nasal chattering from a tree nearby. "What's that?" he whispered.

"Nuthatch." Rusty pointed to a small bluish gray bird working its way down a tree trunk, tapping into the wood for any insects that might have found shelter under the bark.

Rusty identified birch and sycamore trees, each with their unique bark patterns, and oak trees with occasional acorns and leaves still clinging to their branches. He showed Rick where he'd come across a ruffled grouse a few years back, and the place where he'd once spotted a ten point buck.

Each day they'd walk deeper in the woods, Rick timing their outings so as to not wear Rusty out too much. By Friday they'd built up to a long enough trek that they reached the stream that ran along the far end of Rusty's property.

Rusty stood several minutes in silence, watching the trickle of water that remained unfrozen and the bubbles along the edges of ice that covered the stream. At length he told Rick, "This was always Terry's favorite place when he came for a visit."

Rick kept his eyes focused on Rusty rather than the stream and snow nearby. "I never knew that."

"We always had our best conversations here, like we could say anything and the trees and stream wouldn't judge us or laugh at us. We spoke all our dreams here. . . ."

Rusty's voice trailed off. He screwed his eyes shut to block the tears that had risen and now threatened to overflow.

"We haven't mentioned Terry all week." Rick didn't want to push his brother too hard, but he knew bottling things up inside would be worse. "Let's talk about him now."

Rusty thought of all the conversations he and Rick and their Odysseus brothers had shared over the years. They'd discussed it all, girls, drugs, politics, dreams, hurts. There was never any topic off limits, never anything they could not level with each other about. Their lives were open books among each other.

Why then, he wondered, could he not level with Rick now?

He tried to put into words the overwhelming sense of loss he felt, the ache so deep in his heart he was sure no medicine on earth could heal it, how each memory of Terry was so heavy he was sure he'd be buried under the weight, how each image of Terry that crossed his mind stole his breath away and he was sure he would suffocate. He tried to describe the absolute emptiness he felt, how it crushed him to think of a world without his brother and best friend. He tried to open up to Rick the way he always had before; but the words stayed stuck in his chest, unable to work their way up to and through his vocal chords and mouth.

Instead he just told Rick, "I'm not ready to talk about him yet. I will in time."

There was no sense pushing him. Rick changed the subject. "Hey, feel up to tackling your upstairs bathroom while I'm here? We can install the new vanity you want, I can paint, bet we can get that all sorted before I go home."

The upstairs bathroom was one in a long list of projects Rusty struggled to find time to accomplish with the demanding schedule he'd had the past few years. Rick's offer was tempting. "Are you sure you don't mind?"

"We've got the time, let's do it!"

Rusty knew older homes were prone to unexpected difficulties during repairs or renovations, and this was no exception. The new vanity faucet openings didn't line up with the old ones, and Rick and Rusty were forced to run new pipes to accommodate the space difference. The new medicine cabinet they bought to replace the outdated one was too deep, its ability to slide into place blocked by beams that ran behind the opening, so Rusty and Rick chose to update the old cabinet with spray paint and reinstall it. They replaced the bathtub faucets, installed a new shower head, and painted the walls sage green.

"I can't believe we got this done." Rusty surveyed the finished room. "I think I owe you a steak dinner or something."

"Not tonight, Pittsburgh and Philadelphia are up against each other in hockey!"

While Rick watched the two rival teams battle each other on the ice, Rusty received two phone calls.

The first was from Steve. "Just want to let you know I'll be there Sunday, hopefully before Rick leaves."

"No you won't."

Surprised, Steve asked, "What do you mean no I won't?"

Rusty forced his voice to sound upbeat and positive. "I'm feeling much better. You can ask Rick how well I'm doing now. There's no need for you to pull yourself away from Kody and all you've got going on out there to come out here and babysit me."

"It's not babysitting," Steve protested. "It's being there for a friend."

"I know. It's about the promise you made." Rusty set aside the apple pie he was dishing up for Rick and himself. "Steve, you've fulfilled that promise. You've done all you could do or need to do. It's time for you to look after yourself and your own life now."

Fear gripped Steve. If Rusty had not been able to withstand Eliza's abandoning him, how would he ever get through the days ahead? He'd promised himself he would stay by Rusty until any danger was over. In Steve's mind, the danger still remained.

Rusty recognized Steve's hesitation for what it was. "I promise, Steve, I'll be okay. I'm not going to do anything stupid, and if I feel like I'm really struggling I'll call you and you can come out then. Fair enough?"

At last Steve relented. "Alright, I'll stay here, but I'm calling you twice a day."

The second call came a half hour later and caught Rusty off guard. The hockey game Rick was watching was a very tense, pivotal one, and Rick was so completely engrossed in it he didn't even hear the phone ring. Rusty stepped into the front living room where he could hear the caller without the interruption of Rick's passionate outbursts every time a play went in an opposite direction of what he thought it should.

"Rusty, it's Renee."

Rusty froze. He had no clue what to say to the girl Terry had been set to marry.

"I just wanted to call and see how you're doing."

She sounded as lost as he felt. "I'm okay," he told her, keeping his voice as bereft of emotion as he could make it. "How are you?"

Renee had always been direct, one of the qualities Terry had loved about her. She was direct now. "Still trying to find my way. It's a hard road." She paused, Rusty guessed to control her emotions. "I couldn't call you before, but I wanted you to know I'm glad you survived."

"I wish it had been me instead of Terry."

There. He'd said it. The secret he'd carried inside him for weeks. He would not have been able to say the words to Steve, or Dave, or Rick; but Renee, she needed to hear it. Terry should be here. She would understand that.

"Don't ever say that," she ordered. "Even if you don't mean it, don't ever say it."

"Terry had everything going for him. He had a future with you, he loved you so much, he had so many dreams and plans ahead of him. If anyone should still be here, it's Terry, not me."

Renee was crying now; Rusty could hear it in her strained voice, in the catch in her words. "Rusty, Terry loved you. You were his brother, his best friend. If you'd been killed instead of him he would have been devastated, just as you are now. Just as we both are. You're still here. Don't throw that gift away."

It didn't feel like a gift, Rusty thought. It felt like torture, knowing he and Terry should have had their outcomes reversed. He wouldn't argue with Renee, though. She had enough on her plate.

"I'm sending you something in the mail," she was saying now. "I came across a few things I think Terry would want you to have."

Nothing Terry owned would bring him back. Rusty declined her offer. "You don't have to, Renee. Anything Terry left behind should be yours."

"No, I'm sure he'd want you to have what I'm sending. There's not much, but they're things you would value more than anyone else."

"Alright. Thank you." She could send anything she wanted. Rusty would pack them away somewhere where they couldn't crush him, or throw them out altogether.

He imagined Renee alone in Terry's apartment, sorting through the possessions he'd left behind, facing empty space and walls that no doubt echoed with heavy silence. He pictured her wide brown eyes, filled with so much love for Terry every time he saw them together, of how her smile in Terry's presence lit the world around them. Not sure whether it was the right question or the right time, he asked, "What are you going to do now?"

"I have a sister in Phoenix. I'm going to move in with her for a while, find a job out there, try to start over. It's as far away from here as I can get. I think the change would be good."

You'll never move away from the memories, he thought. They'll haunt you wherever you go. He didn't say that, though. She would find out soon enough on her own. Instead he said, "Keep in touch with me, let me know how you're doing."

Rick was still engrossed in the hockey game. He hadn't heard the phone call or even noticed that Rusty had stepped away. Rusty settled into the recliner and faked interest in the final period of the game.

Fifteen

*Breathe, you tell me in a dream, move forward with caution,
do not remain in this stagnant place*

—Sinéad Tyrone, *Breathe*

"Are you sure you're okay with me moving out there?"

Renee listened for any hesitation in her sister Leanne's voice. The move had been Leanne's idea; but Renee knew offering help was one thing, having someone take that offer up was another.

"I've got your room all ready." Leanne sounded excited. "You'll love Phoenix, and we'll have fun together."

"Alright. I've almost finished packing. I won't be bringing much with me, the rest I'm either giving away or storing at Mom and Dad's house."

"Did you fax your resume to the library here I told you about?"

"Yes, and Mrs. Clarke gave me a glowing referral to send with it."

Throughout their conversation Leanne recognized the dull, flat tone that carried through Renee's words, so unlike Renee's normal upbeat, vibrant manner. She still couldn't believe the twist her sister's life had been handed. Encouraging Renee to move in with her was the only way she could think of to restart Renee's life; staying where she was now, with so many memories of Terry nearby, would drown her.

"You stand a good chance for the library job here," she reassured

Renee. "If it falls through, though, there are plenty of other opportunities. Everything will work out."

Renee hoped she was making the right choice. She surveyed the boxes that crowded her apartment, some labeled for thrift store and church donation centers, others marked for her parents' basement where they'd be safe until she settled somewhere.

Her eyes fell on the two boxes off to the side. One was taped closed and addressed to Rusty which she would mail to him today.

The other, smaller box contained photos, perfumes, scarves, jewelry, and other items Terry had given her over the years. This box she would take to Phoenix with her and tuck in a corner of her new room. Maybe she would never open the box. She just couldn't let these trinkets go yet.

"Tomorrow's Kody's first visit to Steve's new place." Sascha told her mother over lunch. "I hope it goes well. The last time Steve took him to the zoo Kody was a little distant with him."

"Are you sure you aren't pushing things a bit with Kody spending so much time with Steve? With all the turmoil in your life these days, Kody's confused. He needs stability. Steve's life is far from stable."

"He's Kody's father, he has a right to see his son. Besides, Steve's changed, he's really trying to have a good relationship with Kody."

"How many times have you seen Steve since he came home?"

Sascha bristled at her mother's insinuation that she didn't know what she was doing. "Enough to notice the difference in him."

Renata recognized Sascha's defensive tone, just as she'd noticed the change in Sascha's demeanor towards Steve in the last few weeks. "You're changing your mind about the divorce, aren't you?"

Sascha hesitated. "I don't know, Mom. Steve's a different person. The accident shook him, not just losing a friend but being there, experiencing it. He's been through hell, and it's hit him hard. He's not so gruff, not demanding. He's not in a hurry to head to the next project. How can he be? The whole band's in turmoil right now. Steve's hurting, he's broken, and he's a bit lost."

Renata leaned back in her chair, lunch forgotten as she weighed Sascha's words and her change of heart. "What happens when he finds his footing once again? What if he goes back to being the same old Steve?"

Even Sascha knew her change in heart seemed crazy. "I'm not turning a blind eye to what's gone on in the past, Mom. I just think he deserves one more chance."

The part of Renata that wanted to protect her daughter from every hurt in life wished she had words wise enough to make her daughter see sense, pull her head out of whatever dream cloud Sascha had stuck herself in, and recognize that people didn't just change, that all of Steve's good intentions were bound to not last.

The part of her that still believed in the magic of love hoped whatever difference Sascha thought she saw in Steve would hold true.

Steve traveled from room to room in the house he had rented, surveying each, making sure everything was clean and ready for Kody to visit. He inspected the bathroom, made sure the toothpaste, shampoo and shaving products were stored in the cabinet under the sink. He hung his jeans and shirt from the morning back in his closet, and straightened the blankets on his bed. In the kitchen, he set dirty dishes in the dishwasher, wiped the table and counters with antibacterial cleanser, and returned the cereal box and sugar bowl from breakfast back into their appropriate cupboards. He picked up newspapers from the living room floor, and removed his new leather jacket from the back of the sofa where he'd flung it the night before and hung it where it belonged on the hook in the entry alcove.

He peeked again into the spare room he'd made into a bedroom for Kody. He liked the train decorated bedspread and curtains he'd bought, knowing how Kody adored trains, and the bookcase he'd loaded with toys and age appropriate books. The room looked perfect; he hoped Kody would like it enough that he'd want to sleep over someday.

The front doorbell rang, and all of a sudden Steve was more nervous than he'd ever been stepping out on a stage as he opened the door.

Steve bent down to eye level with Kody. "Hi, little buddy. Here, let me take your coat."

Thrown by unfamiliar surroundings, Kody drew closer to his mom. Steve backed off and gave his son space. "Thank you for letting me have this time with him." Steve told Sascha.

Sascha's eyes took in the lines across Steve's face and the sadness behind his smile. "Have you slept at all since you got home?"

"Some." Steve held out a box of animal crackers to Kody, having remembered they were his son's favorite treat. "Here, would you like these?"

Kody eyed Steve with guarded interest, then let go of Sascha's hand and reached for the box.

"This chair is perfect for you." Steve led Kody to a child's chair he'd found. "You sit here while I talk with your mom, then you and I can play."

Kody settled himself in the chair, munched on cookies, and watched the cartoons Steve had turned to on the TV.

"Don't worry," he promised Sascha. "We won't be watching TV all day."

"I know you'll be fine with him. I'll be back around five to pick him up. Unless . . ." she stopped herself, suddenly not sure she should take the next step. She studied Steve a moment. He looked worn down, like he carried an unbearable weight. He'd shed his know it all attitude and seemed vulnerable, unsure how to find his way through the curves life had thrown at him. Something inside her melted at the sight of Steve hurting.

She finished her thought, "Why don't you drive Kody home, and stay for dinner with us."

It wasn't a chance, Steve cautioned himself, not wanting to read anything more than general kindness into her words. It was just dinner, nothing else. He accepted, shutting down inside him any thoughts that tried to run too far ahead. "I'd like that."

"Be at our house, my house, at six."

Steve and Kody colored pictures in a coloring book, built towers and walls with a set of connecting building blocks, raced toy cars across the living room floor and, when Kody was worn out, watched cartoons on TV. Steve made macaroni and cheese, Kody's favorite, for lunch, and had another box of animal crackers ready for afternoon. Any apprehension Kody had felt when he first entered Steve's house evaporated; by mid-afternoon, as they watched cartoons, Kody curled up next to his father on the sofa and leaned his head against his father's arm.

The warmth of his son's small body curled up next to him was just the healing balm Steve needed. After all the stress of the last tour, and then the crisis in Cleveland and all the grief and worry that had wrought, watching this innocent little being, part of him, something he had helped create, who had no cares in the world, no faults, no failures, whose only focus in life was eating, sleeping, and having fun, filled his heart with so much love that all of the pain and worry he'd carried inside him faded to the background. Every time some thought of Rusty, or Terry, or anything Odysseus related, tried to enter his mind he blocked it, and concentrated on what was most important to him, the little boy at his side.

Six o'clock came way too soon. Steve did not want his time with Kody to end. Still, he bundled the boy into coat and boots, fit the car seat Sascha had left into his car, and they returned to the house he and Sascha had once shared.

It felt surreal to him to sit in front of the house he and Sascha had bought, fixed up, and lived in for so many years, and to know that he was no longer a part of its story. He felt a foreigner as he walked up the front steps with Kody's hand in his, knocked on the front door and, when Sascha opened the door to admit them, stepped into the front hall.

Rusty was surprised at the size and weight of the box he received in the mail. He guessed at who it was from even before he spotted Renee's name and return address.

He set the box on the kitchen table and stared at it. Then he poured fresh coffee for himself and sat in the family room awhile, trying not to think of the box. When that failed, he returned to the kitchen, slid a knife through the tape that held the box shut, and folded the flaps back.

He placed the knife back in the drawer where it belonged, washed his coffee cup out and the plate from the toast he'd had for breakfast, returned the toaster to its storage spot in a cabinet under the counter, and then turned back to the box.

An envelope sat on top of the contents. Rusty opened it and withdrew a dozen photos of himself and Terry that Renee or others had taken during their shows over the years. He set them aside, choosing to return to them later.

A second envelope contained a few of Terry's ocean drawings. They were much more sophisticated than Rusty had ever realized. Terry could have been an artist after his music days were over. A fresh layer of pain for all that had been lost in Terry tore through Rusty's heart. He slipped the drawings back into their envelope for safe keeping.

Next, wrapped in several layers of tissue paper, was Terry's best leather jacket, the one with a large gothic cross stitched into the back, the one Rusty had given him for his birthday two years prior. He held it in his hands several minutes, savoring how smooth and supple the leather felt under his fingers, before slipping it on. A faint aroma of Terry's favorite cologne still clung to the inner lining. The jacket felt warm and comforting, but Rusty slipped it off after a minute, not sure he could ever wear it.

The leather bound *Iliad and Odyssey* volume he'd given Terry was under the jacket. Rusty picked it up and opened it, reading again the inscription he'd written before presenting it to Terry: "To our own Odysseus, keep on fighting the good fight!"

He placed the book on top of the jacket, sure he would never be able to read it.

At the bottom of the box, each protected in its own manila envelope, were all of the journals Terry had kept over the years.

Overwhelmed at the magnitude of this gift, of all the memories and thoughts they represented, Rusty sank down onto one of the kitchen chairs. He opened one of the envelopes and flipped through the pages of the journal it held, recognizing Terry's careful, neat handwriting. The words blurred before him. Rusty replaced the journal in its envelope, set it back in the box along with the other items, and folded the flaps of the box closed again. He carried the box into the dining room and placed it on a corner chair. He just wasn't ready for its contents.

Clouds thickened and the sky turned whitish gray. Rusty knew from years of watching skies that the light sky would turn a darker gray, and snow would fall by dinnertime. Desperate for fresh air to clear his all too cluttered mind, Rusty slipped his coat on and headed out for a walk.

Without intending to, he found himself walking deep into the woods, past the bend in the trail where the trio of birch trees stood, past the boulder that had always been a perfect resting place where Rusty could gather his thoughts and spot a wide variety of birds, all the way back to the open space by the stream where deer often came for a drink.

This had always been his and Terry's favorite place to talk. This was the place they shared so many dreams, so many hurts, so many stages of life. Every time Terry came out for a visit they would end up here. It had become a ritual, as had the flask of whiskey they always carried with them for these special visits. At the end of their conversations here they would share a toast to life.

Silence surrounded Rusty now. No birds called to one another. No wind stirred, and no leaves or branches rustled or whispered. Even the stream, which a few short days earlier had bubbled when he and Rick had stopped by, was completely hushed by a thick layer of ice covering it.

There would be no more stream side conversations. No brotherly sharing of hopes and dreams, of frustrations and fears. Those times were over.

All while Steve, then Dave, and after that Rick, had been with him, Rusty had held back tears, had tried to display a positive front so they wouldn't worry about him. He had done everything he could to convince them he was alright.

Now, standing at this favored ground, with dead silence all around him, the tears he'd held back while Steve had been with him, while Dave was at his house, while Rick then took his turn, forced their way out. Rusty sank to the ground, leaned back against the large oak that had always stood silent witness to his time here, and allowed his tears to flow unhindered.

"Did you have fun with your dad today?" Sascha asked Kody as she unzipped his jacket and slid it off.

Kody nodded. "We played cars and colored and I knocked Daddy's blocks down." He ran towards the staircase. "Can I go feed my fish?"

"You can feed them later. It's dinnertime now."

Over chicken nuggets and french fries Kody told Sascha, "Daddy's got a room with trains just for me. He told me I could stay there any time I want. Can I?"

"Only when you approve, if you approve," Steve whispered to Sascha. "I wasn't trying to interfere."

Sascha nodded, and told Kody, "We'll talk about it another time. Right now you need to get ready for bed." She turned to Steve. "Would you like to give him his bath?"

Steve looked like a kid who'd just been handed the Christmas present he'd dreamed about most. "Are you sure?"

"Yes. I'll clean the kitchen while you get him ready for bed."

Steve filled the tub with warm water and kids' bubble bath. He and Kody raced the rubber duck against the toy boat over the water, Steve allowing Kody's duck to beat his boat every time. He scrubbed Kody clean, and washed the boy's golden brown hair, relishing how silky soft it was, a sensation he'd almost forgotten.

After the bath, Steve dressed Kody in clean flannel pajamas, combed his hair, then cleaned the bathroom while Kody ran into the kitchen to rejoin his mother. She had taken extra time cleaning their dinner dishes, scrubbing the frying pan with greater care than normal, working extra hard to scrub food stains out of the cream colored linen table cloth that hid stains and scratches the table had suffered over the years, in order to allow Steve extra time with Kody.

"Why don't you read him a bedtime story while I finish here, then I'll come and tuck him in for the night."

Steve stared at Sascha. Was this the same woman who had filed for divorce? Well, he'd grab this opportunity in case it was the last good will offering she extended.

Once Kody was settled in bed for the night, Steve returned to the living room and picked up his jacket. "Sascha, thanks for everything today. You didn't have to give as much as you did."

Sascha frowned. "You don't have to leave, do you? I thought we'd have time to talk a bit."

Steve set his jacket down again, apprehensive as to what she wanted now. Was all the good will today just a front, a cover for what she was about to hit him with next? Whatever the case, he'd best just get it over with. "No, I can stay a bit. What's on your mind?"

Sascha poured two glasses of wine, offered one to Steve, and sat on the sofa. Steve took the chair across from her.

"How are you doing?" she asked. "I mean really, how are you? We haven't talked much about what you've gone through the last few weeks."

Steve drained a third of the wine from his glass. "I'm okay. I'm doing alright."

"You look tired. You're not sleeping much, are you?"

"I'm sleeping enough." Then he stopped. He could never lie to her. "No, that's wrong. I don't sleep very well. Too many images run through my mind. It's starting to get better though."

"Is it?" Sascha peered into Steve's face, into the depths of his eyes. After years of marriage she could read him better than anyone else, especially through his eyes where no emotions could be kept secret. What she read now was a level of pain that pierced their vivid blue. "Is it getting better? From what I see you're holding a lot of grief and hurt inside. If you don't let all of those feelings out, you'll never be able to heal."

Steve weighed her words against his need in the past few years to distance himself from those around him, even those closest to him. For months he'd known he was driving Odysseus too hard, and in so doing damaging his relationship with them and impacting their and his personal lives in the process. He'd only thought of the business end of things, of capitalizing on success and grabbing for more. He had built walls around his heart so the hurt he was causing others would not penetrate deep enough to affect him.

He no longer wanted those walls, or the isolation they'd resulted in around his life. He wanted, no, needed, the people he'd tried to shut out. Lowering walls, and in time eliminating them altogether, would take time and constant effort, he knew; now was a good time to start.

"It's horrible, Sascha. I can't believe Terry's gone. It hurts so much I don't even know where to start."

They talked for two hours, mostly about Terry, cried for the loss of him, laughed at some of the stories, listened to a couple of songs where his drumming was best exemplified and acknowledged to each other how grateful they were to have known him at all. Finally, drained but somehow relieved, Steve stood and slipped his jacket on.

"I better let you get some sleep. Morning comes early with that little guy in the house, doesn't it?" He nodded towards a recent photo of Kody Sascha had set on the coffee table.

Sascha smiled, and in that moment Steve caught how her golden hair shone in the soft light, how her emerald eyes glowed. "He sure does!"

"Sascha, thanks for everything today. The time with Kody, dinner, getting him ready for bed, and the talk just now. You didn't have to do any of that. I really appreciate all of it. It helped me a lot." For a split second he was tempted to lean over and kiss her, just on the cheek, nothing intense. He rejected the thought. She wasn't his to kiss anymore.

Sascha stared at the door several minutes after he'd closed it behind him. Steve was different, he had changed. Anyone would have after a horrible crisis such as Steve and Odysseus had gone through. Was it a permanent change, she wondered, or only a temporary one, to be replaced in time by his usual all business drive? She couldn't predict. She only knew her heart had broken for him tonight, as she watched him with Kody, as they'd talked after, as he'd shown a vulnerability she hadn't seen in him in years. As she switched off downstairs lights and headed for bed, she prayed for the man she'd never stopped loving.

Snow had started falling as Rusty trudged home from his visit to the stream. By dinnertime a fresh storm was throwing down snow at a rapid rate. As much as he loved how beautiful fresh snow made the world outside, he hoped this would be the last storm of the season. He was tired of snow. And cold. And everything else in life.

He heated spaghetti left over from the night before's dinner, and carried it into the family room where he'd built a fire in the fireplace. He tried to watch a hockey game, but without Rick's enthusiastic outbursts the game was dull. In fact, everything on TV was dull. After scrolling through channels for a good half hour he shut the TV off.

The box in the dining room called him so loudly he could no longer ignore it. After fighting against it all day, he gave in at last and reopened the box.

He removed the photos from the envelope on top and examined each one. Some captured Terry's signature drumsticks raised and pointing heavenward at the start of an Odysseus show. Two were of moments when he and Terry played off each other, his back to the audience, he facing Terry, his guitar and Terry's drums pouring out notes and beats at a furious pace, and as Rusty looked at those photos now he could hear the songs themselves run through his mind. One of the photos, Rusty's favorite, was of the end of a show, when Terry had stepped out from behind the drums and joined his bandmates at the front of the stage. In this shot, Terry had thrown his arm around Rusty's shoulder, and he and Terry had looked at each other, the broad smiles on each of their faces memorialized the deep bond of brotherhood between them.

Rusty set the photos aside, and picked up once again the leather jacket that had been Terry's favorite. He remembered the day he'd given it to Terry, how Terry had been so overwhelmed by the gift Rusty could swear he'd seen tears in Terry's eyes. Rusty didn't slip the jacket on this time. Instead, he carried it upstairs and draped it over the back of the chair that stood in a corner of his bedroom.

As he turned to leave the room his eye fell on the pocket watch Terry had given him at the end of their last tour, now sitting on his dresser where he'd last placed it. He picked the pocket watch up, ran his fingers once again over the intricate design on its cover, then pressed the latch and opened the watch. He read once again the inscription on the lid: Brothers to the end. Oh Terry, he thought, if only we'd known how soon that end would be.

All cried out after his time by the stream earlier that day, Rusty shed no tears now. He closed the watch, placed it back on the dresser, and headed back downstairs.

Before returning to the box Rusty poured himself a large glass of whiskey. He carried it and the box into the family room and settled himself in the recliner for the long night ahead. He closed his eyes and inhaled long and deep, steeling himself for the task ahead. Then he pulled out from the box the first of Terry's journals.

This one started with Odysseus' early years, from their first days, learning each other's talents and weaknesses, personalities and likes and dislikes, to their early shows. Rusty found himself smiling, almost laughing, at some of the entries, recalling the craziness of it all, madcap musicians breaking as many rules and protocols as they could get away with, endearing themselves to fans and fellow musicians alike who celebrated the rebel spirit in each of them when life allowed.

He read in the entries from that year and subsequent years Terry's intuitive knowledge of music, from the intricacies of capturing just the right sound at just the right time on percussion instruments, to theory and form, the building blocks upon which each song was created.

Having dreaded all day the fresh pain reading these journals would impose on him, Rusty found himself captivated by each entry, reliving so many moments now lost to them all, their history, the thrill of playing together, the blessing of being able to make a living doing what they loved best. It was all there, all the challenges, all the frustrations, and all the magic. Grateful that Terry had taken the time to write so faithfully, no matter how they'd teased him about it over the years, Rusty read long into the night. Morning would find him asleep in his recliner, a half filled whiskey glass on the table beside him, the fireplace filled with cold ashes and an open journal spread across his knees.

Renee made three trips dropping boxes off at various donation centers. She ran two carloads of boxes to her parents' house for safekeeping and joined them for lunch, her favorite, chicken pot pie, with hot fudge sundaes for dessert.

"I know you hate seeing me leave," she told them as she slipped her coat on, "but I think Leanne's right. Making a fresh start somewhere else will be good for me."

As she drove away, she struggled to believe her own words.

Mrs. Clarke surprised Renee with a collection of Tennyson poems and notepaper with a book theme. "So you won't forget me," she said with a smile.

"I could never forget you," Renee told the woman who had been like a second mother or favorite aunt, guiding her through her work to the point when Renee felt strong enough to step out on her own. "I know I'm letting you down, stepping away from the head library job so soon."

"Hush, child!" Mrs. Clarke interrupted. "You haven't let me down a single day since I've known you."

"I never thought. . . ." Renee closed her eyes to regain control of her emotions. "Life doesn't always go the way we plan, does it?"

Mrs. Clarke hugged Renee. "No, it doesn't. So we make new plans. You go off to Phoenix, have fun with your sister, and start a new life. Please stay in touch so I will know how you're getting on."

Renee's last stop was the hardest. She pulled up in front of Terry's apartment, turned the engine off, and sat for five minutes steeling herself to go inside.

Inside, memories washed over her like the waves of the ocean Terry loved so much. All the times they had sat on his sofa, his arm around her, watching movies. The coffees, dinners, wines they had enjoyed on his balcony in summer. He had spent so much time on the road, they grabbed every minute together they could find, Renee coming to think of his apartment as her second home. Together they had planned and dreamed here.

The apartment echoed every one of her steps now, emptiness swallowing her. She hurried with her task, eager to return to fresh air and open space. Opening Terry's closet, she pulled out two of his Odysseus t-shirts, and the cobalt blue sweater she'd given him for his birthday, his favorite. Burying her face in them, she could still smell his aftershave, his scent. She tucked them into the bag she'd brought with her, as well as the crosses and wristbands from his dresser, and a pair of his drumsticks from the coffee table where he'd left them. That was all she wanted. His parents could keep or dispose of anything left behind.

"Enough," she told herself. "It's over. Let it all go."

Leaving the key on the kitchen counter and a note with his parents' address for the landlord to contact, she walked back outside, drove back home and finished packing. Tomorrow she would fly out to her sister, her brother would pick her car up and use it as his own, and a new chapter in her life would open.

Sixteen

Together we will make it through the dark
— Sinéad Tyrone, *Fall On Me*

The April morning spread sunshine and warmth over Milwaukee. The scent of fresh air wafting in through open windows filled Steve's house, welcome and refreshing after the long, cold winter he and Odysseus had gone through. He thought it funny that, although they each lived in different regions, none of them had been spared the harsh snows and freezing temperatures of the past few months. For a few minutes he gazed out the living room window, mesmerized by how brilliant the sun looked as it reflected off the windows of the houses across the street.

It had been so long since anything in his world looked bright.

Three months had passed since the accident in Cleveland. Steve had resettled his life into the small house he was renting, had learned how to fend for himself with laundry and cooking, and had won Kody over by spending quality time with him, taking him on trips to the zoo and the library, and playing with Kody's various toys with him. His divorce from Sascha had not yet been finalized; still he was starting to build a new life and finding it not as scary as he'd feared.

The only thing not moving forward in his life was his band.

With Terry's passing, Odysseus had been shattered. Three months was not enough time to work through their loss, they were just beginning to move beyond the initial shock. Still, they couldn't stay stuck forever.

"We have to do something," he told Dave one day. "No, I'm not trying to push us too hard. I know we're not ready for anything. I just think if we start having conversations about how to move forward, if we even want to move forward, if this is the end and we go our separate ways. . . ." He allowed his words to drop off, afraid to face that option.

Dave agreed, "We should have the conversation, shouldn't we. Find out what everyone wants to do."

Steve couldn't help himself, he didn't want to wait. He needed to ask, "What about you, Dave? Where are you at?"

Dave pondered the question long after he'd ended his call with Steve. Where was he at? He tried to imagine another drummer sitting in Terry's place. The pain was almost overwhelming. After so many years working together, the hole Terry's absence left in his heart, in all their hearts, was too large to just be covered up, or filled with anyone else's presence.

Steve was right, though. They had to start facing their future. He had no idea what he'd say to Steve, but he knew he'd better start figuring it out.

Entering his music room, he passed the line of Odysseus album cover photos evidencing the band's long history. On the opposite wall hung the two platinum and four gold records they had earned. They'd had a glorious history. If it all was over, at least they'd had a good run.

He sat at his keyboard. Running his hands over the black and white keys, their smoothness felt like fine silk to his fingers, and brought back the exhilaration he always felt when his hands danced across them. He chose not to attempt Odysseus songs yet, but rather turned to classical composers, Mozart, Beethoven, Bach, Grieg, so many masters who had been the inspiration for him ever starting music. Not caring what the future held, playing for his enjoyment alone, he allowed the healing power of music to work its magic, playing through daylight and well past evening.

Rick received Steve's text suggesting a date for a conference call to discuss what was next for Odysseus. He turned to Laurel. "Steve's asking what we want to do about moving forward."

"Isn't it kind of soon to be asking?"

"Not really. If we had any other job we'd already be back to work."

Laurel set a plate with grilled cheese sandwich and french fries in front of Rick, relishing him being home for lunch. This was the longest stretch they'd had together in over a year, and she wanted to make the most of every moment. "True," she admitted, "but other jobs aren't like yours. What do you think you want to do?"

Rick picked up a couple of fries, crinkle cut, his favorite kind, dark golden brown, the way he loved them best. He weighed his words with great care. "We're musicians," he told her. "It's what we do. I can't see any of us choosing different careers at this point in our lives. We'll go back to it one way or another, no matter how hard it is now."

"Do you think Rusty will go back?"

Rick lifted his eyes to meet hers. "I honestly don't know. When I talk with him we never mention Terry, or Odysseus, or music in general. We talk about his house, you and our kids, anything other than the elephant in the room."

Laurel had met Rick through Odysseus. She'd seen all their ups and downs, and the tight bond that held them all together no matter what. She knew their manners, their personalities, and how each one dealt with difficulties. Rusty, she knew, would always hold things close inside him unless someone forced a topic. "Maybe you should ask him about Terry. You know he won't bring it up first."

Rick pictured Rusty as he was the week Rick was there. He put up the same brave, stoic front they all did, kept his focus on whatever he was doing at the moment, buried his feelings deep inside as he always had. It was funny, Rick thought now, for all that Rusty was the most outgoing among them in connecting with media and the public at large, he hid volumes inside himself when it came to personal matters. Even when it was just the five of them sitting around backstage, or in studio, or on their bus, Rusty would only open up to a particular level, and no further. Terry was the one Rusty always confided in.

Maybe Laurel was right. Maybe now he needed to be the one to try to coax things out of Rusty.

As he dialed the phone, he prayed Terry would send some help his way.

"Hey, Rusty, just checking in with you. I haven't talked with you in a week. What are you up to today?"

What Rusty had been up to was staring at the bottom of his coffee cup for the past hour, thinking he should do something constructive but having no idea what and no interest in moving from his kitchen table. He wouldn't tell Rick that, though. Rick would worry and hop the next plane up to check that he was alright.

Instead he told Rick, "I'm looking at plans for a deck off the back of the house. Do I want French doors or sliding glass doors, off the kitchen, or off the family room?"

"Sliding," Rick answered. "Family room. No, make that kitchen. Then you can bring food and drinks to all of us easier!"

"Good point."

Rick chose to dive in to the purpose of his call. "We haven't really talked about this since the accident. How are you doing? Not just on the outside, what's going on deep down?"

Automatic defense walls went up inside Rusty. "Why are you asking? Do you think there's something going on?"

Rick fought the temptation to back off. "I was just thinking, Terry was always the one you confided in. Who are you confiding in now? You have to have someone to talk to."

"I talk to the owls."

Rusty meant it as a joke. Disappointed when it fell fell flat, he admitted to Rick, "I still talk to Terry. It's just a little harder to hear his replies."

There. He'd let that secret out. Let Rick think he was off the deep end. Let them all think he was crazy. It didn't matter anymore.

Rick didn't laugh. "I have no doubt Terry hears every word you say."

Rusty wanted to believe him. "Do you really think so?"

"I do. Rusty, there's so much about the spirit world we don't understand. You and Terry were so close, closer than brothers. No matter where Terry is in the universe now, he would never abandon you."

Even as he spoke the words, Rick found himself believing them. He'd never thought much about afterlife, but it made sense that Terry's spirit would be hovering over them now in some capacity.

Rusty let the words settle into his heart. "Thank you Rick. I needed to hear that."

"Hey, I got a text from Steve a little while ago. He wants to set up a conference call with all of us, just to get us all connected again and start to figure out where we go from here. You might want to check in with him."

Rusty's blood turned to ice. He didn't want any part of Odysseus. Not now. Maybe not ever. "Can you please just tell Steve for me that I'm not ready? Tell him you all should go ahead without me."

"You mean for the conference call right?"

"No. I mean for everything."

Rick's heart sank. "Rusty, why don't you just join in the call? You might feel better with all of us talking."

"No." Rusty shut him down. "I can't, Rick. I'm just not ready."

"Hope you're both getting this warm spell!" Steve started the conference call. "Has anyone heard back from Rusty, whether he changed his mind about joining in?"

Rick shook his head. "He hasn't. I checked with him again yesterday. He told me we should go ahead without him."

"How do you feel about that? Should we move forward, or wait a few more weeks or so for him?"

"I'm all for waiting," Rick told them, "but I don't think a few weeks will do it."

Sadness crossed Steve's face. "He's so stuck. I know we're all hurting, but he's giving up isn't he."

"He was closer to Terry, and for longer, than the rest of us," Dave pointed out, not that they needed the reminder. "Steve, you and Rusty were there. You both have more pain that Rick and I know. Rusty survived, his best friend died. He's got a lot to work through right now."

Steve struggled to block the accident from his mind. "We're all still fragile inside, aren't we. What would you both like to do?"

Dave remembered the feel of the keys under his fingers the last time he played. "I'm all for moving on," he told Rick and Steve. "I know we have a lot to sort out, but I'm all for starting the process."

"We can't live without music," Rick said. "We have to start over. But I want Rusty with us."

"So do I," Steve agreed. "I have an idea on how to get him back on track, but I might need your help."

Steve laid out his plan. Dave and Rick both agreed to do what they could to make it succeed.

After the call, Rick returned to his music room and picked up his favorite bass guitar, the first one he'd played with Odysseus. He'd tried playing music dozens of times since the accident; each time he got a couple of songs in but had no heart to go further. He was so used to Terry's drums pounding a steady beat in his ears; even when he was just home practicing and ran his bass lines he'd play a track of Terry's drums in the background in order to ensure he had the right tempo and accented the right moments in a song. Terry and he formed two legs of the anchor to Odysseus' music, with Rusty's rhythm guitar the third leg. Without Terry, Rick had felt anchorless, drifting through songs without any direction.

Today there was a glimmer of light in the future. Odysseus would find their way back, or at least an element of hope that they would now existed. Rick slipped the guitar strap over his neck, ran his left hand along the fingerboard, caressing it, reveling in the smoothness along its neck and the raised sensation of each fret. The weight of the bass guitar in his hands comforted him. It felt good to return to the music that had seen him through so many of the highs and lows of life. With each note he tested he found renewed confidence that, even despite the pain of losing Terry, he could play music again.

Dave poured himself a fresh coffee, his fourth of the morning, and ran his mind once more over the conference call they'd just finished. He liked Steve's plan for pulling Rusty back into the fold, although he wasn't sure it would work. Still, someone had to try something or they would have to move forward without him, and none of them wanted to do that.

Even if Rusty did make it back, they were still down one drummer. No matter how torn inside he was that Terry was gone, his pragmatic side kicked in and he made a mental list of drummers Odysseus might call on. A quick online search confirmed which ones were available and which were booked for the next few months. He would let Steve know the various possibilities the next time they talked.

Dave then sat down at his keyboards and played around with various chords and single notes, borrowing a bit from a classical piece he'd always loved, testing different tones, setting it in a minor key and adding a metal music bridge. He played around with words, and by dinnertime had the start of a new song which he would dedicate to Terry.

Rusty wandered from room to room in his house, unsure what he wanted to do with the day, not finding anything that interested him, noting various tasks he could accomplish if he felt so inclined: clearing boxes and leftover pieces from projects that had been stored in one of the spare bedrooms of his house, bookshelves to install in the living room, and carpeting to pull up and hardwood floors to restore in two spare bedrooms.

None of those tasks motivated him, though.

He was recovering well from his injuries, his lung and chest still ached if he overexerted himself and he still lacked the same level of energy he'd had before the accident, but overall he was fine. At least, he was physically well.

The nightmares were another story. By day, if he heard loud sounds, whether from TV or radio or outside, he would jump. Television was especially problematic; the action shows and movies he used to enjoy carried a lot of car crashes and near crashes, and he found he could no longer watch those programs. He tried listening to music but so much of it, whether from Odysseus or other bands they had known and worked with, made him think of Terry.

Nighttime was worse. He stayed up as late as he could, until his eyes could no longer stay open and he thought it was safe to retire for the night. Exhausted, he would drop off to sleep right away, only to be startled awake in the middle of the night by cars flying through glass and horrific noises of metal grinding and twisting and bodies crushed in the middle of it all.

He would lie awake for hours after the nightmares, panicked and sweating, terrified to close his eyes again.

Bright sunshine streamed through Rusty's kitchen window and called him outside. He obliged, finding the spring air warm and sweet scented. He strolled the yard closest to his house, noting tips of spring bulbs pushing through soil, soon to be blooming with yellows, reds, and oranges. Three robins scouted for worms in his soil. The first signs of spring, their red fronts were always a welcome sight, and this year more than ever. Rusty was tired of winter, tired of cold.

In truth, he was tired of life.

He returned to the house, heated chili left over from the night before, took a couple of bites out of it, then set it aside. Even his favorite meal couldn't capture his interest today.

The phone rang. Rusty debated whether he would answer, and in the end picked it up.

"Hey, Rusty! How are you doing this week, brother?" Steve's voice greeted him.

Their shared Cleveland experience had forged an even deeper bond between Steve and Rusty. Steve was the one person on earth Rusty was glad to hear from today. "I'm alright," he responded. "And you?"

"Doing okay. Hey, what are you doing May fourteenth?"

Rusty didn't even have to look at his calendar. "Nothing. Why?"

Steve whispered a quick prayer before answering, "There's a big metal show going on in New York. Dave, Rick and I will be playing. We were hoping you'd join us."

Rusty sidestepped the invitation. "What are you going to do about drums?"

"Dave thought Allen Barnes would be a good choice. What do you think?"

Rusty knew Allen from being on the same show lineup several times over the past few years. He was a good drummer, not as good as Terry but acceptable. "You'd be okay with Allen."

"There's one other thing we need. We need you," Steve told him. "We can't go on without you."

Rusty thought of the guitars hung on their racks in his upstairs music room, and of the White Rose guitar in her stand in the family room. He hadn't touched either since coming home; the truth was, he had no intention to. He had to make Steve see that now.

"You can," he told Steve. "You have to. I'm not coming back."

Steve could not accept the resolve he heard in Rusty's voice. He understood where Rusty was coming from, but he was not about to let it end there. "Rusty, I know it's hard to think about moving forward, but you have to. Terry wouldn't want you to just stop the music. He'd want you to go on without him."

"Steve, I haven't even touched my guitars since Cleveland. I can't even think of picking them up. I won't be ready for a very long time. You need to have someone come in and take my place."

Steve refused to believe Rusty could give up music so easily. He'd seen for years the passion with which Rusty played, it was too much a part of Rusty's heart, of every cell and fiber inside him. Pushing any harder now, though, would get him nowhere. "I hear what you're saying, Rusty, but don't let this be your final decision. I'll be in New York in a couple of weeks. I'm going to stop up and visit you, if that's okay. We can talk more then."

"You can visit here any time. I won't change my mind, though."

Steve hung up, disappointed but not surprised. He knew his plan would be a hard sell where Rusty was concerned. He wouldn't give up.

A glance at the clock indicated the day was farther gone than he'd realized. Sascha would be here in an hour to drop Kody off. Steve had chicken nuggets and macaroni and cheese planned for dinner, and books and videos ready for the evening. Tomorrow, he planned to take Kody to the zoo before returning him home.

His phone rang, Sascha's number appeared on the screen, and apprehension struck him. Kody had had a cold earlier in the week; Steve hoped Sascha wasn't calling to tell him the cold was worse and Kody wouldn't be coming after all.

"Steve, I was just wondering, is there any chance you'd have dinner here tonight? I know you were looking forward to Kody staying over, but, well, it would be better if you wouldn't mind coming here."

"Is it his cold? Is he worse?"

Sascha almost laughed at the panic in Steve's voice. "No, it's nothing like that. Everything's fine. I can explain more tonight."

Steve exhaled, relieved. "Okay, sure. No problem. Want me to bring anything for dinner or dessert?"

"No, we're all set. Just bring yourself."

After they hung up, Sascha prayed she was doing the right thing.

The return address on the envelope Rusty received in the mail didn't register at first. The scrawled handwriting could have belonged to anyone. Some letters like that made Rusty suspicious; fans might somehow find their way through the layers of security that surrounded his life and send God only knew what through the mail. The envelope was addressed to Russell Morgan; at first Rusty didn't even recognize his full name. It had been so long since anyone had called him Russell. He opened the envelope and drew out the single sheet of lined paper.

"Dear Uncle Rusty," the letter started. Uncle? My God, thought Rusty. Someone from my family actually found me? He read on. "We haven't met. I'm your brother Harold's son. I've followed your music a long time, although my dad won't let me go to any of your shows. I hope someday he will. I heard about your accident, and I wanted to let you know I'm very sorry. I hope you will be okay, and that I get to meet you someday. Your nephew, Luke."

Rusty stared at the letter a long time. He tried to picture what Harold would look like now, paunchy and bald headed, he guessed, just like their father. From the return address, he could see Harold still lived in the same town they'd been brought up in. Harold never was one to stray far from their parents' wishes and orders. Of all his siblings, Harold was the one to give Rusty the hardest time, criticizing everything Rusty did, what he wore, and most of all what music he played. Harold was the spy in the family, always running to their parents to tell every time Rusty smoked or swore.

So, Harold had a son who loved Odysseus? Good! The thought that Rusty could torment Harold through Luke was pleasing, he savored the feel of it.

Then he wondered, if Luke knew about the accident, the rest of their family must as well. He'd never had a phone call, or card, or anything from any of them. Not that he'd expected any reaction from them, but Luke's letter, and confirmation that the rest of them ignored Rusty still cut deep into his heart.

Rusty thought about sending a response to Luke but decided against it. If Harold got the mail first, Rusty's answer back would end up in the trash. He thought of tracking down a phone number, but if anyone other than Luke answered they would just hang up. Luke might have a social media account but Rusty was staying off social media for now, not ready to see or respond to posts about Terry.

In the end he folded the letter, slipped it back into its envelope, and tucked the envelope into the top drawer of his desk for safekeeping.

Steve arrived on time with a carton of ice cream, some chocolate sauce and whipped cream. "I thought at least I should bring dessert."

Sascha accepted the package with a smile. "Kody will love this."

Kody came running around the corner shouting, "Daddy! You're home!" He wrapped his arms as tight as he could around Steve's legs.

It's not home, Steve thought, but didn't try to explain complicated matters to his son. Kody would understand in time.

Dinner was a simple meal of spaghetti, salad, and garlic bread. After dinner Steve played a game with Kody while Sascha cleared the dishes, then they had their ice cream dessert before Sascha gave Kody his bath. Before heading to bed, Kody curled up on the sofa next to Steve so Steve could read him a book.

After tucking Kody into bed, Sascha returned to the kitchen where Steve was rinsing the ice cream dishes and loading them into the dishwasher.

"I'll do that," she told him, motioning for him to join her at the table. "Sit down a minute. I want to talk to you about something."

Here it comes, Steve thought. I should have known she wanted me here for a reason.

Sascha fixed her eyes on Steve's and plunged into her words before she lost her nerve. "You've changed these past few months. You're different than you were before Christmas. At first I thought it was the accident that changed you, but I don't know, it seems to go deeper."

"I've been pretty horrible the past year or so, taking so many people for granted," Steve admitted. "I've learned my lesson. I don't want to be that person anymore."

"You've been so wonderful with Kody these past few months. He talks about you all the time, you know."

Nothing in the world could have made Steve happier than to hear that.

"I was thinking, maybe we should hold off on the divorce."

There. The words were out. Sascha prayed she wasn't making a huge mistake.

Steve was stunned. "What? Are you sure?"

Tears rose in Sascha's eyes, and the words she'd been so afraid to say rushed through like the Niagara cascading down its cliff edge. "I think so. Oh Steve, I don't know. I never really wanted a divorce, but I couldn't stand the way you were treating me and Kody. I don't know if this change in you will last or if it's just temporary until you're back on the road, but I'm willing to take another chance on us. Kody needs to have his father around more."

"Is this only for Kody's sake? Sasch, if this is only for him it won't work. There had better be something to hold us together besides him, or we're doomed."

"No, it's not just Kody." Sascha brushed away the tears sliding down her cheeks. "Steve, I've never stopped loving you. If you promise me you won't go back to the way you were before, I'll tear up the divorce papers now."

Steve rose from his chair, crossed over to where Sascha sat, and kneeled in front of her. "Sascha, I almost lost you and Kody once. I swear on everything I own, I swear on my life, that I will never run that risk again."

Sascha opened the bottle of prosecco she'd bought on her way home and poured a glass for each of them. They curled up on the sofa and finished the bottle while watching the divorce papers turn to embers and ash in the fireplace.

The next day Steve packed his belongs up and moved back home with Sascha and Kody. The day after, he visited Rusty.

"You look better than you did the last time I saw you," Steve teased when Rusty answered the door.

"Ha! That's not hard!"

Over coffee Steve told him about the canceled divorce and moving back home. As they toured Rusty's property, Rusty pointed out which plants were poking though soil or sending out new buds. All while they chatted an uneasy wedge rose between them, each of them knowing what the visit was for. When they returned to the house, Rusty confronted Steve head on.

"I'm not ready to return to the band. I'm not ready for the show you mentioned."

Steve would not give up. "Don't you miss music? Damn, Rusty, you used to play nonstop! You always had a guitar in hand. You breathed, ate, and slept music!"

Rusty stared hard at the spot in the corner where his White Rose guitar stood. Terry's image floated before him, as it always did, every day, multiple times every day, each time causing a fresh wave of pain to slice through his heart. God, did the pain ever end? Did it never lessen? He was quite sure the heartache would follow him the rest of his life. Return to music? First he had to return to life, to breathing without the breaths catching in his throat, to getting through several hours in a row without wishing he could join Terry wherever his friend's spirit now resided.

He pulled his gaze back to the brother now so intent on dragging him back to the world of music, the world that could never be the same, the one he was sure he could not survive without his best friend. For the first time he noticed the deep lines etched across Steve's face, and the pain that filled Steve's eyes, and knew Steve's pain was as heavy as his own.

Rusty wished with everything in him that he could turn the clock back to the Cleveland show, to the week before Cleveland, to the months on the Odysseus tour bus that had been so tense, almost combative. Maybe if they could do those days over, he could change the course of events and Terry would still be alive.

But no, courses, once set, could never be changed.

Rusty asked Steve, "Do you ever wonder what sin we committed that was so horrible we are now exiled to torment for the rest of our lives?"

Steve was sure he knew what Rusty meant, but he played dumb, waiting for Rusty to voice his feelings further. He knew exposing what lie deepest on Rusty's heart was the first step in healing. That was just one of the lessons Sascha had taught him the past several weeks.

Rusty continued, "Did you ever wonder what god we pissed off that we would be so cursed now? Why us? Why Terry? Why was our cab the one to be hit? Why did Terry have to die? Why do we have to be the ones left to find our way through this hellish nightmare? Couldn't another car have been hit instead? Couldn't the accident have been held back altogether? What god is so angry at us that we are now banished to a world of sadness we will never be able to escape? No matter what we do the rest of our lives this will haunt us. I know I'll never get past it. Will you? I mean, you, me, Dave, Rick, even Renee, I don't see us ever getting to a place where it doesn't hurt when we think of Terry, and we will think of him every single damned day, right?"

"Yeah, we'll think of him every day," Steve had to agree. "I don't think it will always be this painful, though. I have to think we'll have better days somewhere down the road. And don't we owe it to Terry to move forward? He'd kick our asses if we let this be the end of all our music, all the phenomenal music he had a hand in writing and sending out into the world. Renee's starting to rebuild in another place. It's terrible for her right now. But she'll find her way through to another dream. Dave and Rick and I know we can't just sit around and do nothing, we need the art, the creative process, the music itself to give us a reason to get up every day and not feel like we live in a black hole."

Rusty turned back to the guitar standing, waiting, in the corner. "Yeah,

I get that. For you three moving forward is the right thing. Music is the right thing for you. Even Renee, moving away and giving herself a fresh start, that's all good. I just can't do that, though. I think of music, and my mind automatically goes to Terry, and I can't see how I will ever get past that. The dream is shattered and I will never be able to pull it back together. You three have to understand that, and have to go on without me."

Steve's heart broke for his brother. He wouldn't push anymore, although he still had one card to play. "Alright Rusty, I do understand and I won't force you. But here, here's a couple of tickets to the show. Even if you're not up on stage playing with us a lot of people would still love to see you."

After Steve left, Rusty stared at the tickets he had set on the kitchen counter. All he could think of was how Terry would have loved that show. So many of their friends were on the bill, the music would be explosive, and the parties afterward, they'd be epic! Terry wouldn't have missed this for anything, even if he wasn't up on stage with the others.

Rusty recalled the words in Terry's journals. So much of what Terry had written was positive. Life was always beautiful to Terry, even when filled with challenges and disappointments. Terry lived for the fun in life, reached out for all he could grab hold of, never let a day go down sad or empty.

What would Terry do if he had survived and Rusty was gone? Rusty had no way of knowing. He was sure, however, that Terry would find a way to go on, with or without music.

"No, Steve," Rusty lied to the empty room he stood in. "I don't miss music. I can't do it. It hurts too much. But you're right about one thing. I can't spend my whole life stuck like I am. I do have to find my way forward."

He stepped into the family room and picked up his White Rose guitar. Where she had always fairly leapt into his arms in the past, now she hesitated, unsure of her welcome. Before, she had always felt warm, comforting, now she felt distant and cold. Rusty knew he had changed, and not she. Too many memories were tied to her, memories he would take a long time in being able to embrace.

Without testing a single note, he carried the White Rose upstairs, stored her in her travel case, and banished her to a corner of his music room with the other guitars now deemed useless.

He then threw some clothes in an overnight bag and drove to the Massachuetts shore.

It wasn't hard to find Terry's favorite spot; Rusty had been there often enough. He parked his car, walked to the point where Terry always stood, and gazed out over the ocean. He remembered Terry's awe over the constant movement of the waves, how mesmerized he was by their ever returning nature, how the endless expanse of water before them made so many of life's problems seem tiny, insignificant.

Below the cliff edge where he stood, hundreds of jagged rocks protruded from the ocean's blue waters. For a flash of a moment, Rusty wondered how it would feel to cast himself down upon them, let fate take him, and join the brother he missed so dreadfully.

Standing face to face with Terry, he knew his brother would be furious. With or without music Rusty could not let go of life. He would not disappoint Terry that way.

Rusty stood a long time at the cliff edge. Even for early May the air felt chill, wind gusts buffeting him from time to time, almost pushing him over the edge as if some invisible hand had a plan for him. Gulls swooped in and out in wide, erratic circles, their plaintive screams echoing in his ears long after they wheeled away.

The ocean before him was as wide open as the future he faced without Odysseus. Endless options crossed his mind. He could learn a landscaper's art and tend gardens and lawns for a living. That would be fun. He could drive limousines. He'd always been fascinated by photography, maybe he could take that up. Perhaps he could learn the art of cabinetry or carpentry, and make a living off the feel of wood under his hands, something that would give him great satisfaction.

He had no idea which way he would go. He only knew what he had to do today.

Rusty allowed his thoughts to roam wherever they wanted as long as he could, until the cold air buffeting him became impossible to stand in any longer. Then, staring out at Terry's beloved ocean, he raised the flask he'd carried in his jacket pocket.

"This is it," he spoke out loud. "This is where I leave you, Terry. I don't want to say goodbye. I will never forget you. Thank you for all the laughs, all the fun, all the music. Thank you for being my brother."

He drained the flask of its contents, then pitched it as far as he could into the ocean, watching it float for a brief time then sink. He returned to his car, stayed at a motel nearby that night, and the next day returned home, sure he would never visit the ocean again.

The last of Terry's journals waited on the coffee table for Rusty to open it. Best get it over with, he thought, figuring that was the last step in putting the Cleveland tragedy behind him and starting to move forward.

In this journal Terry had chronicled the last tour, all of the shows that rose to heights beyond anything they'd experienced before, the night Mike and Janice became engaged, and the shows that didn't quite hit the mark. He'd recorded Steve's outbursts and moods, writing with care to try and show Steve's good sides as well, maintaining as much of a positive view as he could.

A week after Tim Caldwell's passing, Terry had written this entry:

I've thought a lot about it, this past week. What was Tim's legacy? What is ours? To say it's our music is an easy answer, and true to some extent, but there should be more. Architects leave buildings behind. Artists leave paintings, authors leave books, musicians leave music. Those are pieces of work, and they may be important, or relevant, or beautiful; but they speak little of the persons who created such works. Do I want to be remembered for how well I played music, or for something more vital?

Tim went through so much in his life. Two divorces. What did they teach him? What did Dave learn through his divorce? What will Steve learn? Rick's on a better track in his marriage, and I pray to God I will be as successful in my marriage to Renee. What's made Rick more successful at this than Steve, or Dave, or Tim?

I remember when Tim lost his young son due to illness. It just about broke him. He turned to drugs for a while, but in time he pulled himself out of that and rebuilt his life. He rebuilt it again after each of his marriages failed, and after his first label dropped him and his band a decade ago.

I remember talking with him once about the space between notes, and all the various meanings people have attached to that phrase. Was it the rests built into the score of a song? I thought so at first. Or was it the silence surrounding the notes that gave the notes more impact? I told Tim I thought it was the breaks in our roads that life threw at us, that stopped us from playing music for a while but in the end we always came back to the notes and the lyrics. In the end we agreed all three answers were right.

Tim's ability to keep pushing on – I think that's his legacy, the same as it was Odysseus' in the book by Homer. That's what I want my legacy to be as well.

Terry's journal ended there. After that they'd been busy finishing the tour and returning home, where Renee and Christmas had been his focus.

Keep pushing on. Oh Terry, Rusty thought, if you only knew how hard that is without you. But maybe you do know. Maybe you see us from where you are now. I'd like to think that, anyway. If you do, show me how to move forward. Show me how to push past all the pain and make a fresh start.

Rusty's eyes fell upon the tickets Steve had left for him. Somehow he felt Terry was urging him to attend. He decided he would, if only to see some of his friends. If the show proved too hard to stomach, he would just leave.

Luke learned about the show in New York through social media. Odysseus would be there with a new lineup. No information was given as to who would be in the band, just as there had been no information regarding Rusty's health beyond the statement released a few weeks after the accident that he was recovering at home. Luke had no idea whether Rusty would be back with the band, or at the show in any capacity. He only knew he had to be there himself, in hopes that he could meet his uncle at last.

Luke researched the cost of show tickets, airfare, and hotels near the concert venue. He checked the balance in the savings account his parents had started for him years ago, and worked out a plan for how he could cover the shortage through odd jobs around town. After dinner, he presented the information to his father.

"I know it's a lot to ask," he admitted, "I know you don't want to see him, but I do. It means more to me than you know."

Impressed as he was with all the detail Luke had put into his request, Harold still shook his head. "Someday you'll understand better," he told his son. "For now you'll just have to trust my judgment."

Luke didn't rage against his father, or allow the tears in his heart to become visible. He only sank, defeated, into the armchair across from where his father sat. "Haven't you ever wanted anything this much? Haven't you ever wanted something so bad it tore you up inside to not get it? Please, Dad. I swear if you take this trip with me I'll never ask for anything again."

Luke's words, and the anguish behind them, opened a crack in the corner of Harold's heart where he'd relegated any thoughts concerning Rusty and the years so long ago when his parents had gone through such turmoil. As memories rushed through he saw it all, the angry confrontations, the slammed doors, the pleading on both his brother's and his parents' parts. He saw something else as well, something that caught him off guard, made him catch his breath.

The looks on his parents' faces then were the same as they turned on Luke from time to time now. When his hair was too long. When his clothes didn't suit their tastes. When he raved about the music he loved, the cd he'd just bought, the next band coming to town, or his desire to learn an instrument, any instrument, he didn't care, he just wanted to be a part of the music scene.

What had those harsh looks accomplished, Harold wondered now. What had all the arguments resulted in. Harold had always believed his parents had been right, and Rusty horribly wrong. Maybe, in retrospect, his parents were the wrong ones. Maybe Rusty hadn't been such a bad person, any more than Luke was now in incurring his grandparents' harsh judgments.

Harold sized up the young man seated across from him. Luke was a good kid, a little obsessed at times, a little stubborn, but polite, and with a kind heart. He pulled in good grades and complied with all their rules. The worst Luke had ever done was be independent, his own person and not a mirror image of what everyone else thought he should be.

Maybe that independence and courage should be rewarded and not discouraged.

Harold glanced once again over the report Luke had brought him. "If we go to New York, think you could fill me in on what your uncle's been up to all these years?"

The night of the show, Odysseus took their turn with Allen Barnes at the drums. Mack Michaels, a friend of theirs from another band, filled the rhythm guitar spot in Rusty's absence. Their performance was solid, and the support they received from the audience and their metal brothers alike overwhelmed them.

As he scanned the audience, Steve saw what he hoped for. When they had a break between songs he drew Rick over to Dave and told them both, "He's here."

"Are you going to go ahead with your plan?" Rick asked.

"I have to. I can't leave him broken like he is now."

Dave asked, "What if he refuses?"

"I won't put him on the spot for too long. If he refuses, I'll just say 'maybe next time' and move on."

Rick and Dave both nodded agreement. "Go for it," Rick told Steve. "I hope it works."

Steve took a deep breath, whispered a quick prayer, and stepped up to the microphone. "I hope you're all having as much fun tonight as we are. I know the organizers of this show did their best to gather the best metal musicians they could for you all tonight.

"There's one musician we couldn't get, though. When we tried the timing just wasn't right. He's in the audience tonight, and I'm hoping, if you all give him a lot of encouragement, we just might get Rusty Morgan to join us for a song or two."

At the mention of Rusty's name, the crowd went wild with cheers.

Rusty glared at Steve and shook his head. He mouthed, "No. I can't."

Steve had anticipated that. He told the audience, "Now, I can see where Rusty's sitting, and I can tell you he's hesitating. I get that. We guitarists are kind of funny animals. If someone called me onstage to play one of their guitars, I wouldn't do it. We like to play our own guitars, know how they feel in our hands, how they respond, how they will sound. So Rusty, if that's why you're hesitating . . ." Steve stopped and reached for what a stage hand was holding out to him, "here's your White Rose, all tuned and ready to make some music with you."

Steve placed Rusty's guitar on a stand near the stage front, thankful to the neighbor who had snuck it out of the house and delivered it to him earlier that day.

Rusty was trapped. The audience was applauding and whistling, sending him as much encouragement as they could. Even some of their musician brothers had stepped out by the curtains and were cheering him on.

He had no choice.

He stood, stepped up to the stage, and picked up his guitar.

"I hate you," he whispered to Steve.

Steve smiled. "I know you do. You can kill me later. Right now, you're here. You know the song I want, Whispers In The Dark. Allen on drums, Rick on bass, the rest is all yours. I'll join you on the double notes at the end."

The lead notes felt odd to Rusty as he started out. By the third bar, though, the spirit of the song had captured him, and he gave it all he had in him. Something about this song always grabbed hold of his heart and moved him to tears. Tonight, he played with eyes closed. Terry's image floated in front of him, and he had to fight to hold his tears back.

When Steve joined him on the double guitar notes towards the end of the song, something else rose inside Rusty. The power of music and the bond of brotherhood he shared with the rest of Odysseus kicked in, took over, and Rusty felt he'd returned to where he belonged. Even Allen on drums felt okay. The peace Rusty had sought for months filled him again.

The audience gave Odysseus a standing ovation when the song was done. Later on, all of their metal brothers would shower praise and congratulations upon them.

Rusty stepped next to Steve and whispered, "Thank you. I needed this."

"I knew you did." Steve winked. "Play another song with us. Your choice."

The show had ended, the crowd had largely dispersed and musicians were packing up to head for home or whatever parties they had planned. Two figures approached the backstage, one young, one much older.

"Uncle Rusty?"

Rusty turned to the voice and found a thin teenager dressed in black jeans, a black shirt, and a wild, uncontrollable head of red hair. "Luke?"

"I hoped you'd be playing tonight!" Luke's green eyes shone wide with excitement and awe at meeting his hero.

"I almost didn't." Rusty nodded to the person behind Luke. "That's not your father is it?"

"Yes. Dad, I told you Rusty would be glad to see us."

Rusty wasn't sure glad was the word he would use, but he wouldn't correct the only person in his family who was on his side. He held out his hand. "Harold, it's been a long time."

"Too long. Russell, I'm sorry I've let so much time go by. I don't even know how to apologize."

For a split second, Rusty was tempted to let his brother hang in the wind. He couldn't do it though. "It's okay, you're here now, that means a lot. And please, it's Rusty! If you call me Russell I'll have to take all kinds of crap from these guys!"

Steve, Rick, Dave, and Allen stood off to the side, ready to leave but not wanting to rush the family reunion taking place before them. Rusty spotted them and told Luke, "Look, I have to go with these guys tonight. Are you and your dad staying over? If so, maybe we can meet up for breakfast tomorrow and have a good long talk."

Luke looked at his father, who nodded consent. "That would be great, Uncle Rusty."

The Odysseus brothers stepped outside as the venue attendants started turning out the lights. While others felt the night was ending, to Rusty it felt like the night was a new beginning.

The Space Between Notes:
The Poems

A word about the poems:

This project started with poems. The poems eventually inspired the novel.

Some poems in the early part of this section are love poems, reflecting the relationships between some of the characters in the novel, Steve and Sascha, Rick and Laurel, Terry and Renee.

Some reflect the challenges touring musicians face.

Some deal with loss and grief.

Towards the end of this collection are poems specifically relating to, and paying tribute to, the musicians who inspired this project.

I hope you enjoy them all.

Table of Contents

The First Ancestral Language
For Every Artist Striving
Beyond The Lights
Of Lyrics and Notes
Silent Conversation
Trees Reflected
Brotherhood
God's Tears
Somewhere In Between
We Watch Through Eastern Window
Beneath A Golden Moon
Waiting Out The Storm
Some Mornings
This Road Carries No Outlets
Unrepaired
Mazes and Labyrinths
Tiny Star Hamlets
Of Partings And Returns
If I Had Known
If Only
The Space Between Notes
Fragmented
Early Morning
Memories Stirred
Dream Keeper
Set A Steel Door
Picking Up The Pieces
Five Hundred Pound Load
Climbing Machu Picchu
Releasing Your Spirit
Still Standing

Behind The Mask
Two Guitars
Three A.M. World
Empty Space
Building Blocks
You Hide Among The Trees And Flowers
Beyond The Veil
Smooth Round Stone
Not Mine To Keep
Rose Light Healing
Moment In Time
Calming Voices
Breathe
Filling The Empty Cracks
Fall On Me
Faith Walking
To Dream Again
A Million Pieces
Looking for the Lost
Wanderer Released
Four Simple Notes
Stream-Side Dreams
Still The Band Plays On
Dreams Kept Alive
Every Dream
Celestial Viewpoint
Legacy
You Among The Stars
You Shine A New Light

The First Ancestral Language

Something so honest
so pure
music at its deepest core
pulling the strings of my heart
setting them to dance
or cry

most ancient of tongues
music speaks
what my ancestors spoke
long before ancestral records
were kept

this is church
spiritual language
so deep no words are needed
the holy comes through
instruments as old as time
as fresh as this morning's sun

secrets of my soul
poured forth
soaring through your notes
to the heavens themselves
collected and treasured
by the creator
who spoke music
into our hearts

For Every Artist Striving

It was always there
the passion
the drive and desire
to deliver music
that transforms lives
true artists hold that
within their hearts
their highest calling
the dream that keeps them going
through the lean times
the darker days
the bruises and deeper wounds
from which they must heal

and if your lives
were sometimes checkered
and demons and lessons
tough to fight through
you willed yourself
to pay the price
and push forward
the prize of dreams realized
the goal you always pursued

Bend your head
over your instrument
caress the tools of your craft
close your eyes
and turn your face skyward
pour everything in you
into the pursuit of your dreams

in those simple movements
your observers feel the magic
as you cover
scars and bruises
and make the world shine
one more time

Beyond the Lights

Look beyond the stage
beyond the laser lights
and pyrotechnics
behind the amps and instruments
through the words
and fancy riffs

to the hearts and souls
of those who craft the music
of our lives

they are gentle souls
rough exteriors
with soft hearts
that feel every heartbreak of life
and transform so much pain
into notes and words that shine
like jewels for us

harder hearts
could not create such magic

Of Lyrics and Notes

Rain cascades down
on cars and people outside
while here in the hotel lobby
where I am safely ensconced
I try to find the sun and warmth
that will carry me through the day

Bright lights and soft ambiance
soothe but do not satisfy

my mind and heart need something more
something that penetrates
the corners of my heart
that remain fragile
in need of deeper light

I turn to the only healing
I know will work
notes and melodies
lyrics and chords that stir my heart
without me ever fully understanding
why or how

Rain outside continues
while here in the lobby
my spirit is no longer dampened

Silent Conversation

Rose early
to catch a sunrise with you

    in truth we hadn't gone to bed
    friends and beers too tempting
    to turn away

boulder seats
we settled on
hard and cold
but the air around us
was new dawn soft

gulf water lapped
near our feet
songbirds and gulls
called morning greetings
to their friends
half moon appeared
a ghost unwilling
to surrender his domain

    I would have spilled all my secrets
    confessed my entire soul
    to you that morning
    if you had asked

Few words passed between us
as we watched the morning
take hold
perhaps none were needed
the bond of brotherhood
a finer language
than any we could speak

Trees Reflected

Here was the difference between us

we both looked out
on the same melting snow filled yard
I saw mud and broken branches
strewn throughout from winter's wind storms
you saw the dozens of pine cones
adorning the top of my pine tree
went into a lengthy discourse
on the wonders of pine cones
amazed at the design of them
their invaluable nutrition
packed into such intricate designs
I reminded you they were death traps
squirrels threw around the yard
for us to slip on and fall
you laughed and replied
it was all part of a silly squirrel game

I still saw mud and flooding across the yard
you caught sight of how
our trees were reflected
in the ice melt ponds
marveled at the contrast
between black wood reflection
over silver ice and white snow

I saw sky
you noticed the shapes in clouds

you always saw beauty
in landscapes
in sounds
in people
while I saw the ordinary

Brotherhood

United
in this world of one night stands
and hotels all the same
lonely nights
and long drives in between
we give the audience what pleases them
make it look so easy
they have no clue
the nights we push past tiredness
the nights heartache sets in
crowds always energize
carry us through

but when those crowds are gone
and we're left on our own
we stand together
band of brothers
drawing strength from one another
know each other's secrets
share each other's fears
passion for our craft
the thread that binds us

God's Tears

I see behind the layers you build up
to hide behind
the hair
the piercings
tattoos and leather
I hear behind
the wall of sound
the screaming metal
and pounding drums
I see inside
where you are real
the brokenness
the fears
I see it all
through fresh formed tears
I cry for you
though you don't see
think you're beyond my love though you're not
I follow wherever you are
all the lows and highs
Somewhere
behind the long hair
behind the leather and tattoos
behind the wall of sound
beautiful souls
with cracks and holes
shine before me
I reach through the layers they hide behind
my love flowing
like streams newly released from winter freeze
don't mind
if they don't turn my way
the love never ends

Somewhere In Between

It all looked so brilliant
a million pieces of gold
shining just out of reach
we could grasp them
if we pushed hard enough
stretched far enough
so we pushed and we stretched
fueled by our passions
caught up in our dreams

No one ever sees the
thin ice sign
until they're drowning

We've seen both sides
from dirt poor
sleeping on floors
existing on peanut butter and crackers
to soaring among the stratosphere
gold records on walls
gold lining our pockets

these days I wonder which is better
as I count relationships lost
calendars with no empty space
aches in my muscles
matching the ache in my soul
I wish at times
we could have landed
somewhere in between
where stars glittered overhead
and the landings below us were kind

We Watch Through Eastern Window

Dawn breaks
soft white
on a grey, snowy morning
I lie in bed
make no moves
careful to let you sleep

watch your breath,
my world,
rise and fall
as gentle as the dawn
as hushed as the snow
falling outside

your long lashes
dark against your cheeks
soft feathers come to rest
on hallowed ground
light pink blush
like the roses
you tend in our garden

too light, too fragile
to be an anchor
yet anchor you are
keep me grounded
settle my moods
calm the seas
that rage within me
safety net
that catches when I fall
full moon
to light my darkened path

if I knew which gods
to thank for sending you here
I would lay a hundred bouquets at their feet
sacrifice a thousand doves
burn incense of the finest blend

you stir
I place an arm around your waist
we watch through eastern window
as another day is born

Beneath A Golden Moon

Beneath a golden moon
we drink wine
and dream a future together
lunar eclipse that blocked our view
now passed
clear light shows
what I almost lost
what is worth saving
illuminates my path home

It scares me sometimes
this deep river of love
that rages at full flood stage
through my heart,
failing you this river would drown me

Wrap my arms around you
together we dance
underneath a field of diamonds
I pledge my heart to you once more
willing to take the risk
face my fears
guard this treasure
at all costs

Waiting Out The Storm

Lightning and thunder
break into my sleep
startle me awake

You are still under Morpheus' spell
undisturbed by the storm
I shift closer to you
my back pressed against your front
your arm still across my shoulder
where you placed it
as we'd first drifted off to sleep
after our love making

Your arm is a secure anchor now
under which I take comfort
as rain pelts our windows
lightning illuminates our walls
thunder shakes our house
I envy your deep sleep
and count the spaces
between flash and crash
it seems hours before the silence
between each grows longer
and the storm moves away

Some Mornings

Some mornings
I rise and watch the sun
send healing fingers across
emerald green grass
watch tender branches
dance a light breeze
listen to chickadees
exchange animated chatter
with one another

and wonder how you are

This Road Carries No Outlets

I want to walk an easy road
where sun shines
not relentless, bearing down hard
but soft gold warming skin and soul
and shade trees cast a gentle cooling shadow
across smooth even pavement
where a bubbling brook feeds into
a clear blue lake
bordered by meadows of wildflowers
and tall green grass
tossed by a light breeze
and song birds accompany me
on the left and the right

I do not want to travel
this road I am on
narrow lanes of rough broken pavement
steep ascent which
upon reaching the top
plunges me back down
into another dark valley

This road carries no outlets
no turnoffs by which I can escape
I can only follow where it leads
trust the road will not fall away
that if I stay the course long enough
the road will ease
and I will once again be safe

Unrepaired

Not every broken item
can be repaired

the antique compass
you presented me on my birthday
fell a long distance
shattered on rocks
below my hiking trail
distraught, I gathered every piece
spent countless hours
trying to fit each fragment into place
no glue on earth
could hold the multiple pieces together
and even if they could
its usefulness was forever marred
by scars too deep to be erased

So too my heart carries scars
too deep to be eradicated
cannot be restored to its former glow
fragments no longer fit
as they once did

Mazes and Labyrinths

Troubled by this complex
series of avenues
my mind is fixed
on running over

I cannot find the keys
to open locked doors
struggle to find answers
to complex problems

Light at the end
of the tunnel
is denied me

No matter how often
I travel these blind alleys
searching out the right path
that will grant me release

Each turn
leading to another
stone wall
another dead end

Until I come
to the end of myself

Let the road take me
wherever it will
understanding life's journey
is less right path wrong path

But more
a series of lessons
knowledge gained
heart and spirit transformed

Finding peace
no matter what road
my mind may wander

Tiny Star Hamlets

Stars
come to earth
light the dark night
through which I travel
tiny clusters
scattered across
sleeping landscapes
constellations
with no names
galaxies wheeling
across their own universes
too small
and unimportant
for discoverers
to pay them any mind

I imagine
their terrain
warm and smooth
welcoming to sojourners
such as I
in need of rest
and soul healing
and the peace that comes
from slipping through life
unnoticed

I wish
I could turn this vehicle
off highways
pull into one such
tiny star hamlet
undetected
while the rest of the world
rushes by

Too many people
depend on me
staying the course
so I ride past
unnamed towns
whose inhabitants sleep
in comfortable beds
secure in worlds
more starlit than mine
wish for just one night
I could trade places with them

Of Partings And Returns

Sun breaks through clouds
over ocean
below our vantage point
causing a thousand diamonds
to glitter upon rippled surface
twinkling against blue and steel
wind driven waters

Shore receives ocean
time and again
no matter how often
ocean pulls back

sometimes they come together
gently
their embraces soft
their partings easy
sometimes they hurl
angry words at each other
their violence thunderous
explosive
causing the ground beneath them
to grumble
sometimes they cry
over their partings

always
no matter the anger or tears
shore forgives
opens arms
and takes ocean back
always ocean
faithfully returns

I wonder
if our story
will be the same
no doubt there will be times
our anger flares
we have already experienced
tearful partings
and will surely face them again
I will fail you
or you may let me down

Will we always
welcome each other back
forgive transgressions
remember our love
and let that passion
rule above all
will our love story
shine like diamonds
against life's background

I watch ocean depart
and then rush back
unable to leave shore
theirs the ultimate love story
and hope
as I kneel before you
pledge my love
and offer you my future
our story
like ocean and shore
will be never ending

If I Had Known

If I had known
the last time I saw you
would be the last time
I would have shared with you
a memory of a special time
would have found a reason
to make us both laugh
would have complimented you
on any one of the unique
and wonderful things you did
would have told you how
you make my life
bearable and beautiful

would have told you
I loved you

If Only

If only -
empty words
now that the crisis has hit
wishes sent out
for a different outcome
that the universe
cannot possibly answer
still they clog my mind
split my heart in two
scream through
the void inside me
you've left behind

What might have been -
if only's vacant cousin
all the potential now lost
all the dreams
that will never come true

I stare into the darkness
of a world without you
horrified at loss's magnitude
too overwhelmed
to shed any more tears
shock freezing me
inside and out

If only
fills my mind
like an oven timer
whose buzzing cannot be stopped

The Space Between Notes

In music
as important as
the notes themselves
enhancing the tone
and volume played

is the space between notes
the pause
the break in sound

I never expected this break
never wanted this pause
would rather have had
all our notes run together
forever

Impossible
to find meaning
or enhancement
in this unexpected space
so hard to know
how to string
these notes together now

without you
the string
that held them connected

Fragmented

Try to push through
this layer of sadness
it does not budge
never gives an inch
clings to me
like my sweat drenched shirt
at the end of a show
like the hair that sticks
to my face and arms
back and chest
hurricane winds would not clear
these clouds away
low and heavy
they hang over my skies
wherever I go

They say time heals
I have not found this
no distance of time
separated from you
lessens my pain
everything lies shattered
on the ground
I pick the pieces up
examine each one
each shard glitters in the light
but when set back down
each piece looks flat
lifeless
I gather the fragments
into a box
set the box in a cupboard
try to move on
the box calls me back
pins me down
I am frozen

Early Morning

Early morning
I lie in bed
listen to the world around me
come awake
birds sing
house floorboards creak
I think of calling you
need your help on a project
have a new joke to share

Then the last remnants of sleep
fall away
my mind clears
I remember you are gone
another day without you
stretches before me
I rise
and make other plans

Memories Stirred

Memories stir
this late in the day
darkness a cloak wrapped
around body and mind
each memory a dim candle
that briefly illuminates
a corner of my mind
a spark to momentarily
warm my heart

I run my mind's hands
over each one
feel its smooth edges
and those of rougher texture
test each memory's fragrance
and weight

Listen close
to each memory's song
played across my heart strings
some notes comfort
some cut a deep line
soothed only
by the medicine of tears

Each memory
marking a point in my life
personal constellation
shining against the dark night
guiding my way

Dream Keeper

Standing oceanside
on grassy knoll above rocky bluff
your favorite vantage point
I watch waves roll in
retreat
return
constant breeze drives whitecaps
to shore
sends seagulls off course
wheeling away
flying back into headwinds
to regain their route
they think it all an amusement ride
I hear them laugh
in the face of the strongest gusts

Recall so many times
we stood here
deep in thought
deep in conversation
voicing our dreams
casting them to the breeze
I liked to imagine
the wind grasped them
dispersed them to the atmosphere
where they circled the globe
before returning to us
fulfilled

You were my dream keeper
the safety deposit box
where I entrusted my thoughts
and all of the impossible dreams
I dared to hope for
you held them close
always believed with me
never once betrayed me
you always had my back

Now where do I take my dreams
who will safeguard them
who will dream along with me

Winds have grown stronger
buffet me until I find it hard
to stand against them
I return to my car and drive home

Set A Steel Door

All cried out
I have no more tears to shed
only a stone cold heart
dead inside
I stare hard at the trees and sun
outside my window
hear birds chirp and sing
find I don't care about any of them
don't care about the coffee
or pastries
friends and family set before me
go through the motions
of drinking and eating
they watch for that
I will satisfy them
will shower and dress
make small talk and work
try to not think of you
although you will haunt
my every step and thought
set a steel door against my heart
enter a new day
without you

Picking Up The Pieces

Your favorite photo crashes to hardwood floor
glass shards are thrown in a dozen directions
two of them scratch the faces
in the photo you treasure most

People no longer here
captured forever on paper
as they remain captured in your heart

Time doesn't heal as everyone says
although the cutting pain softens
and grief resides subdued
in the corner of your heart where you relegate it

You pick up the shattered glass pieces
throw them away
place the photo in a new frame
restore it to its place of honor on your desk
and move on with your day

It's as simple as that

Five Hundred Pound Load

Learn to walk
with a five hundred pound load
strapped to my back

I can't do it
fall under the weight
each step I take

strain to shoulder the burden
I cannot breathe
cannot move

cannot stay immobile
inertia not an option
I continue to stand

each time I rise
I stand a little straighter
take a few more steps

learn to walk
carrying a five hundred pound load
it's an acquired ability

Climbing Machu Picchu

Every morning
as I drift towards consciousness
under the warmth of nighttime blankets
Machu Picchu comes to mind
image of rough trail
and towering, crumbling steps
looming large
striking fear in my heart once again
vice-like grip freezing my blood
mind overwhelmed
terrified

Each morning I force myself
to swing legs over edge of bed
lower feet to ice cold floor
slip out of the warm shelter
of nighttime's embrace
face that climb to Machu Picchu's top
face the fear of sliding off rickety steps
and crashing, broken, to the ground

The image never fades
the stairs never grow easier
some days I reach the top
some days I fail

At Machu Picchu's top
all I find is ruins
reminders of what once was
what can never be again
it's all changed, irretrievably broken
I struggle to find beauty
In the midst of stone cold, rock hard walls
search for sunlight and warmth
pray for blessings

Some days I find what I seek
some days I leave empty handed

Every morning
I start the climb again

Releasing Your Spirit

Tibetan prayer flags
waving in light breeze
colors faded
edges frayed

I remember the day
you brought them to my house
hung them on a lower branch
of my birch tree
colors resplendent
against white bark
I worried weather
would erode their crisp beauty
you explained as they disintegrated
their spirit was released
to the universe

I wonder if now
your spirit has done the same
been released
to the world around me
the warmth in the sun's rays
fresh scent in rain
brilliant hues in flowers and foliage
if now you are the ocean waves
that kiss the coast

Still Standing

Skies have cleared
storms have stopped swirling
wind has blown itself out
now only a few breezes
send gentle currents that stir a leaf here
a branch there

broken branches
lie strewn across my landscape
a patio chair has overturned
a string of miniature lights
has been ripped from the shrub
it was wound around
I have no idea where my wind chimes
were flung to.

In truth
there was no windstorm
my yard, when I look out on it,
stands intact.

The storm was in my heart
aftermath of the upheaval
caused by your passing
no tree left untouched
no furnishings undisturbed
nothing left where it once was
nothing unbroken

I pick my way
through the debris that remains
know some things must be thrown away
some, although damaged,
stored in containers
they are too much a part of our story
to be completely let go of
some items can be refashioned,
reworked.

I remember seeing aerial photos
of a neighborhood
ravaged by a devastating tornado
belongings flung in every direction
houses obliterated
yet in the neighborhood park
where playground structures
had been reduced to rubble
a lone maple tree stood.

I am that maple tree.
The storms have passed,
I am still standing.

Behind The Mask

I.

Hear how they shine
these notes I twist and bend
to suit my songs

they are pieces of my heart
I set on the line for you
words I cannot put into language

can only speak through my guitar
each note a whisper
a cry

a language safe for me
volume a protective barrier
behind which my true self hides

II.

Strap my guitar across my body
it becomes an extension of myself
it is me

its wood and wires my arms
distorted cries my breath
pounding beat my heart

III.

A heart can break
in a million pieces of shattered glass
strewn across the floor

I gather each piece
send it back across the universe to you
through my guitar

each piece shining
a million shades of light
my heart exposed in the safest way I know

tears turned brilliant
passion channeled into power
explosion of sound a wall

hold outside world at bay
disguise my heart
let no one see inside

IV.

Late night
audience has left
stage and surroundings abandoned

we dance a slow waltz
notes wailing across night air
slicing through darkness

you are my solace
when the rest of the world
has retreated

and I stand alone
doubts and fears my companions
held at bay by your chords

Two Guitars

Alone
at center stage
I feel unmasked
vulnerable
exposing my heart

Solo lines at first
I am grateful
when drums kick in
minimal anchor
against which I can stand
while pouring my heart out
through the notes I play

these notes are my tears
my heartache released
as the faces I've lost
rise before my eyes
ghosts soaring
through spotlight rays
I close my eyes
but ghosts are not so easily dismissed
continue to float
across the black screen of my mind

At the point I fear
I cannot finish this song
your guitar enters
accompanies me
note for note
us playing in tandem
tonight you are my salvation
brothers standing together
against a world
neither can survive alone

Three A.M. World

Three a.m.
all around me sleep
the rest of those
who have exhausted themselves
giving their all for others

I slept as well
until you inhabited my dreams
called me forth
from your world beyond mine
memories so alive
I swear I could grab handfuls
and hold them close

Each memory
breaks one more piece
in a heart I thought had already
completely shattered
each night I am surprised
to find one more fragment
falls to the ground

Tears slide from my eyes
to the pillow beneath my head
I stay silent
fearful of waking others
they have their own grief
a dark black thread
that binds us close
they deserve their rest
I allow that
shift my pillow to find
an un-damp place
and fail

Daylight will find me
taping my heart back together
bright smiles and humor
for all to see
tonight is yours
I allow your spirit
to dance with mine
in the three a.m. world
only broken hearts know

Empty Space

Empty space
where I would normally see you
on stage
another knife
plunged through my heart

It doesn't get easier
as people tell me it will
each night out
a fresh wound
impossible to heal

I strain my spirit
to feel your presence
sure you are somewhere nearby
you would not leave me here alone
my partner in crime
my brother

Play my guitar
with all my heart
every note screams out for you
demands you answer
cries when our pleas
go unheard

Building Blocks

Wake up
heart still beating
lungs still breathing
daylight lightens my walls
casts pale shadows
where light touches candles
and photo frames on dresser

I rise
shower and shave
brush my teeth
slip on whatever jeans and shirt
are within closest reach

Downstairs
I brew coffee
stare into refrigerator
realize I'm hungry for bacon and eggs
and the fried potatoes
you taught me to make
salt pepper and a pinch of sugar

After eating
I walk my land
recognize bird calls
my companions as I pass
familiar trees and bends in the path
spot a location
where a bench for meditation
would fit nice

Air hangs heavy
when I return home
find myself at cross purposes
undecided
force myself to choose a path
pick up a craft
do something constructive

Building blocks
are stacked one upon another
one step
one hour
moving forward happens this way
block upon block
moment by moment
day after day

You Hide Among The Trees And Flowers

Sun reaches its fingers
through the trees in my orchard
warms the branches
inside their outer shells
soon buds will appear
then blossoms
then fruit

stalks from flowers
long given way to winter
spread lace patterns
on fresh fallen snow
sun shining on them
is absorbed into their roots
energy gathered
for the season of release

You hide
among the trees and flowers
enticing my spirit
to play tag with you
I can almost hear your laughter
in the wind
but my spirit is tired
not interested in games
only healing

You move to the window
through which I view my world
singular white light
reflecting off wood
I feel your touch
soak it up
like the dish sponge in my hand
drinks water

Store this feeling away
for days when the sun
shines less bright
and your spirit
will feed me warmth

Beyond The Veil

Wall of mist
from morning rain
throws a grey curtain
across my nearest tree line

I cannot see the woods
beyond the grey
know trees and shrubs are there
and the shed where the garden tools are housed
and the stream where the ducks play
they are invisible though
and silent
no sound to confirm their presence
rises out of their grey cloak
no shadow to hint they still stand

I know you are here
cannot see beyond the veil
that separates us
cannot hear your words
no shadow of you
crosses my sight line

my only resource
the one confirmation I have
is faith
and that as shaky at times
as the aspen leaves still clinging to branches
in a late autumn breeze

Smooth Round Stone

Release comes
in a dozen different ways
each one so subtle
you hardly notice it happens

I walk the woods on my land
follow where rabbit tracks
cross from left to right
then disappear in the thicket

Listen to drumming on a dead tree
signature sound of a woodpecker
downy I think
picture the black and white bird
with small red patch
long before I see it

Turkey tracks appear
in the open space around a curve
where I know they will be
deer prints are found
in the mud by my stream

The air smells clean in these woods
whisper of branches and leaves
soothing
stilling the anxiety my heart
has carried so many weeks

The peace in these woods so powerful
I would sit here for hours
sleep in this spot
soak in the healing balm of this place
until my soul has had its fill

Time presses in
I have places to be

Smooth brown stone
appears in my path
I pick it up, examine it
feel its coolness
and light heft in my hand

Say a prayer
as my fingers memorize
its roundness and surface
set the stone at the base
of the birch tree you always admired
in time I will add more

Not Mine To Keep

Release you
into that world beyond mine
other side of the veil
that separates physical from spirit
temporal from eternal

I would cling to you
if I could
tie your spirit to mine
force you to stay

you are not mine to keep

you walk with angels now
forcing your spirit
to walk with me
would deprive you of a better joy

I open the doors
of my heart
loosen my hold on you
imagine your spirit soaring
so high above me
I can no longer feel you here

hold you to your promise
we will someday be reunited

Rose Light Healing

Morning
soft like a prayer
light from the east
casting rose shadows
on my western thicket
cardinals call to each other
from nearby trees
robins forage open spaces for food
air still cold from the night before
I warm my hands on my full coffee mug
allow the peace of this moment
to seep into my body
fill my soul with quiet
rose light healing broken cells
bar any thoughts
that try to break this serenity

seagull circles overhead
brilliant white in morning sun
watching him I think of you
soaring distant heights
you always soared
so high above the rest of us
we could never keep pace
with where your mind drove you
we were just grateful
to be along for the ride
basking in the glow
of your brilliant light
I wonder now what your eyes see
what fills your mind and heart

then shut my thoughts down
I am not yet ready
for this easy morning
to be broken by memories
that do not comfort
light has turned from rose to gold
bottom of my coffee mug now exposed
I inhale deep
fill my body with one more
long healing breath
before refilling my mug
and turning to the day at hand

Moment In Time

Sometimes
even while my fingers
traverse the landscape
of my guitar strings
while the notes
are dancing through air
as they have time after time
the beauty of a song
catches me off guard
strikes some chord
deep within me

and all of a sudden
I find myself
living two worlds
the visible one
still playing the song
that triggered my heart
and the private one
emotions full to overflowing
a memory
a never forgotten voice
a moment in time
captured in word and tune

I forget
for that moment
the crowd exists
I become one
with my guitar
and the tune at hand
if I were standing
in the middle of an empty field
playing to only
the ground and the air
my feeling would be the same
pure rapture
complete fulfillment
utter joy

Calming Voices

Quiet
evening falls
across my house and yard
no trill of birds
from within trees' sheltered branches
lawn fades from green to black
lights warm my living room
shine amber in dark corners
tonight I choose
to leave sleeping electronics be
and spend my time
in silent meditation
my thoughts running the gamut
from the morning's rose gold sunrise
to hours spent honing my craft
at times so much more dream
than tangible success

I try
to keep realistic perspective
although occasionally
shadows creep in
and the path I'm on
is enveloped in fog
my faith that I'm on the right road
less strong
now night has fallen
and doubts multiply
like the nighttime creaks and groans
that disturb the silence
of my sixty year old house
by early morning hours
I have shaken off my doubts
as my house has settled its voices
and my trees outside
have shaken leaves and limbs
in winds now subsided

Breathe

Breathe
you tell me in a dream
move forward with caution
do not remain
in this stagnant place

I want to comply
tired of the dark clouds
and invisible weights
pinning me to desert ground
no nourishment there
no growth
solitary roads that stretch forever
unbroken

I listen hard to your words
I always have
you have never steered me wrong

Voices crowd my mind
try to convince me
my direction is wrong
scream out to be heard
above each other
try to hold me back

I do not want to be waylaid

Your image drifts
in front of me
I try to keep your pace
you are so far ahead
I gain no ground
can never reach you

It was always so
time after time
you noticed my struggle
slowed your pace to match mine
kept time with me

Breathe
you whisper to me now
move ahead

I comply
anxious as always
to do your bidding
and make you proud

Filling The Empty Cracks

Early morning
grey clouds tinged
with pink and gold
hover over my trees
last night's snow has left
vanilla frosting over my land
soft, clean
covering winter's scars

The air is silent
save for the whisper of leaves
when an odd breeze disturbs them
and the gentle running
of the stream that edges my land
and the cardinals
that call and answer each other
off in the woods
to the left of my house

The peace
of the scene before me
penetrates into my heart
I allow it to fill
all the empty cracks inside me
savor its taste
revel in its embrace
know my day will be alright.

Fall On Me

Standing alone
can be so hard
no one to hold you up
when walls cave in
and the floor threatens
to fall away

You struggle to be strong
to carry the loads
life throws at you
but you are no rock
and some burdens
not meant to be borne alone

Fall on me
I will be the wall
that will not collapse
the support beam
that will hold you up
together we will
make it through the dark

Faith Walking

Easy to sense your presence
when rays of light
stream out from underneath clouds

so much harder
to feel you near
when I need you most
behind the scene where doubts and fears
threaten to shake my confidence
as I prepare to step out
and follow the dream
you inspired

I am desperate
to see your smile
hear your voice
feel your hand on my shoulder
reaffirm your never ending
belief in me

I have no choice
have to move on without you
although I have no idea how
every lesson you've taught me
flashes through my mind
I search every memory
for the one that will carry me through

Faith
one of your favorite words
I cling to it now
as I step out
no longer seeking evidence
that you are nearby
you are in me
wherever I go

To Dream Again

Dreams
such fragile things
like ours, when we finally gave them breath
dared to dive off the high board
into the fray

dared to believe our dreams
could come true

they shone so brightly
for a brief span of time
like a perfect 4th of July
so much excitement packed
into a few brief hours
friends, food, and libations flowing
from sunrise to sundown
air hot but not sweltering
capped off by endless exhilarating fireworks

the next morning
life was quiet again, flat and dull.

Did our dreams end with you?

I rise
watch morning come alive
in the eastern sky
try to dream again
hope a foreign feeling in my cells
try to not extinguish its delicate spark

will myself to pick our dream up
and try to give it new life

A Million Pieces

A million pieces
all that's left inside of me
too much pain
too many heartaches
grief a crashing wave
barreling over me
throwing me under time after time
until I can no longer catch my breath

Time to leave
I scan once more familiar surroundings
feel that when I step outside
I will be leaving you behind
forever
I want to stay in this building
keep you close by
cling to our last remaining connection
thread thin though it may be

I know what I must do
pick up my bags
walk outside
face the future
one last deep breath
and I take those necessary steps

The night sky shines with extra light
crisp winter air
adding clarity and brilliance
to stars overhead
my gaze is locked on them
even as I move on
their glow illuminating
the parts of my heart
I have tried to hide away
warmth from their light
seeps into me
or is that warmth you
demonstrating you are still here
a million pieces
become a million shining jewels
each one meant to strengthen
and heal

Looking for the Lost

Sometimes I seek you
among the waves you cherished
sure your spirit rides
their never ending swells
where you stood so often
mesmerized

Sometimes I search for you
among the trees
where you always listened
for the words hidden in the breeze
always sought to understand
the depths within them

Most often I am sure
I will find you
carried on the air of music
your smile shining among individual notes
your quick feet dancing
to the beat of the drums
your heart still alive
in the soaring, wailing riffs
of our guitars

I know you are there
I listen hard
for the stories you still long to tell
the lessons you call me to learn

I gather each in my heart
and wait for our next encounter

Wanderer Released

Beautiful
and sad
I can only think of you that way
having never known you
only your photos
and limited parts of your story
I see you as shattered glass
reflecting broken sunlight

Some glass
cannot be put back together
no matter how strong the glue
I think most days
you wandered through life
a lost spirit
not yet released to go home

I will hold to the hope
you and your beloved
are once again side by side
watching over those you love
no more pain
only peace

Four Simple Notes

Four small piano notes
ring out clear as crystal
pierce the dark
like a full moon
illuminates a harvest field

and with these four notes
I am drawn back
to when we first met
to a time when all was bright
and we were living our dreams

we had it all back then
the laughter
the camaraderie
you teaching me
and me soaking up every lesson
like a sponge

the brotherhood
that existed among us all
our own solid unit
strong against a world
that could be so harsh and cold

those same four notes
pierce my heart
as our history unfolds in my mind
the crash
the fall

broken
we reunited
held each other together
as best we could
no glue could repair us
no surgeon's sutures

only those four notes

and we owed it to you
to move forward

I hear those four notes now
echoing through night air
see how far we've come
our body of work
since our shattering

prisms casting rainbows
albeit smaller
our individual pieces
could never compare
to your greater light

I play those four small notes
and the ones that follow

and the ones after that

and beyond

Stream-Side Dreams

The stream that crosses
the back end of my land
lies frozen, covered in clean snow
that fell all day in heavy bands
those bands have shifted east now
skies have cleared
stars call me out to commune with them
I decide to test the snowshoes
Christmas brought me
recent snows have built a two-foot depth
have no idea where I will walk
but eventually find myself here
as I always do

You always loved this spot
how many times did we end up
by this stream
on your visits here from the city
away from people and noise
it always seemed a safe haven
a place to let our guard down and be real
the trees would keep our secrets, we knew,
the rocks that lie scattered along the edges
would never tell
the stream would carry our words
but its language
rushed or whispered
was undecipherable to anyone traveling its borders
we revealed so many fears here
so many losses
so many hurts

and every dream we ever had
thoughts so fragile
we didn't always understand them ourselves
although we always understood each other's thoughts
like we were one heart and mind
separated into two bodies
we needed each other to complete our dreams

So hard to dream now
I would give all this land
and everything I own
if you could return to this place
share one more stream-side conversation with me
but you have crossed over
to a place I cannot yet follow
I lean against the large oak
whose toes cool themselves in the stream
at summer's height
think those toes must feel the same ice
I carry inside since you've gone
through naked branches I see stars smiling down
wonder if they are you
if it was your voice I heard
calling me forth
I test this thought
try to share my latest dream with you
though the words stay stuck in my throat
the same place they've remained lodged
these last five months since you left
it will always be this way now
I know

no more stream-side conversations
no one left to believe in my dreams
I will have to face future roads alone
which I will
I promised you that

I draw out the flask of Jack Daniels
I had tucked into my jacket pocket
our tradition on each of our visits here
raise a toast to you
listen hard to the silence around me
willing you to whisper through the trees
toss one patch of snow up through spirit wind
cause a deer to appear
move the snow owl I know resides in the maple
across the stream from where I stand
to give out one brief hoot
no response comes my way
as I turn back for home
I wonder if I will ever have the courage
to visit this stream again

Still The Band Plays On

Close our eyes
we still see your face
your smile
your haunting eyes

Still hear your voice
a constant loop running
over and over
through the air

Space where you once stood
still feels empty
no replacement
could shine as you did

Still we play on
push past the hollow core
we carry inside
to the music you always inspired

Each note, each word
played for you
played with you
your spirit driving every step we take

Dreams Kept Alive

Look up to the heavens
as my guitar
and the cello beside me
open your song
I can almost see the stars
shining overhead
a million diamonds
glowing over a city
now dead

can almost feel all over again
the hope you built into your songs
the dreams still alive
when all else seemed lost

you still call me to hope
and to dream
to push past deep wounds
and shine like the stars

feet still bound to stage
I allow my spirit
to soar with yours
beckon yours to soar
through my guitar
stay connected with you
though we are now
of two worlds

as the lone cellist
kept hope alive
while the city around him
was fallen

Every Dream

You knew my heart
from the very beginning
from when we first met
you read what I didn't even
fully know I carried inside

My dreams
must have matched your own
for how else would you
have worked so hard
to make them come true

In your hands
the dreams shone like diamonds
like all the stars in the universe
gleaming
shimmering
so beautiful I hesitated to touch them
for fear they would turn to dust

They remained gold
turned out so brilliant
even now I am amazed
at how they materialized
how they still shine
after so many years
their magic has not diminished
when I stand back and take the long view
of what we've accomplished
I am still awed
and humbled

You have crossed over
to the other side
will you from there
still read my heart
still find ways to hand me my dreams
or am I now on my own
where my feeble attempts
to make my dreams come true
can never match
your masterful touch
your uncanny ability to succeed
where I no doubt would have failed

And how am I now
to repay all you've given
to return to you
the blessings you have showered on me
a thousandfold

Celestial Viewpoint

Reclining on lounge chair
by the fire pit in my yard
flames from earlier in the night
reduced to glowing embers

I study the skies
undimmed
no city lights to interfere
vast expanse of fairy lights
winking down at me

You loved those stars
knew so many of them by name
fit their constellation pictures together
while I struggled to find
the Big Dipper

I try to remember
all you taught me
about the stars
about the universe
novas, nebulae, galaxies
about so many other things
history, humanity
your brilliant mind captured so much
but always sought to understand more

I soaked up every word you said
absorbed as much as I could
before it evaporated
try to recall it all now

most of it gone
all that remains is the feeling
me astounded by your beautiful mind
wishing with everything in me
I could have those moments back
record your words
so I could hear them forever

that's the hardest part
knowing I've lost
your unmatchable mind
those lofty ideas that set you apart
made you stand out
fueled your dreams
which you in turn handed to us
the magic of it all
the majesty

you must be so happy now
seeing the universe
from your spirit world perspective
glorious beyond any words
you could speak
I can imagine you
jaw dropping
taking in such heavenly sights
your heart would be racing
a thousand beats a second
your mind whirling
trying to take it all in at once

and you standing with God
understanding now
from your celestial viewpoint
the mysteries you so often
begged God to come down and explain
I imagine your conversations with Him
wish I could be there
to see a child's wonder
spread over your face
for no matter your age at passing
you would still be a child
in deep, reverent awe
at God's knee

the thought of how happy you are
pleases me
I will cling to this image

Legacy

Stare out
over sea of crates and cables
lighting and pyro equipment
scaffold rigging
and stage platforms
all being readied
for tonight's show

workers scurrying
like so many ants
all methodical
purposeful
carrying out the visions
you handed us
as only they know how

musicians and singers
warm up backstage
ready to play their part
in the experience
set to unfold tonight
each of them cognizant
as always
of the dream
you laid out for us

and what of me?

as I watch
your presence
presses down hard

an ever present shadow
angel that guides
every one of my moves

some days your hand
is gentle upon me
a brush of air
a feather
today it feels a heavy weight
comforting to know
you still guide our ship
but my longing to see you
face to face

to walk down a hall
in your presence
or laugh over coffee with you
overwhelms

your lyrics
run through my mind
the brilliance of them
the power
your creative genius
miles ahead of anywhere
anyone else would have taken it
days like these
I am humbled
to even be a part
of your grand design
every fiber and cell within me

desires to let your music
shine like the stars
I am happiest
while performing this task
joined with the cast of performers
you assembled
we know our parts
and revel in playing them

we are your legacy
and those who will follow
we will keep safe and keep alive
the jewels you crafted
as long as your hand remains

as for me
I sit in the silence
of a rear section seat
watching preparations unfold
mindful of every word
you spoke to me
every lesson you taught
as much a singular part
of your legacy
as the group as a whole

I know my part
I will play it well
as long as you promise
to guide me

You Among The Stars

Each note
like a thousand fireflies
floating through darkness
a million stars
piercing the night
your brilliance shining through
with each movement of your hands
intensity etched on your face
passion pouring forth
you and your guitar as one
you made it look so easy
you made it sound so beautiful

I would give everything I own
to have you back
I do not have that power
or that right
you reside now among the stars
your magic fingers once captured,
and speak to us
through the songs you left behind
or perhaps
if we are truly blessed
through our dreams

we remember you always
we cry
we move on
carry you and your songs
wherever we go
forever still a part of our lives

You Shine A New Light

You always were
one to shine a light
on the paths of those around you

I have grieved for you
no matter how long you lived
your passing
would have been far too early

so hard to face the world
without your smile
your infectious spirit
your unending optimism
I struggle every day
with all we have lost

Until you touched me
and I understood

you had reached all your heights
accomplished things
far beyond anyone's imagination
lit a million candles
that shine through the dark
like glittering stars

You had one more
path to illuminate
one candle which you
could not light from here

You had to leave
to show us
we have more strength than we knew
could find our way down blind roads
could survive
the darkest days

and someday
when it's our turn to pass
you have already
gone down that path
and will leave your light burning
to guide our way

Acknowledgments

I am grateful for the help and support of many people in completing this book, but most notably for the following:

Beth Bales Ostrowski always creates stunning covers for my books. In this book, she has gone far beyond my hopes and created a cover that completely captures what I had in my mind and heart. As always, Beth, I am grateful for your artistry and your friendship.

Chris Macry, thank you for the use of your guitar for the cover, and Jacki Bruder, thank you for the phenomenal photo of that guitar.

Steve "Doc" Wacholz, thank you so much for the drumsticks that grace the book's cover.

To J.P. Sexton, thank you for your wonderful words in the foreword to this book.

To my test readers, Ann, Patrick, Dave, Chris, Kevin, Danica, Marian, and Larry, thank you so much for your time, comments, and support. Your faith in this undertaking kept me going many nights when the struggle was especially hard.

Danica, Cindy, Arlene, and Terry, I am so grateful for your belief in this project, and your support through the spiritual path I walked while writing this book.

Amanda and Elizabeth, thank you for all of your encouragement and support and for listening to all my stories along the way.

I am blessed with numerous friends in the writing community, in the poetry community, and in general. I won't try to name you all here, for fear of leaving someone out ... but please know I am grateful to each and every one of you.

About the Author

Sinéad Tyrone is a Western New York author with two novels and two poetry collections published. Her novels, *Walking Through The Mist* and *Crossing The Lough Between*, are set in current day Ireland and cover the crises, challenges and celebrations in the lives of a band of Irish musicians. Her poetry collections, *Fragility* and *A Song Of Ireland*, cover a wide range of subjects, the latter containing poems that relate to her travels throughout Ireland. Her poems have appeared in the anthologies *The Empty Chair, Beyond Bones III*, and *A Celebration of Western New York Poets*. Find out more about Sinéad at www.sineadtyrone.com.

Made in the USA
Monee, IL
22 May 2023

33992117R00184